A NOVEL BY
JAMES W. HALL

A Warner Communications Company

WARNER BOOKS EDITION

This Warner Books Edition is published by arrangement with W. W. Norton & Company, Inc., 500 Fifth Avenue, New York, N.Y. 10110

Cover illustration by Punz Wolf
Cover design by Irving Freeman

Warner Books, Inc.
666 Fifth Avenue
New York, N.Y. 10103

A Warner Communications Company

Printed in the United States of America

First Warner Books Printing: December, 1988

10 9 8 7 6 5 4 3 2 1

UNANIMOUS ACCLAIM FOR

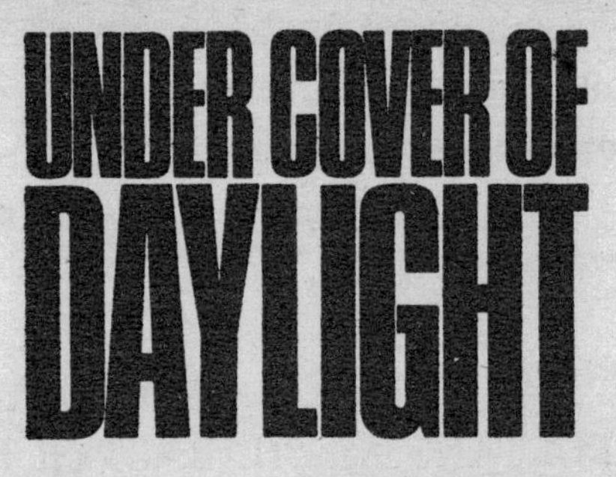

"TOUGH, TAUT... FINE STUFF... the characterizations leap off the page."

—*New York Daily News*

☆

"IT STARTS GOOD AND IT STAYS GOOD, RIGHT TO THE END."

—*Chicago Tribune*

☆

"MASTERFUL... MORE THAN JUST AN ORDINARY MURDER THRILLER."

—**United Press International**

☆

"PICTURE THIS, THRILLER FANS... a cold winter night and this hot book set in South Florida, and the heat alone of your fingers turning the pages will make sparks. Read *Under Cover of Daylight*, and make your own little revenge against winter."

—**National Public Radio**

more...

☆

"TRULY CHILLING. *Under Cover of Daylight* is unquestionably one of the finer novels I've read recently."

—John Katzenbach, author of *First Born* and *In the Heat of Summer*

☆

"HALL MAKES PLACE AND CLIMATE AS IMPORTANT AS CHARACTER IN BUILDING THE POWERFUL EFFECT OF THIS ACCOMPLISHED NOVEL.... Hall's characters, people of heart and soul with real-life combinations of strengths and flaws, are so sharply evoked as to be almost physically present. The sex scenes, graphic and strong and often lovely, are particularly effective."

—Publishers Weekly

☆

"AS THEMATICALLY DENSE AND ENVIRONMENTALLY LUSH as any other living thing that grows in this region of overripe beauty. There's no blocking the rush of feeling that surges over the people and the places that Hall has brought to life in Florida."

—Marilyn Stasio, *San Jose Mercury News*

☆

"HALL JOINS THE ELITE CREW (HEMINGWAY, ELMORE LEONARD, TOM MCGUANE) WHO HAVE USED THE FLORIDA KEYS AS A BACKDROP FOR MUSCULAR MEDITATION. Via language as fresh as tropical rain, narrative as deep and swift as a sea current, and the crackling pull of love/hate between rich, strong, believable characters, Hall makes this captivating, exciting tale uniquely his own."

—*Kirkus Reviews* (starred review)

☆

"EXCELLENT... the real pleasures in Hall's book are the sensual ones of place and people. It's the honest feel of the Florida Keys, with all their menacing rhythms and contagious lassitude, that Hall nails down so well."

—Carl Hiassen, author of *Tourist Season*, for the *Raleigh News and Observer*

☆

"A GREAT FIRST NOVEL... hard-hitting, nuts-and-bolts prose, effectively picaresque characterization, periodic sex and violence, and a wonderful cinematic climax embellish a largely realistic plot."

—*Library Journal* (starred review)

more...

☆

"MASTERFUL . . . GREAT READING. . . . Murder, drugs, and sex help rivet the reader's attention. Hall's imaginative and literary power reward that attention on every page. . . . The authentic sense of place will delight "Miami Vice" fans. Against a tropical background, a fascinating cast of characters moves through a plot both terrifying and heartwarming. You will finish it well satisfied, but also wanting more."

—***Tampa Tribune***

This book
is dedicated with love and admiration to
STERLING WATSON

Very special thanks is also due to
Les Standiford and Captain Alex Kitchens
without whose help
this book would not have been written.

There is the calmness of the lake when there is not a breath of wind; there is the calmness of a stagnant ditch. So it is with us. Sometimes we are clarified and calmed healthily, as we never were before in our lives, not by an opiate, but by some unconscious obedience to the all-just laws, so that we become like a still lake of purest crystal....

HENRY DAVID THOREAU
A Writer's Journal

UNDER COVER OF DAYLIGHT

July 1966

Standing in front of his dresser mirror, the young man pointed the revolver at his reflection. He held it there until the waver in his hand had subsided. He closed his eyes, drew in a deep breath, and brought the revolver down.

After he had replaced the pistol in the tackle box, he slid it back onto the shelf and shut the closet door. He went into the bathroom, washed his face, brushed his teeth. Outside, he stood on the veranda for a moment, looking out at the ocean. A flock of pelicans glided past, a few yards above the water. He watched them till they were out of sight, then walked down the long rutted road to the highway.

He came to the highway just as the Postal Service Jeep was pulling away from the mailbox. He opened the mailbox and quickly removed the package. There was a birthday card taped to the lid of the box. He tore that open. It was an accordion card. A fisherman in a rowboat had hooked a small fish which was about to be swallowed by a bigger one, and on like that as the accordion opened until the last fish was twice as big as the fisherman's boat. The printed message said, "Have a Whopper of a Birthday."

There were two black-and-white photographs inside the envelope, too. In one a balding man was holding up a salmon in each hand. He was smiling. In the other a graying woman was holding a salmon bigger than either of the man's. She smiled as well.

The young man studied each of the photos for a moment, then opened the package. There were two hand-tied flies in the box: one a replica of a tiny field mouse, the brass hook curving out of its belly; the other a bright imitation of a dragonfly. "Take a shot at these," said the note. "Happy Nineteenth from the frozen North. All our love. Wish you were here."

It was an hour before he got a ride. He had walked almost five miles up the highway by then. The driver was a tourist from Michigan, driving a rental car. He drove with one hand while he pawed with the other through a stack of photographs. He held each one up in turn for the young man to see, then took a long look at each of them himself. The man had been charter fishing in Islamorada for the last month. He'd been after snook mostly, but he'd also gotten tarpon and permit.

The man didn't seem to notice that the young man did not talk. The young man looked politely at each photograph, nodding the same way each time. By the time they reached the outskirts of Miami, the photographs were exhausted and the man began to concentrate on the thickening traffic.

At a light in South Miami, without any announcement, the young man got out of the car. He walked quickly down a side street until he found a phone booth.

He stepped inside it, closed the door, and brought the phone book up. He turned the pages till he came to the proper one, ran his finger down the list of names, stopped finally on the name he was after. He stared at the page for a long time, then let the phone book fall back to the end of its chain.

From his back pocket he withdrew a street map. He unfolded it and studied it for a few minutes. He peered out at the street sign near the phone booth and spent more time looking at the map. After refolding the map and putting it back in his jeans, he stepped out onto the sidewalk and began walking.

He was wearing canvas boat shoes, no socks, a dark green T-shirt. His hair was sun-scorched blond and cut in a flattop. He was an inch below six feet and gristly thin. His arms and face were deeply tanned. His dark blue eyes seemed focused on some distant point, practiced in scanning the horizon for some subtle disturbance.

With long strides he walked out of the small shopping district, across Dixie Highway, and along the perimeter of the university. Past the practice fields and parking lots into the shady neighborhoods of Coral Gables.

It was five o'clock when he reached a curvy, narrow street that ran along the edge of a golf course. The young man glanced down the street and then turned and retraced his steps for half a mile to a small park where there were a few swing sets and a long slide. He sat in the shade of a live oak, watching a black woman in a white uniform entertaining a white child. After an hour the two of them left, and he was alone as dusk came on.

At eight-thirty, as the darkness settled finally, he rose and returned to the curvy street. He cut through a vacant lot and walked along the rough of the golf course. Staying near the thick shrubbery, he made his way to a one-story white stucco house with a tiled roof. Light came from the patio doors, and there were the sounds of dishes and silverware from the open kitchen window.

The young man crouched behind an oleander shrub about ten feet from the patio and watched the lighted windows. Once a child's voice called out the name of some pet, and an hour later the young man could hear a woman's voice as she chatted on the phone while she paced in front of one of the back windows.

At around ten o'clock the house went dark, but the young man continued to stare at it. It was an hour and a half later when he heard a car arrive around front, and a few moments later the front door slammed. A light came on in the living room, then the kitchen. The young man stood and edged closer to the kitchen window, pressing his back against the rough side of the house.

A fat man in a dark blue suit was in the kitchen. He had black, shiny hair that was parted in the middle and a small mouth with fleshy lips. The man dropped his keys on the kitchen table, took off his suit coat, and let it fall to the floor. He poured himself a tea glass full of scotch, and before the young man could move away, the fat man lurched out of view and suddenly swung open the kitchen door and walked outside.

The young man flattened himself against the wall, and the fat man stood on the paving stones a few feet away and poured some of the scotch down. He turned away from the young man, mumbled to himself, and walked across to the patio, which was partially lit from the kitchen light. The fat man stood for a moment next to a chaise longue, then bent over and vomited into a flower box.

When he was finished, he wiped his mouth on the sleeve of his white shirt and lot himself down carefully into the chaise and took another belt of the drink. The young man waited for a few minutes more until the fat man seemed to be dozing, his glass on the patio beside him.

He opened the kitchen door carefully and slid inside. He stood there and looked around the kitchen for a few moments, then picked up the man's suit coat. Inside the breast pocket he found the fat man's wallet. He took the man's driver's license out and inspected it.

After a few moments he put it back in the wallet and replaced the wallet in the coat and dropped it again on the floor. He took the keys from the kitchen table and walked back outside and walked over to the chaise.

He grabbed the fat man by the front of his shirt and hauled him upright. The man giggled. But when he was on his feet, he stiffened and drew back and peered into the young man's face. The young man turned him and prodded him forward with one hand, gripping the fat man's shirt collar with the other.

The man stumbled ahead, saying nothing, wavering as he walked. The two walked around the side of the house and came to the driveway. A '65 Buick coupe was parked there, its grille buried in the hedge. The young man gripped the man's collar tightly and looked down at the smashed-in front right headlight on the Buick. He took a deep breath.

The young man turned the fat man around, leaning him against the passenger door.

"I don't know you," the fat man said, uncertainly.

The young man stepped back a step and cocked his right fist to his shoulder and slammed the fat man flush on the nose. The man sagged, and the young man held him against the car while he opened the passenger door. The fat man was perhaps twenty, thirty pounds heavier. The young man got the door open and muscled the man into the seat. He closed the door and stood still, breathing hard, listening.

He got into the driver's seat, fumbled with the ignition key, jammed it finally into the slot. Glancing back at the house, he started the car. He backed it out the drive, hitting the power brakes too hard and making a small screech as the tires hit the pavement.

He looked again at the fat man's house. A dark figure was standing in the shadows on the front porch. Maybe a stone statue, maybe a child, a large dog. The young man put the car in gear and carefully pulled away.

The fat man came to in about ten minutes. The car was stopped at a red light, the intersection empty, streets empty in every direction. A black man sat outside the office of an all-night gas station, listening to his radio, looking at the Buick.

The fat man blinked, stared at the young man, then across at the gas station. He had the door open and was in the street before the young man could step on the gas. The fat man was running into the gas station, waving his hands, stumbling. The black gas station attendant watched him come toward him, then rose from his chair and hurried inside the office.

The young man pushed the shift lever to park, threw open the door, and ran after the fat man. He caught up to him at the door to the gas station office. The black man had a small-caliber revolver pointed at the fat man, and sweat had broken out on the black man's forehead.

"Come on, Dad," the young man said as he put his arm around the shoulder of the fat man, taking a twisting grip of his underarm. He said to the black man, "One too many. Celebrating my birthday."

"Get on out of here, the both of you," the black man said.

"Help me," the fat man said. "This guy's kidnapping me." He tried to wriggle free of the young man's hold.

The young man shook his head at the black man. "He gets like this."

"He surely do," the black man said.

The fat man broke away from the young man's grip and ran back toward the car. Halfway across the gas station lot he stumbled and fell to his knees.

The young man trotted over to him, dragged him up, and together they staggered back to the car. The fat man was breathing very hard, sweating heavily. Again the young man pushed him into the car and came around and got behind the wheel.

"Who are you?" the man said, out of breath.

The young man said, "If you try anything like that again, I'm going to kick the shit out of you. Just sit there."

"I know," the fat man said, tilting his head, his eyes focusing on the young man's face. "I know who you are."

The young man was silent, driving carefully, keeping the Buick at the speed limit.

"It's the anniversary," the fat man said. "I know that. You think I'd forget?"

"Shut up," the young man said.

"You don't think I've suffered, is that it? Is that what this is? You going to torture me, get even, is that it?" The man mumbled to himself. "Tell me. You're the kid, right?"

The traffic lights were behind them now. It was just a long strip of highway with packing plants and a few motels, and then they came to Florida City and hit the rougher asphalt road running through the Everglades down to Key Largo. There were no other cars. The sky was clear. The young man kept the car at seventy.

The fat man screamed for help. He turned in the seat and yelled into the wind back toward Miami. The young man nudged the car up to seventy-five.

"I got a family," the man yelled at him.

The young man turned his head and stared at the man.

"I can give you money. I got money. Whatever you want."

"I want you to know," the young man said. "Know how they felt."

"You'll get prison," he said, all menace.

The young man smiled and pushed the car on. "I'll take what's coming to me," he said.

"I was just your age, for chrissakes," the man said. "It was a careless mistake. A kid's stupid mistake."

The car was up to eighty by the time they rounded the long curve and came up to Jewfish Creek Bridge. The car hurtled up the ramp of the bridge, left the ground briefly, and the undercarriage banged on the other side. The fat man grabbed for the door handle. Sober as hell now. Adrenaline sober. Night air, going eighty five through the dark sober.

The young man's foot drove deeper into the accelerator pedal, and he watched the flash of guardrails, saw Lake Surprise appear, the car slewing right, a tire slipping off the edge of the pavement, catching in the shoulder, twisting the wheel from his hands, and he didn't try to recapture it, and the Buick rammed through the guardrail, sailing out into the water. The young man thinking, Yes, this is exactly right. Exactly as it should be. Yes.

There was the short flight, the pounding drop, the spray of glass, the sledgehammer to his chest. The warm water of Lake Surprise flooding in. And he lost consciousness.

When the young man woke, he heard the faint wail of sirens. Water was up to his shoulders. His chest ached, ribs burned. He climbed out the window, slogged around the car to see about the fat man. A wedge of glass had opened the man's throat, and his head rested on the back of the seat. Dark syrup rose at the gash. If he wasn't dead just then, he was about to take wing.

The young man went back to the driver's side and leaned in and hauled the fat man across the seat, head lolling, and he wedged him behind the steering wheel. Then he swam and waded two, three hundred yards through Lake Surprise to the mangroves. And climbed into them. Wet, hurting, nothing numb, not the least in shock. Feeling every mosquito sting.

He stayed for the whole show. There was nothing dramatic about it. Just men working, figuring out. A physical problem with winch, long cable. Cops wading out with the ambulance boys. No one looking around for a passenger. Just another drunk who'd lost control.

He watched it all. And finally, an hour or so before dawn, it was over. They were gone. Lake Surprise was calm. It went from oily black to gray to green. An early-morning fisherman arrived in his skiff and began casting into the shadows along the shoreline a mile away.

The young man worked his way through the dense mangroves up to the highway. He was having trouble taking breaths; his hands were shaking. There was blood coming from somewhere inside his shirt. It was only a three-mile hike back to his house, but it took him two hours.

1

Thorn watched her standing at the shore, up to her ankles in Lake Surprise. The moon had laid down a wide silver path across the water, and a light breeze was blurring patches of the glassy surface. For the last few minutes Sarah Ryan had been standing there, gazing out at all of it.

Not turning around, she asked, "So what's the ceremony?"

"There isn't any *ceremony,*" Thorn said. "I just sit here, try to be quiet."

"You don't get in the water? You don't *do* anything?"

Thorn sighed. Maybe it'd been a mistake bringing her. She'd wanted to come since he'd known her—

what?—a little less than a year. Soon as she found out about his ritual, she wouldn't leave it alone. Started hinting around that June. By the first of July she was out in the open about it. Take me along. I won't bother you. I'll participate, do whatever you want me to. OK, so he'd let Sarah, his lover, come along. Maybe to tell her the details, fill in blanks he'd not even revealed to Kate. He had thought they were ready.

But who showed up? This other Sarah. Sarah-the-Public-Defender, cross-examiner of cops, used to prying open clamped mouths. Intolerant of lazy emotions. Breezy and tough. And what he'd planned on saying, the confession he'd been rehearsing for weeks, had gone cold and quiet.

Still looking out across the sound, Sarah said, "Well, *I'm* going for a swim."

"Look. Point is, this is my one day a year. Like going to the graveyard, flowers on the grave. Like that."

"The overexamined life is not worth living," she said. "Haven't you heard of baring your soul and getting on with it?" She turned and the moon gleamed in her dark hair.

"I've heard of it," said Thorn.

Sarah shook her head and said, "And then there's the theory of swimming your way to mental health. Getting out there, exposing yourself to the waters."

She peeled off her khaki camp shorts. No underwear for Sarah. The T-shirt next, and she was there naked in the moonlight. Full moon. Two hundred yards from U.S. 1. The cars rumbling across the grating on Jewfish Creek Bridge. She let Thorn take in her silhouette. She was tall with wide shoulders and thin limbs. And had a gawky gracefulness to her movements, like a fashion model slightly out of practice.

"Watch out for lemon sharks." Thorn felt himself hardening for her.

"Let them watch out." She hesitated for a moment at the shoreline, took a deep breath, and waded out into Lake Surprise, into the meadow of light from that heavy moon.

Thorn watched her float on her back. Her breasts breaking through the calm surface. Her pubic hair sparkled. Maybe this was her game. Shake him awake with a little splish-splash, some serious treading of water.

He shifted on the army blanket, dusted away a mosquito singing in his ear. The repellent was already wearing thin. He steered his eyes away from the glisten of Sarah Ryan, following that path of light across the mangrove-rimmed bay to where it veered west toward Mexico.

Would she swim so easily there if she knew the blood that water was spiked with? Thorn had shuddered when Sarah first grazed her toe across it, but he'd said nothing. He had not been able to touch that water himself for twenty years.

Twenty years he'd been coming out here on the fifth of July to sit beside the bay. Twenty years. It sounded like a jail term. Twenty to life. That was about the sentence he might've expected if he'd turned himself into the sheriff.

Maybe he should've done that. Maybe that way the guilt would be gone, and Thorn, thirty-nine years old, could walk away from all of it, back into the world, debts paid. This way was turning into a life sentence. A sentence with no period at the end.

Sarah was gliding out farther, on her back, the water

bubbling quietly at her feet. It seemed that she was trying to let him have his time, his little meditation, get it over with. Or maybe she had caught the doleful vibrations of the place. The ghosts. The ghosts of Quentin and Elizabeth Thorn and one Dallas James. Fat, drunk, puke-scented Dallas James.

Thorn watched Sarah Ryan. She was still on her back, the water bubbling up from her quiet, efficient flutter kick. It glittered like silvery foam. She swam farther out into that warm bay, making a lazy circle near the spot where it had happened.

Thirty-nine years before, Quentin and Elizabeth had been driving home to Key Largo from the Homestead Hospital. Thorn was twenty hours out of the womb, still four hours left to get him back to the Keys so he'd be officially, by local custom, a Conch. To give the boy roots.

Maybe *roots* was wrong. *Suction* was a better word. This island didn't grant much purchase. Limestone and coral just under the couple of inches of sandy dirt. It was just a long, narrow strip of reef really. And with a little melting at the North Pole, one good force five hurricane, it would be reef again. But Conchs had suction. They could hold on to places where no roots could burrow in.

The custom was important enough to Quentin and Elizabeth to steal away from that hospital after midnight against her surgeon's warnings. She'd had a C section. Fat little Thorn, ten and a half pounds, stalled at the hatch.

There were four hours left. No hurry. The drive back down to the Keys took only half an hour. It was July 5, 1947.

Everything Thorn knew about that night had come from the *Miami Herald* article. Dr. Bill had saved it till Thorn had asked one too many questions about his real parents' death. Dr. Bill had led Thorn into his study, where the newspapers were spread out on his desk. And Dr. Bill had gone outside to whack his machete at a rotted limb while Thorn, thirteen years old, read and reread. Nothing to soften it. The same clean surgical cool Dr. Bill had about everything. Read this. This is all that's known. Outside chopping at punky wood while Thorn grappled with it.

July 5, 1947, had been a clear night. Hot like any July. Light breezes from the southeast. Oh, Thorn read everything else before letting his eyes take hold of the headline about the Thorn family. The weather. The sports, the Reds Reject the Marshall Plan. Three-cent first-class stamps. Today's Chuckle. A story about a young couple getting married. She says, "No," not, "I do," at altar. Changes to "Yes," but then he says, "No." Thorn read that.

Finally, there was only one article left. Thorn, picturing it as he read, taking the gray neutral journalism and brightening it with detail, fixing it in his imagination forever. Whenever he recalled it after that afternoon, it came up like this. It was a clear night. Twenty miles of two-lane highway, along the bed of an old railway line. You could reach out either car window and touch mangroves, said the old-timers. Narrow and dark, an empty stretch of asphalt. Thorn was asleep in Elizabeth's lap. Sleeping with the rhythm of her breathing and that old car humming along.

Coming from the other direction, in his old man's

Studebaker, barreling home from Key West, was twenty-one-year-old Dallas James. A couple of his friends in the back seat. Everybody giddy from bourbon and Coke. A girl at Dallas James's side. A nice girl from his university graduating class who didn't know the ride was going to involve Key West and back to Miami in one day, and all that drinking and hooting. She was Doris Jean Parish. All of it was in the paper. She was the one blew the whistle. Next day she blurted it out to her daddy. Good Catholic girl, couldn't survive overnight with all that guilt.

That night Dallas had been telling a story, a long one, and he was looking back over his shoulder for reactions. Bourbon and Coke, a long joke, caring more about the laughs, impressing the two in the back seat and Doris Jean than about whose headlights he was straying into.

Quentin Thorn swerved off the shoulder, over the low bank, and out into Lake Surprise. No choice. Into those headlights and the tons of steel behind them or into the moonlit water of Lake Surprise. Surprise, surprise. There'd been only four feet of water at that hour. Tide was out. But with heads flattening against that steel dashboard, a birdbath would've done fine.

Thorn had bounced around in there, coming finally to lodge atop his mother's suitcases in the back seat. And as the black, warm water of Lake Surprise seeped into the car, Thorn squawked probably, the water rising to cover his parents' faces, peaking finally a few inches from where he squirmed.

Dallas James stopped his car, got out, looked over the situation, gave his morals a quick workout, and got everybody back in the car and drove off.

In the second clipping, from a few weeks later on, Dallas had had his moment in court. His story was that this other car was weaving, Dallas honked, veered to avoid it, and the new father, new mother, and their infant of their own free will sailed into that lake. The judge allowed as how there had been enough tragedy already and, seeing how Dallas was from a good family and all, was inclined to give him nothing more than a stern look.

Not Thorn. It had simmered in him for six years, but he had finally done it. And now he was here, serving his indeterminate sentence, his hard time out among the innocent. Very cruel, very unusual. And this was visiting day at the penitentiary. Mr. Thorn to visit Mr. Thorn.

Sarah was coming ashore. Thorn watched her wake arrive before her, stirring among the mangrove roots. And she waded up to the bank, the moon glazed her body.

"You done?" she asked, the gold water falling from her, standing a couple of yards away.

"I guess *so*," Thorn said.

"What were you thinking about just now?" She stooped and pulled her towel from her large straw bag, began patting herself dry.

"Your hair."

"Before that?"

"Your skin," he said.

"Oh, come on, you know what I mean."

"About this place," Thorn said. "Lake Surprise, dark, serious things."

"But you're not going to tell me about them." She spread her towel out beside him and lowered herself onto it, leaned back, propped on her elbows. Moon tanning.

"My voice is failing me at the moment."

She said, "Maybe I should get dressed, help you get it back."

A transfer truck rumbled from the highway, heading south with supplies. In the Keys everything had to be shipped in; even fresh water was piped down. The only natural resources were fish and balminess.

"Maybe you should," Thorn said.

"Am I being sacrilegious, naked in the graveyard?" She smiled at him and moistened her upper lip.

"Yeah," Thorn said, "but I like it."

"We could swim," Sarah said, the smartass gone from her voice now. A regretful tone that almost matched his mood. "It did me a world of good."

"No, thanks," Thorn said.

"I hear it's good in the water, all that buoyancy."

"No," he said. "I just want to stay a little longer. Like this. Nothing fancy."

"I'll shut up."

"Yeah." Thorn let himself look at her again. "And there's nothing wrong with the buoyancy at my place, is there?"

"No," she said. "Nothing at all."

2

It was a two-foot sea, overcast. Noon on Sunday. Time to start thinking about Monday, the week. Sarah was rocking easily with the light chop on the second level of the tuna tower, alongside Kate Truman. Sarah's long black hair snapping, skin not feeling yet the sunburn she knew she'd gotten. It had something to do with the blue-eyed Irish in her, bred for gloomy skies, layers of clothes, a heavy gray mist on the moor.

Sarah leaned forward toward Kate and half shouted into the wind, "I'm running out of company names."

"Wait a minute!" Kate unrolled the plastic windshield for the tower platform. The two of them snapped it in place. Now, with the breeze cut off, Sarah felt it, the prickle on her cheek, a puffiness beginning.

"I'm running out of names," she said. "I come up with one, it's on the computer already. It's a janitorial service or a shop sells popcorn. Crazy things."

"How about Wood Rat Enterprises?"

"Not businesslike. It should sound like it's for real."

"Well, you'll think of something. What's the big worry about corporate names anyway? You worry about the oddest things."

"I'm worried about all of it. But the only parts I can focus on, you know, are the small parts."

They were only a mile offshore, the fiber glass twenty-footers were all around them, Aquasports, Makos full of Miami snorklers headed out to the reef, chopping up the quiet water.

"I know," said Kate. "I know what you're going through."

"This Port Allamanda thing. It's not like the others, all this cash. And you can bet Grayson is going to be damned curious to know who beat him out. I want to shield you better than I've been doing."

"Well, you're the expert on that."

"Kate, I keep telling you. I'm no expert. On any of this."

"You're doing a hell of a job. You worry too much. It's going to give you something."

Captain Kate lined up on the wind sock rigged up on her dock, that and Carysfort light seven miles out. One hundred and twenty degrees took her into her own channel. Two degrees off either way and you'd be walking ashore across limestone beds and the backs of stingrays.

Kate cut back to half throttle; their wake caught up with them and rocked the boat lightly. In the narrow homemade channel, a hundred yards offshore.

"I'll get the lines," Sarah said, moving toward the ladder.

"Whoa. Let the lines rest." Kate backed off another notch, took off her dark fishing glasses, examined Sarah.

Sarah tried a smile, said, "I'm just paranoid. It's just a phase." She gestured down at the cockpit. "It gets to me sometimes."

Most of the fifty bales of marijuana were stored inside the cabin below, but four were in ice chests out in the sunny cockpit.

"Hell if it doesn't get to me, too. It'd be damned strange if it didn't. And my granddaddy smuggled rum most his life, and my daddy made his share of midnight runs. I keep telling myself it's my heritage, but that doesn't seem to help much." Kate rubbed her eyes, pinched the bridge of her nose, smoothed her forehead upward.

Kate said, "But we've gone over this. Again and again. Ends and means, the higher good. I can't see anything new to talk about. If there's something else, some way of doing something, change things around, anything you can think of that would take the pressure off, say the word and we'll do it. Buy the land some other way. Sell melons along the road. I don't care what, rob a Brink's truck. You come up with something better, tell me."

"No," Sarah said, suddenly sleepy and sheening again with sweat now that the breeze had stopped. "I just feel guilty, getting you involved in this."

"Hey, now." Kate smiled at her, leaned against the seat. "I got *you* involved. It may be your contact, but it's my fight."

"Let's don't bullshit each other," Sarah said. "I come to your meetings, like the stuff I hear, offer my legal services, and two months later I'm talking you into running dope."

Kate looked off at a passing dive boat headed for Grecian Rocks. "You didn't hypnotize me, hon. I'm a big girl. You think I hadn't thought of bringing in some bales before you showed up? Only reason I hadn't tried it before was if I went in with anybody down here, the whole island would know the next morning. As it is now, the gossip is we're a couple of sweethearts. Spending nights together on the boat."

Sarah laughed.

"I swear to the Lord above," Kate said. "Sweethearts, that's the word going around."

Sarah shook her head, grinning her thanks.

"We'll make it," Kate said. She winked at Sarah. "Two more fifty-bale trips. There's the million. And that's it. Walk away. Use the rest of our lives earning forgiveness." She took hold of Sarah's shoulders and straightened her up, looked up into her face. "But listen, this is *my* passion, *my* fight. You can drop this in a second and I'll sure understand. Think about it."

A rumble came from the south, growing quickly thunderous.

Kate pushed the throttle forward, making for the dock. Sarah scuttled down the ladder, cursing.

"Too late," Kate called to her as the roaring mosquito plane passed above them, twenty feet, clipping the mangrove tips, its contrail of blue diesel smoke and Malathion settling down, drifting into the mangrove shoots along the shoreline.

Sarah fanned the fog from in front of her, holding on to the chrome railing as she worked her way forward. Kate reversed and cut the wheel hard so the starboard side nudged up to the dock.

They set the spring lines. Sarah got her straw bag from the cabin, took her spinning rod from the rod holder behind the fighting chair, and jumped across.

"He flew right over us."

"He'll be back in about five minutes, fifty yards east. The bugs have been brutal lately. All this rain."

"Could he see anything?"

"What? Ice chests? That's Jerome Billings. I know his daddy. Known the boy all his life. He's a friend of Thorn's from high school. That boy must see more goings-on than God Himself. I never heard a peep of gossip out of him either. What's he going to see?"

The Sabrosa Seafood truck was parked under the gumbo-limbo beside Kate's back porch. Sarah hated this part. Her Spanish wasn't up to anything subtle, anything going wrong, the wrong amounts, a canceled deal. But it was Armando, good-looking in his orange tank top, who'd been the pickup the last two months. His English was better than Sarah's Spanish.

The mosquito plane was on its next pass, so Sarah waited under the thick tamarind tree until the poison had broken up. Armando joined her and nodded hello, both of them fanning for good air.

"How you live here with poison gas?" Their first personal conversation. She didn't want to prolong this, encourage anything more than just official exchanges. But she feared being abrupt.

"I live in Miami, but this is awful, no?" Her Spanglish.

"Oh," he said, checking her out now, lingering at the open throat of her work shirt, a flash of cleavage perhaps.

She said, "In Miami we put out enough poison at ground level."

"OK," he said. "That's OK."

"You *listo a pesar*?"

"*Sí.*"

"Well, *vamanos*."

Armando carried the first bale inside the styrofoam cooler. He dumped it in the back of the seafood truck and waited around for a minute or two in the shade, making eyes at her. Then back to the boat with the empty cooler, loaded the next one, and brought it ashore. The process was slow, but to any passing boat it would appear that someone was merely unloading a hefty catch.

Sarah hated it. The exposure was so great. Down the hundred-foot dock, thirty yards up the terrace to the canopy of trees, Armando making the trip fifty times. She stood in the shade during the whole ordeal, her eyes panning the horizon, her hearing fine-tuned for any passing plane. Their only concealment was their brazenness.

* * *

After showers she and Kate sat on the front porch, the Atlantic spread before them. Rum and Coke. Sarah's face coated with a layer of aloe jelly, fresh from Kate's yard. Just snap a leaf in half and smear it on. She rested her hands cautiously in her lap. Everything stung. Already the itch. Every time, no matter how thick the sunblock.

"Going to see Thorn?"

"Thought I would."

"This is his special weekend."

"Yeah, I know," Sarah said. "He took me along Friday night."

"He did?" Kate took a sip of her drink, eyeing Sarah.

"I asked him, and he said yes, and took me along."

"I'm amazed." She set her glass on the wicker table. "So, tell me about it. The ceremony."

Sarah smiled. "That's what I thought. But it wasn't anything very special. Sit out beside Lake Surprise, swat mosquitoes, pee in the shrubs, rewire the central nervous system. Just a lot of quiet. Staring at the dark."

"Not very sympathetic."

"I hear sad songs all week. I guess I don't have as much sympathy as I should."

Kate said, "Well, the boy's gotten better about it. Was a time his going out there every year made me mad, like he just couldn't let it go. Mournful, mopey."

"Losing parents like that. It couldn't be easy."

Kate gave her a curious look and said, "He never knew them. Dr. Bill and I took him in, he was only two weeks old. Oh, I don't know. I always thought he'd made it all into more than it should be. Let his grief steal him away. Like he was glorifying them too much."

"They weren't worth glorifying?"

"They were good people. Normal people."

"But they were his parents," said Sarah. "It doesn't matter if they were good or normal or what."

"Now you're sympathetic."

"I am. And I'm not."

"He tell you how it happened?"

"He hinted around," Sarah said. "But no, not much."

"His folks, coming home from the delivery room, a drunk kid ran them into the bay. They drowned, Thorn got bruised up pretty bad, and the kid went free."

Sarah swirled the ice in her drink, shifted in her chair.

"And Thorn? How old was he when he found out the details, the drunk getting off?"

"Just thirteen, fourteen."

Sarah nodded, considering it.

In a moment she said, "How'd he react? What'd he do?"

"Nothing," Kate said, her eyes on the horizon. "Oh, maybe he got a little more quiet after that. But he was always quiet."

"If somebody killed my parents, I don't know what I'd do."

"What *could* you do?" Kate said. "Dr. Bill and I, we were angry for a while. I think the doctor stayed angry for years. We even talked to a lawyer about it. But there was nothing to do."

"I'd want justice. Somehow. I would've located the

guy, confronted him, camped on his lawn, done something."

"No," Kate said, bringing up a hazy smile. "You think you would, but you wouldn't. My God, you and I are having trouble justifying smuggling that grass."

"I don't see it," said Sarah, "just letting something like that go."

"Thorn did," Kate said. "Goodness, is this a public defender I'm listening to?"

Sarah said, "You defend enough of them, you get cynical, you develop an appreciation for vigilantes."

Kate leaned away from Sarah and appraised her. "What in the world are we arguing about?"

"Nothing," Sarah said. She repeated it, almost a whisper.

Kate said, "I don't see you two, you know. I have trouble putting the two of you together. In the same room. Talking. Or anything."

Sarah swallowed some of her rum and Coke, raised her eyebrows. Smiling, she said, "I'm not right for your boy?"

"You're a city girl. I like you, but you come around here and I feel the screens vibrate. The Geiger counters all go berserk. Something's always humming ninety miles an hour with you. Maybe you act like Miss Placid, but there're those little pulsing arteries running up into your temples. Like it's all you can do to keep from screaming out something."

"The arteries, those are to keep the brain going," she said. "Occupational hazard."

Kate took a sip of her drink, carefully as though it might burn her lips.

"On the other hand," she said, "you seem to be helping Thorn come back to earth."

Sarah was silent, looking out at a brown pelican coasting low across the smooth Atlantic, its belly nearly skimming the surface.

She said, "I'm not sure I want that responsibility."

"He'd slunk off," said Kate. She stared down into her drink. "What's it called? Burned out?"

Sarah swung her head around. "Thorn! Burned out?"

"Well?"

"Look at me. Look at my face." Sarah let her expression go slack. "This is burnout. You get burned out from working too hard. Not from sitting around." Sarah smiled again, shook her head. "Thorn's something else. Stoned on silence. I don't know what, but it's not burned out."

Kate said, "Whatever it is, you seem to be having some effect. He's been coming around a lot lately. Talking. Got a haircut last week. First time since I can't remember when. And you won't believe this. He's coming to the public hearing Thursday night."

"Well, that *is* something," said Sarah. "At least that'll make three of us against the project."

"I wouldn't count on him cheering or stomping his feet. One step at a time." Kate fanned a mosquito away from her face. "But he does seem . . . I don't know what it is. Energized."

"He might be coming down with something," Sarah said.

"Yes," Kate said, a faint smile forming, "it looks as if he is. And he's very concerned about his looks all of a sudden. What do you suppose that could be?"

Kate held out her glass for a toast. Sarah clinked hers to it.

Sarah said, "You still don't want to bring him into this? Tell him what we're doing? Have him help with the dope?"

"We're managing."

"You don't think he'd approve," Sarah said. "What? He's too moral?"

"No," Kate said, "he'd help. But it would be for the wrong reason. You do something like this, take these risks, get your hands dirty, it should be for the right reason. Because it's worth doing whatever it takes to protect your home."

"You mean if he helped, it'd be because he loved you, wanted to protect you? Like that?"

"Yes," said Kate.

Sarah said, "That seems like a pretty good reason to do something to me. 'Cause you loved somebody."

Kate, watching the pelican make another pass, said, "I think of him as something of an artist. Those flies he makes." She took another sip. "They're not like anybody else's. I know that may not mean much to you, but, well, he's got something. A vision. Something." Kate watched a mosquito hover over her arm. She let it land and set its drill. With her fingernail she nudged the mosquito back into flight.

She said, "I'm just full of jabber today. Sound like a proud mama. It's this rum. You made these too strong again."

Sarah said, "So, tell me." She settled back into her chair. "Thorn says there aren't any other women in his life. I find that hard to believe."

"Oh, my," Kate said. "This *is* serious."

3

Sarah was wearing one of Thorn's T-shirts, a long gray one that came to her thighs. She had pulled a loaf of rye bread out of his refrigerator, put it under her arm, and was still poking around in there. She tore off a handful of grapes and popped them one by one into her mouth. While she chewed, she let the refrigerator door shut, opened the bread, and took out the top slices.

Thorn watched her, liking it all, liking her in that shirt, her hunger, the way her hair had not recovered from their lovemaking. Her skin, chapped by the sun. Most of all, he liked the way she seemed to be at home here in his one-room house.

"You don't have a toaster?" She didn't look back at

him but seemed to know he was watching, seemed to bask in it.

"I'm not much of a toast eater."

"I guess not." Sarah fiddled with the dial for the oven.

"Oven doesn't work either," Thorn said. "Just the back left burner."

"How quaint."

Thorn propped himself up on his elbows to give her a look. She smiled over at him, a somewhat drowsy one. In the fluttering light from the two hurricane lanterns her skin seemed coppery. A trick of light, for her skin was pearl white. A refreshing change for Thorn, even slightly exotic in this land of tans. He liked to watch his sunburned hands move across her white flesh. An eerie arousal.

Thorn asked, "How many burners do *you* have?"

"Four," she said. "And all of them work."

"Yeah, I can vouch."

"No, you can't, Thorn. Don't get carried away with yourself."

He let it pass. No reason to square off. Maybe she was right; they were cooking on less than maximum heat. Still, it was hotter than anything Thorn had ever known.

He said, "You are free in direct proportion to the number of burners you can do without."

"Well, if you want women to keep making house calls, you're going to have to upgrade your appliances."

"I thought you-all came for the view." Thorn rolled out of bed, came across to her.

A skeptical tilt of head, she said, "Withered, shriveled view that it is."

"It has its moments," said Thorn as he reached out and pulled her into an embrace, his skin still damp.

"Hmmmm." She hugged him hard, cartilage in his spine popping.

"Want to smoke another one?" He spoke into her shoulder, pressing his thigh into the subtle parting of her legs.

Stepping out of the embrace, she said, "I don't like people who smoke dope anymore."

"Me either," Thorn said. "But you couldn't call what we do smoking dope. Not exactly."

Sarah said, "I only smoke it with you. I thought you liked it."

"I like it OK. Take it or leave it. I thought you liked it," Thorn said. "Till you showed up, I hadn't smoked any for years. I still got a half a lid from 1978."

They smoked a joint out on his balcony, looking off at Blackwater Sound at the metronome blink of a channel marker for the intracoastal. A jet headed into Miami, also blinking, timing its beat to the channel marker. Thorn felt himself warming inside, the loosening of some clenched part of himself.

"For someone who doesn't smoke it, you always have the best shit," Thorn said, letting the smoke out gradually as he spoke.

She leaned forward in the oak rocker and took the joint back. Before she took her turn, she said, "One of the perks of working at the courthouse. The only perk, come to think."

"Hell of a perk. Perks me right up. Better than having all four burners going at once."

"It's good," she said, "but it's not that good."

"Do all the public defenders do drugs?"

"Ex-hippies. Every one of them. The state's attorneys are the worst. Judges, too. I know a couple of judges, they'll pitch a fit if you're prosecuting somebody for inferior dope. They sniff the stuff, shake their heads. They laugh prosecutors out of their office. Tell them to bring in some serious dope if they want a conviction. They do all this in chambers, and in court they'll just drop the case soon as a PD moves to dismiss."

Thorn smiled to himself. Out here in the night air, talking about things from the larger world. Not tides, not the migration of fish or the latest hot spot. A conversation, like he supposed normal people had.

Sarah said, "I can understand that. Got to draw the line somewhere. They got their pick of so many cases a day, why not just burn the guys bringing in the potent shit?"

"Hard to believe. Hard to believe," Thorn said. He paused, watched the marker light blink. Said, "I got to get you and my friend Sugarman together. I told you about him. Only black cop in the Keys? Well, this is his. Know how you can tell which ones are the drug dealers on the highway?"

She shook her head.

"They're the only ones doing the speed limit."

Sarah smiled, said, "Guys at work'll like that one."

"And Sugarman calls it the Veranda Act. The act that keeps you waiting out on the veranda while they flush all the dope down the johns. Funny guy, but he has no idea. Got no sense of humor. Everybody's always laughing at what he comes out with, and he's there saying, 'Huh, what, what's the joke?' "

"I like him."

Thorn said, "He'd like you," and slid his hand tightly down her shoulder, collarbone, ran his hands across the sides of her breasts, barely a touch at all. The worn cotton of the T-shirt was silky against his palms.

Sarah said, "He the one with wife troubles?"

"She's young," Thorn said. "And she's white. High school cheerleader marries all-county fullback. I don't think she even knew he was black till the summer after they were married."

Sarah told him that what he was doing felt good. Thorn's hand beneath the T-shirt, fingertips dialing her nipples, listening for the fall of tumblers.

Her eyes closed, she said, "You make these chairs?"

"No, Dr. Bill." He kept his fingers there, hovering, feeling her nipples rising against his palms.

"You called him that? Doctor?"

"Yeah. Everyone did."

"And Kate, what do you call her?"

"Always so many questions," Thorn said.

"It's a bad habit," she said. "My job."

She handed the joint back, and Thorn took his hands away from her, sat back in the chair, and drew in a harsh, deep drag and held it tight.

He let it out and handed her the roach. He was starting another surge. Blackwater Sound shimmered like licorice Jell-O. He felt seventeen. Foolish, on the edge of a panicky laugh.

"Well," Sarah said. "Dr. Bill made nice chairs. Nice chairs for a heart surgeon. The Cadillac of Cardiologists is what Kate calls him."

The dope didn't seem to be hitting her. Thorn heard her voice seem to come from out in the mangroves, out toward the channel marker. It sounded so cool, saying all the syllables, a radio voice, enunciating. It troubled him a little. He wanted her where he was.

He jumped as her hand touched his arm and lit up a welt of gooseflesh there.

"You perking, Thorn? You off somewhere?"

"I'm here," he said, hanging on, gripping the cypress armrest, his toes curling down for a hold on the porch.

"We could stay out here."

Thorn couldn't muster more than a nod. She stood up and sat down astraddle him. She crossed her arms in front of her, took hold of the T-shirt, and pulled it off. His face suddenly in the cool hollow between her large breasts. Thin-armed Sarah with heavyweight breasts. You never noticed because of the drapey styles she wore. But there they were. And there was Thorn, wondering who she was, who this beautiful, smart woman was, devoting so much time to him.

"I'd like to meet your parents sometime," Thorn said.

"OK." Nothing showing in her voice.

"I mean it," Thorn said. "I'd like to meet them. I'd like to see where you live. Visit you at work. Take you to lunch, pick you up after work, take you home. Everything."

"All right," she said. "Sometime soon. I'll give you the grand tour. Show you my turf." She smiled.

"Soon would be nice," Thorn said.

She massaged his scalp with her fingertips, his neck, a light touch, then a deep rub into the shoulder muscles. Thorn wasn't feeling seventeen anymore, much younger than that, younger than he'd ever been.

She drew parallel lines down either side of his spine, then under the wings of his shoulder bones, both hands into his armpits. Coiling the damp underarm hair into a single strand, drawing it into a tight spike, doing one armpit then the other. Thorn cooperated, his hands behind his head, exposing that hair for her. He felt himself reviving, rising into her darkness.

"I like you," he said.

"You should," she said. "I'm likeable."

It rose, and neither of them had to guide it into her. She made a small adjustment of hips to let it into the liquid flesh. He watched the channel marker across her shoulder, brought his rhythm closer and closer to it. Syncopation.

They were kissing. No borders. The channel marker still guiding his beat, even with his eyes closed. They *were* comfortable chairs. Accepting all the contours of his squirms. Her strong hands held his face, guided his mouth onto hers. Drew him against her mouth, tilted his head to an angle where their lips meshed perfectly. Thorn had never kissed this way before, such a sinking away, such a disappearance. His tongue becoming hers.

He had always been awake before. Alert behind closed lids. But this, the way her mouth seemed to draw him out of himself, this was kissing. This was why people kissed.

She was coaxing him deeper, drawing him upward. His hands still gripped behind his neck, holding himself in his own full nelson, her nipples now dragging across his cheeks and mouth, left, then right. A growl rising from him, the biting pain as he asked, and some gland within him grudgingly complied, to release for the third time that evening. And she beginning to whip her hair across her face. Arching back, and he hugged her, hugged his face into that damp hollow between her breasts, holding hard and letting go.

Afterward she looked down at his head as he buried his face between her breasts. She was not smiling anymore. Nothing in her face at all. She stared into his sun-bleached hair for a few moments, then lifted her eyes to the night sky. Her right arm still hugging him to her, keeping his face hidden against her chest, while she bit at a flake of cuticle on her left hand. Eyes roaming through the bright stars.

"You could open a practice down here." Thorn finished lacing his boat shoes. Looked at Sarah sitting at the table, plucking grapes. She'd finished her pan-fried toast already. The dawn was casting a bright wedge across the wood floor.

"Thorn," she said, a patient warning.

"There's plenty of sleaze down here need defending."

"And what?" she asked him, holding her coffee cup just below her face. "Live here at Walden Pond. Cook on one burner?"

"I'd consider a microwave, you move down here."

"You're just letting your androgen do your thinking. You know you don't want a woman living here. You're the Gandhi of Key Largo, a loincloth and sandals and one burner. Introduce a blow dryer into this monastery and you'd freak."

"I've been considering the virtues of blowing dry."

"It's better visiting you."

Thorn said, "Who am I, your once-a-month stud? Fish and screw and get back to the city?"

"I wouldn't call you a stud exactly," Sarah said, smiling. "Thorn, Thorn. Let's just go with it, one step at a time."

He said, "What's Kate been telling you about me anyway? That I'm some hermit? Don't get involved with me?"

"She tells me you're a guy who's made himself a paradise out here, making lures for the best bonefishermen in the world, and you're happy for the first time in your life."

"I've been happy lately." Thorn smiled at her. "It's an interesting feeling. Grows on you."

She stood up from the table, brushed crumbs of toast from the lap of her dress. "Well, I'd be happy to hear more. I want to know you. You know that. I'd like to hear the unexpurgated saga of Thorn." An awkward smile.

"That's nice. I like that."

"I'm interested," she said.

"That's nice," Thorn said. "I like it when you're interested. You turn me on when you're interested."

"Not now," she said. "I'm cutting it close as it is."

Thorn watched her gather her clothes. Roosters were

waking in his woods. The air was already changing from balmy to muggy. He watched her pack her things in her oversize straw purse.

Thorn said, "Maybe this is it. What if this is as unexpurgated as I get?"

"There's more to you. I know there is."

"OK, I'll work on it, come up with something spicy."

"The truth'll do fine," she said.

"I don't know," said Thorn. He moved over to the doorway, stood there, his eyes straying to the bay. "Maybe anonymous is better. You stir things up, go dredging around, things can get murky."

"We're at the point," Sarah said. "Either we get to know each other better, or we stall out, start sliding away from each other."

"Yeah," Thorn said. "I guess we are." He scratched at his beard, looked at her there on the edge of his bed, the straw purse in her lap. "There's a couple of things I could tell you," he said. "It'd help you know me better."

"Yeah?" Her hands laced in her lap, as if she were about to lift them to her face and pray.

"I don't want us to stall out," he said.

"Me either."

"OK," he said, nodding his head. "Next time. I show you mine, you show me yours."

She released her breath, stood, and came across to him. "Now you're all serious again," she said. With a finger at each corner of his mouth, she drew his lips into a smile. She put a quick, dry kiss on his cheek. "I'll see you Thursday night, the wood rat meeting."

He backed away a step, said with a grin, "When you and Kate are finished saving all the wood rats, what then? Buy them all little leisure suits?"

"Oh, God," she said, rolling her eyes. "Not you, too."

He followed her outside and stood out on the porch and watched her walk downstairs and get into her Trans Am. That car bothered him. It didn't suit her. Too flashy, too powerful. He waved to her as she swung the car around and started out. He listened to the V-eight rumble down his road and kept listening until he lost it in the general highway noise.

4

The Key Largo Elementary parking lot was filled. Kate parked her VW convertible on the grass out near the highway. Top down. Thorn asked her if she wanted to leave it like that. She looked up at the clear summer sky, said, yes, she'd just had the top repaired from the last public meeting. This way, if someone slashed anything, it would be just the seats.

Thorn walked between them, feeling spiffy in long pants for a change, an ironed shirt. Nodding at folks he knew, catching some of them with distressed looks as they saw Kate.

She had her silver hair back in a bun. Wore a white cotton dress and carried a yellow legal pad. Her bifocals were pushed up onto her forehead. And on his other side, Sarah. Tonight dressed like a lawyer. White long-sleeved blouse, sleeves rolled up, black straight skirt, black pumps. A no-nonsense expression. Her hair barely under control with three barrettes.

They entered the auditorium. A stage at one end, with a basketball goal cocked up above it. The big room also served as the cafeteria, and Thorn smelled the scent of fried food.

"Where are we on the program?" Sarah asked.

Kate said, "Near the end."

Thorn asked if that was good or bad.

"Both," Sarah said. "By then the hooters are warmed up. Or drunk. And a lot of people have gone home. But at least she'll have had a chance to hear the other speakers."

"Not that anything'll be new," Kate said.

They took seats in the last row. Chairs for seven-year-olds. Thorn had already been working up a case of awkwardness, and now these pint-sized chairs. His was yellow. He tried to find the right position in it. But the back kept catching him just below the shoulder blades. Sitting up straight, turning to the right, crossing his legs, finally settling on a forward lean, his elbows on his knees. Player on the bench ready to go into the game.

Thorn recognized some people from high school days. And there were retirees, some boat captains he knew. Lots of people he assumed were realtors because they all seemed to know each other and they were dressed for church.

Four men with bandanna scarfs and headbands and

grimed T-shirts took the chairs right in front of them. One of them still wore his leather sling, hammer, and measuring tape. The one in front of Thorn had a red beard. He set a six-pack of Miller on the floor at his feet, tore three cans loose, and passed them to his buddies.

Sarah took a deep breath, fanned her hand in front of her nose. Thorn sat back in his chair.

"End of the pay period," he whispered to her. "Low on Brillo."

"Mr. Natural lives on," she said, loud enough for them to hear.

Redbeard glanced over his shoulder, saw Kate. He leaned forward and whispered down the row to his buddies. While one by one they checked her out, redbeard twisted around and took in Sarah, then Thorn. Gave her a beefy smile.

"Want to move?" Thorn asked her.

"It'd be the same," she said.

At seven the program began. By seven-thirty Thorn's shirt was soaked. He had tried every position he could in that chair and was coming around for a second attempt at each one. Kate had stayed unmoving, her feet flat on the floor. Memorizing, it seemed to Thorn, the words of that first speaker.

For thirty minutes it had been Philip Grayson, a smug, compact guy, making the case in his patronizing Yankee voice for the group of investors trying to build Port Allamanda. Allamanda was a condominium community, but not just another hundred-unit glorified apartment complex. This was a small city. Over four hundred acres. A thousand units, complete shopping center, banks, a couple of marinas, a golf course. Fifteen miles of internal roads, its own sewage plant.

But the particular issue tonight was wood rats. The Key Largo wood rat had been designated by the federal government as an endangered species, and its last major stronghold in America was in the hardwood hammock where Grayson's investors wanted to build Port Allamanda. And the county commission had assembled to hear the will of the people.

Thorn knew wood rats. They weren't anything one way or the other to him. He'd caught one coming up the stairs of his stilt house once, lured by his shrimp gumbo, he supposed. Thorn had shooed it off, and that was that. And he'd come on them in the woods, seen them squirming back under their bed of leaves when he approached. He had no case for or against them. And was having a little problem warming to the issue.

Grayson had shown charts and graphs, aerial views, making his point that the wood rats wouldn't be wiped out. A lot of the tract in question would stay just as it was, with only minor variations, wooden walkways and one or two roads. His organization was willing to comply with this and that regulation.

Grayson made little jokes, calling the wood rat cute, saying he could understand why so many people were so worked up about such a cute thing. And then finishing up by saying how you had to weigh all of this very carefully. Weigh the future of the Key Largo wood rat against a new library, a new public park with a lighted baseball field, and not to mention, and here he paused, the first pause of the night. Gazing out at the crowd with his sharp metallic eyes. Not to mention, weighing that wood rat against jobs. Jobs!

The guys in the row in front of them stomped and cheered. And the rest of the audience joined in. Grayson gave a friendly wave and took his seat in the front row.

Thorn leaned across Sarah as the applause was dying and said, "Now how can you disagree with a guy like that?"

"Exactly," said Kate.

One of the county commissioners introduced the next speaker. The commissioners all sat at a cafeteria table off to one side of the podium. Two women, three men, making a show of taking notes.

This speaker was a local realtor, a young blond woman, her voice quivering a little from talking to five hundred adults. By that point it was standing room only. She started in on the U.S. Constitution, about how there were people among us tonight trying to take away our guaranteed property rights. She got from there to Communists and about how her husband had been wounded in Vietnam and now here she was doing her part. She finished up by describing an afternoon a couple of years earlier, when she'd been living in a mobile home park and she'd come into her baby daughter's room and found a wood rat in the crib with the little girl. Her voice almost broke as she recalled it. "That's the creature these people are trying to get you to give up the Constitution for."

Thorn glanced across at Kate during the applause. She was looking off at the wall of the cafeteria, at the posters left over from the spring semester. Crayon kids swimming, snorkeling. Blue and green parents in their boats catching sharks. The colors were the bright, fantastic primary colors of the reef.

Next it was a retired high school biology teacher with a New York accent. At first the row of carpenters in front of Thorn seemed edgy, ready to hoot. Then the teacher got past his preamble and into his proposal.

"You want wood rats? How many you self-appointed consecrationalists want?" he asked. "How many is right? You give me a figure and set aside an acre of land for me and I'll start a wood rat factory. Give you any number you want." He got the laughter he'd been after. Redbeard put his fingers in his mouth and made a piercing whistle. "Five hundred? A thousand? I dare you people to give me a number. What would it take to keep you happy? All I need is a number and I'm prepared to be the Henry Ford of rodents. Solve this whole damn dispute."

Sarah was tapping her foot, staring at her lap. Kate still looking at those posters. Thorn couldn't help smiling at Henry Ford, though he had enough sense to look away as he did it.

It was ten o'clock before Kate's turn came. Thorn was leaning against the back wall by then. Near the water fountain. Sarah had gone out to the breezeway and come back in several times, standing out there with the smokers, trying to cool off. Maybe half the original audience was left. Redbeard had gone out and come back with two more six-packs. Giving Thorn a look as he came back in.

So far there'd been only one speaker against the project. A seventy-five-year-old man. First off, he'd told the crowd how old he was and told them not to scream at him when he spoke his mind or else he might have a heart attack right there and his death would be on their hands. Then he started a ramble about how bad the fishing was now compared to forty years ago. How he used to pull ten-pound snappers out of bays and sounds that were dead empty now. About how there was a time you could cast off any part of the coastline from Key Largo to Key West and foul-hook your supper. He could remember when you could drive along the highway and look out at the water, before all the motels and those other things. He tried twice to say "condominium" and gave up.

It took him fifteen minutes to run dry of memories.

There was a stir when Kate walked down the aisle to the podium. One of the bandannas said something, and the crowd around him laughed. Thorn went over, took his same seat.

Kate introduced herself, said she represented a coalition of groups. She aligned her notes on the podium, took off her glasses, and set them on her notes. She glanced over at the posters again and came around in front of the podium.

Her pale blue eyes seemed twenty years younger than the rest of her. Silver hair back in a bun. She had a boxy but delicate face and had probably been considered a beauty for a few years when she was young. Now, at sixty-five, she was a serene but plain woman.

"Most of you have made up your minds already," she said, her voice fuller than Thorn had ever heard it.

Redbeard called out, "So whyn't you shut up and go home?"

Thorn nudged him in the back, and redbeard twisted around and gave Thorn a menacing look.

Thorn said quietly, "I want to hear this."

"Most of you," she said, "most of you are good people, thoughtful people. You've looked at this and you've decided. Between wood rats and libraries, we'll take libraries. We'll take a broader tax base. Growth. We're for human beings, not rats."

"Damn right!" one of redbeard's friends called out.

"I understand that. But I have just one question." Kate paused and looked back toward Thorn's section. "When are you going to be ready to draw the line? When will it be that someone will walk into a room like this and say, 'I'll trade you a library, I'll trade you a couple hundred temporary jobs for your last lobster'? Is that when you'll say no? Not lobsters. We *like* lobsters. Or make that sailfish. Or put in there grouper, snapper, trout. You name it."

"Sheeit," said redbeard to his cronies. "I'd trade my damn wife for a steady job."

Kate said, "This year it's wood rats. And you say, yes, we'll part with our wood rats. We'll take the library. We got bills and taxes, so we'll take jobs. Next year what'll it be? And five years from now? What I want, and what a whole lot of people like me want, is for all of us to draw the line here. Right here."

Thorn nudged redbeard again as he started making farting noises. His buddies rooting him on. Redbeard didn't even look back at Thorn. Thorn's chest tightened. His hands were sweaty.

"You heard Mr. Grayson call them cute," Kate said. "I wish to God they *were* cute. I wish they had big, dewy eyes and a button nose and long whiskers and they had a name that made them sound cuddly. But they don't. They're just simple, ordinary rodents, nothing special about them, nothing cute either. The only thing remotely special about them is that there are only a few hundred of them left on earth.

"Mr. Grayson's the one that's cute. He's coming in here, representing people you've never seen, people you won't ever see 'cause they're the kind of people who arrive in helicopters. They like this island. They think it'd be nice to live here for a week or two whenever it suited them, have a penthouse looking out at the ocean, have that penthouse and make a little money at the same time. And you can bet these people wouldn't care if that piece of land had the last bald eagles living on it. They'd still be in here trying to get you people to give away those eagles for a handful of jobs.

"I'm here to tell you I don't think that's cute," Kate said. "I think this gentleman's walked up to you and said, 'Can I trade you an ice cream cone for your baseball glove?' and you've looked at your old glove, one you've had for a long time and not given much thought to and you've looked at that cool, beautiful ice cream and you've said, 'Sure, of course.' "

She went back behind the podium, took hold of the sides of it, and leaned forward to the crowd.

"Tomorrow, after that ice cream cone has become something else entirely, you're wondering what's become of that glove you used to play with. That one you were planning to hand on to your kids. And then there'll be an afternoon your son or daughter asks you if you want to go out and pitch the ball and you start looking around for that glove and then you remember. You don't have it anymore. You traded it. You didn't think anything of it.''

Redbeard said, loud enough for the whole room to hear, ''What the *hell's* she talking about?''

Thorn took a handful of his hair, dragged his head back, and whispered into his ear, ''Let my mother finish her talk and then you and me'll go out in the grass.''

Thorn let him go, and redbeard scooted his chair halfway around, sized Thorn up, and said, ''You got it, asshole.''

Kate, looking back at Thorn, her eyes sending him signals. Thorn crossed his arms across his chest and smiled to her. She said, ''We've got numbers, facts, charts. We can show your taxes are going to go up, not down. We can show how many more cars there'll be between you and the grocery. How long the lines are going to be at the bank and the drugstore. We can tell you just how small the trickle coming out of your faucet will be as soon as they tap into the lines. But this whole thing isn't numbers. It's not numbers at all.''

Kate came around in front of the podium again, brought her legal pad and glasses with her. Faced these people.

''And it's not wood rats. And it's not condominiums, libraries, or jobs.'' Kate looked at Grayson, over at the county commissioners, out across the room of faces. ''This is about ice cream cones. Baseball gloves.''

Thorn and redbeard marched out to the dewy grass, Thorn's blood shining, fired by Kate's voice, not afraid or angry, just a pleasant warmth spreading through him. As they were squaring off, redbeard's friends gathering, Thorn noticed the size of redbeard's thick, vein-laced wrists, and he chuckled to himself. Her speech hadn't been *that* good.

Redbeard dropped his tool belt in the grass nearby, growled, and took a karate stance. Thorn swallowed, stood his ground, and brought his hands up. He fended off redbeard's first two punches and connected with one good right hand. Redbeard managed in the next few seconds to hit him with two jabs. And brought from somewhere out of the dark a roundhouse left that scattered new flecks of light into the sky. It was then that Billy Mason, an off-duty highway patrolman, broke it up and lifted Thorn up off the ground. Helped him dust off and guarded him till the carpenters sauntered away.

By the time Kate and Sarah made it through the departing crowd and reached the Volkswagen, Thorn's lips had begun to swell and he was sucking on a deep slice on the inside of his cheek.

He was sitting in the back seat, replaying the short fight, trying to fashion it into something noble. Kate and Sarah stopped before the car, regarded Thorn.

Kate said, "Will you look at this?" She shook her head and laid her hand on Thorn's shoulder. Gave him a light squeeze. "I inspired somebody anyway."

"Our hero, out winning votes," said Sarah. "Doing what he can for the cause."

Thorn tried to smile. Through his puffy lips he said, "The social skills are a little rusty. Give me time."

Kate said, "Might want to work on keeping the left up, too."

As they were getting in, Sarah made a retching noise and hauled up from the floor of the passenger seat a clear plastic bag. Dead rats.

Kate took it from her hand and held it up so the lights from the parking lot shone on it.

"Three brown rats," she said. "One wood rat."

She and Sarah looked at each other for a moment. Kate shook her head sadly and got out of the car, walked back across the parking lot, and dropped the bag into the school Dumpster. Sarah and Thorn were quiet. Thorn watched Kate come back across the dewy grass.

She started the car, and Thorn shifted sideways, resting his legs across the back seat. Sarah glanced back at him as they got under way. She smiled at him, but Thorn saw something in her face, a slight lift in her eyebrows, a flush that made him uneasy, as though his boxing workout had somehow aroused her.

A mile down the road Kate pulled the pins out of her hair, shaking her head to let the wind work it loose.

5

Kate Truman cut the thirty-two-foot Chris-Craft to an idle, still coasting forward, following the pathway of moonlight toward the east, out toward the shipping lanes. It'd been over a week since she'd had the boat out with Sarah, longer than she liked to leave the boat out of action, but everything was smooth, engine running without a murmur.

She took the big Chevy out of gear, watched the depth finder print out the bottom. The graph paper showed 60 feet, a gradual dropping away, then, as the vessel finished its coast, a plunge to 105, 110. The wall. Just east of Conch Reef, seven miles off Key Largo. Stacks of yellowtail, shadows of computer ink on the paper, marshaled just across the precipice, the larger ones halfway down the ledge.

"They're here," to no one.

She shut the engine off, went forward, and released the anchor. The current was running hard to the northeast. The stern would swing around, and they could lay their chum line right out across the edge of the wall.

Wary for a while, but after some glass minnows, a little macaroni, some menhaden oil, those fish would devour anything she dropped overboard. She'd seen nights the water had turned yellow with fish.

She made the anchor line fast. Alone, she might have stayed up on the bow, admiring. Moon still big, flat calm, a splash from flying fish or ballyhoo. Always something going on below the surface. She could use some of those Atlantic negative ions or whatever it was that granted you the peacefulness, the full, deep breath. There seemed to be a name for everything these days. Everything just biology and chemistry or a little trigonometry. Even the tranquilizing ocean, even tracking down the fish, all named, numbered, binaried.

But tonight she wasn't alone. Her anglers for the evening, Laurel and Hardy, or what, Gomez and Fernandez? The skinny, sweaty one handled the conversation; the fat one probably a Marielito, six months ashore, whispered. All he did, whisper, whisper. Maybe he'd had to sell his voice box for passage over.

Both of them in their black, shiny shirts. The Laurel one wearing mirror sunglasses, in case the moon flared up. Rings the size of brass knuckles. Street shoes. A diamond earring, for godsakes. Ten o'clock at night and dressed for the disco. She should have just turned them away at the dock. "You can't come aboard a fishing boat looking like Al Capone's nightmares."

Those people. Who bought all the black, shiny shirts before the new wave of Cubans arrived? It wasn't like she had anything going on against Cubans. There'd been Cuban fishing down here, living here all her life. But these new ones. They behaved by some other book.

The one with English had wanted to go yellowtailing. He'd called her up at home and said he wanted her to guide. Wouldn't be persuaded that yellowtailing was off. Very slow. Everything on the reef had been slow for most of June. Some Guatemalan freighter had run aground on Alligator Reef, and in the weeks that the tugs had been pulling at her, the water had gotten so milky all up and down the reef line, the fishing had died.

She told him no. She wouldn't take his money for just a boat ride. She was a billfish guide anyway. No meat fishing unless it was for Thorn and her, groceries. But with charters, it was strictly catch and release, except for the occasional trophy fish.

The Cuban wouldn't let go of it. Said he was down from New Jersey, came all this way to catch his favorite fish.

"No," she'd said. And she gave him the names of a couple of others she knew could use the work.

He'd said, "I want the best." And she asked him right back who had referred him to her.

"I forget her name," the Cuban had said. "But I have yellowtail once a long time ago, and I never forget it. It's a savory fish, the best. I like the best."

"Try one of those others. One of them'll find you fish."

"It was Roxy. Or like that. Said she was related. In Key West, where we eat breakfast."

"I have a daughter, Ricki."

"This is the one, then," he said, sounding in a hurry now to get past this name business.

"Ricki recommended me?" she said. Not like her, not at all.

"Say you always get fish. Yellowtail, anything."

"Well." Weakening.

"We'll not be trouble. Pay in front. Don't worry about us."

"All right," she'd said, only because of Ricki. 'Cause she wanted to see who these guys were Ricki would recommend her to, after all this time. Even a little touched that Ricki would give her name. Yes, touched. Otherwise, she'd already begun building a case against this guy.

She put the chum bag in, sprinkled some elbow macaroni overboard. Poured a half gallon of menhaden oil over. Watching the slick spread across the calm surface. More whispering, the big one hunched over his companion, a real speech this time. Neither of them particularly interested in the chumming.

When she was finished, she turned and motioned at the big guy, who was looking over the side, holding on to the rail. She asked if he was OK.

"He is unused to being on the water," said the little, skinny one. His mirror glasses full of moonlight. His hook nose the shape of a shark fin.

"Where does he usually fish?"

"I undertand what you mean"—this with a trace of José Jiménez. "He is catching fish most times before from bridges."

"Tell him if it gets any calmer than this, you could putt on it."

The short, curly-haired one spoke out loud to the big man. It wasn't Spanish, not Cuban, not Puerto Rican, nothing remotely Spanish. She'd heard the real thing all her life. This was something else.

She spilled some more macaroni onto the flat sea. Hands sweaty now. Not concentrating on the path the chum was taking. Eyes scanning, searching out lights. The two of them were watching her when she turned. She couldn't read their looks. The little one was wiping his hands on the seat of his dark pants. Then he clasped his hands and stretched them inside out.

He said to her, "All that shit in the water, doesn't it bring in sharks?" He'd taken off his mirror glasses, was holding them in his hand.

"It brings in yellowtail first," she said, shifting the bucket of glass minnow slush to her right hand. She felt a queasy shake begin in her stomach, sending a wobble into her legs.

"But the sharks," he said, smiling now with his eyes. The moon shining up his earring. "They come around, too. I want to see that. I like sharks. I like the idea of sharks."

The big one was staring at him.

"Let's catch us a goddamn shark. Forget this yellowtail shit." His accent gone. Just American, plain, flat, maybe Ohio, maybe Indiana. It was a hobby of hers, placing accents. With all the tourists, you got so you could hear it.

"I'll get the rods," she said, fighting with the wobble.

"This is them here." The little one motioned at the rocket launcher. It held two rigged yellowtail rods. Just that brass hook knotted onto twelve-pound test, no leader. Bahama rigging.

She said, "Those are bonefish rods. The yellowtail tackle's in here." She moved toward the cabin, not waiting for his permission. Pretending it was all going according to plan.

"Stay out here with us," the little one said, something new in his voice now. A little strain, something frayed, a whine but with anger in it.

"I'm getting the other rods."

"You're fucking staying out here in the fucking moonlight where I can fucking see you."

Where did they come from? Holsters under those tight nylon shirts? Two blue-black pistols, darker than the night around them. The big fellow was starting to bob around now, impatient, as if the boat were rocking or something. His pistol bobbing with him.

"I don't know about you, Irv," he said. "I don't fucking know about you sometimes."

"You got that right, boy. Call me unpredictable. Mr. unfucking-predictable."

"I don't like it, man. I don't like changing the plan in the middle of the things."

"Hey." The little one stepped over to him, watching Kate. "Hey." He slapped the big man on the cheek, half-playfully. "You got to learn to improvise, buddy.

You gonna ever learn how to be creative, you got to start letting go. Got to go with the flow."

"Which way's the flow fucking going, is what I want to know. I'm here, man, going with the fucking flow, and then the flow starts going somewhere else, you know. And it makes me a little nauseous."

"Everything makes you puke. You got puke for blood." Never taking an eye off Kate.

She'd run through her alternatives already. Dive into the cockpit, find her .38. Dive overboard. Rush them. Overboard seemed the best. But all that moonlight. Talk them out of whatever it was. She thought she knew what it was. Not much chance of talking somebody's hired help out of their job.

The panic had gone, the shiver in her legs, like stage fright. Now that the curtain had swept back, and here it was, her nightmare come alive, she was composed. The same practical calm that overtook her when the big reel was spinning, a marlin running. Slow-motion calm. Do this, then this.

"You're a pretty woman, you know that? For an old hag. How old are you anyway? Sixty-five, seventy? Gone dry, I bet, and me without nothing but reel grease in my tackle box. Hey, wouldn't that be just right? Screwed the charter boat captain with reel grease."

This man, Irv, took a couple of steps toward her, a little flounce, a cocky tilt of head.

"You like me? Even a little bit? It's all it takes with me, just to like me a little bit, and I supply all the rest. You know? I make a big impression on most of the women."

He'd closed to just a yard from her, his big partner

edging up behind him. Kate thought something was wrong with those eyes, some failure to focus, a glaze. Maybe drugs, maybe worse.

"You ever thought you're maybe upsetting the balance of things, doing a man's job like this? You know, yin and yang, when it gets out of whack, man, things start spinning. You start getting the white in the black and the black in the white, you're headed for big fucking trouble. Yin and yang, man, that's the thing where the white fish is chasing the black fish, or the black one's chasing the white one. Depends on how you look at it. But lady, if you were born yin, you fucking well stay yin. You don't get a shot at yang till the next go-round." The big guy had moved up to Irv's shoulder and was craning forward, staring at him.

"I hope you know what I'm talking about 'cause it'd be a shame for the last words you ever heard to be confusing. You should always understand the last thing you hear before you die, 'cause otherwise it starts the whole karma thing off on the wrong foot. Know what I mean? Do you?"

He'd lowered his gun. Kate straining to hear any nearby boat passing, or voices out there in the ocean, men fishing who might hear a scream.

"I had a mother, an old fart a lot like you, and she strutted around just like you. She wanted to have what a man has. You know what that is? What a man has. I'll show you. You've forgotten 'cause you're so old."

Only because it was in her hand already. She had no idea that five pounds of decomposing glassy minnows would hurt anybody; it was more a matter of making a statement, not being shot down with a bucket of ground-up fish in hand. Most of the goop went on the big one, but a lucky handful rode in on the little one's inhalation. He was looking down, trying to get his tight black pants unzipped. A mouthful of decomposing fish parts instead.

While he coughed, waving his pistol, she grabbed one of the yellowtail rods, gripped it like a baseball bat, and lunged it at the big one's face. The tip found his eye. Bent him over. She whipped the rod around and slashed at the little one, the boss, caught him on his upraised forearm, threw the whole thing at him, and scrambled to the cabin. Her .38 was in the first-aid drawer.

She got it open, heard the yelling behind her.

She ducked behind the swivel seat and fired at the door. The goddamn gun bucked so, she wasn't sure where the shot went, didn't know how to correct for the next one. She heard the big guy moaning about his eye.

She reached up for the microphone to the shortwave, nothing shielding her from the cockpit door but that swivel bucket seat. There wasn't much of a chance she'd come out of this. She'd made her peace, all that, years before, when the doctor died. But this wasn't just dying. This was something else.

She squeezed off another round, this one at his hand waving around the edge of the door. She heard him go. "Whoowee." A kid taunting. Then ducking his smily face around the corner of the door, and she jerked another round at that. Again too late.

Kate squeezed to her left, just to change the angle, make it harder on him. Maybe she could stay out here all night, three shots left, a standoff. Hope the echo of her shots had made it ashore.

But he was there again, standing fully exposed in the door. She fired twice, but he'd already jumped aside. Still mocking her, her sluggish reflexes. She had that one shell. But with two of them, she knew it was finished.

He was mumbling now. Something he meant to sound like Japanese. Something to raise her hackles, to haunt her, spook one more shot from her. Out there in the dark, his sidekick whimpered, as he did this phony Oriental gibberish.

Kate duck walked back to the swivel chair. She wanted a straight-on shot this time. Her knees ached, the squeak of her boat soles on that scrubbed deck.

His mirror glasses came around the corner, hovered, staring at her. She aimed carefully this time, cradling the .38 with her left hand, and exploded one of the shiny disks. The guy whooped, dropped the glasses. Another trick.

The click on six. Then the skinny one looked around the edge of the cabin door, smiling at her. In the movies they always threw the gun when it emptied. But they always missed. She did it anyway, aimed it at that smile in the moonlight, slung it like a throwing knife. It clattered across the deck.

The only thing left was the flare gun. She'd chance the fire, chance anything at this point. It was in with all the Coast Guard things and charts, the plastic whistle, a compass that had been the doctor's as a boy. She scrabbled among the junk, knowing it was taking too long, but not stopping at this point, going on through with it, the action completed, the statement made. It was there at last, the fat cartridge inside it, the gun broken open. She snapped it closed. An old lady, suddenly feeling fifteen, ready for this smily bastard.

As she turned, he disarmed her. That quick. He smiled at her and pinched her cheek. He went back to the cabin door and pitched the flare gun over the starboard side. This time she waited for him to return. She held the wheel with one hand, still captain of her vessel.

A breeze stirred through the cabin, ran cool across her damp shirt. She could hear the slap of the tide against the hull, feel the strain of the anchor line. The fishing would have been good. The silt from the grounded freighter seemed to have settled. Repairs well under way, everything settling back into place. The ocean, the reef, the fish, the powdery bottom.

Captain Kate Truman looked into his face. His painful smile.

"Lady, you ready to see this thing I got to show you? I know you're going to love it. The girls are just crazy about it."

Irv pressed the barrel of the .44 to her right shoulder joint, jammed it deep into the dry meat there. She didn't try to squirm away, and she kept her eyes on his, not daring him to shoot, but watching him, almost curious.

Milburn started the engines from the upper deck, and as they got under way, Irv kept her pressed against the control panel with the automatic. He didn't like those eyes. But he gave her back a look, trying to make it as hard as she was giving him.

When they were up on plane, the wind cooling things off, Milburn skimming them toward where they'd anchored their own boat, Irv fired a round into that shoulder joint. He didn't want her dead yet. He did it more to close those eyes than anything. He wanted her alive when he screwed her. He might be a little hard on women, but he wasn't any goddamn necrophiliac.

The gunshot surprised him, how loud it was, and he took some powder burns on his hand that scalded like shit. But her head fell back, and when he drew the barrel back and let her go, she slid down the panel to the floor.

When he'd finished with her, he stood up and cinched his pants. Her eyes were still closed, but he could see her staring wide-awake back of those lids. He let his singed hand dangle down with the .44, aiming it vaguely at her deflated old chest.

Irv was feeling sleepy. All that ocean air, all the excitement. His face was heavy, felt like Robert Mitchum's must feel, full of bags.

He looked down at Kate. He'd decided not to dump her body after all. Milburn would freak, but Irv'd decided to let her relatives and friends find out just how weak she'd turned out to be. Coming on like some old Conch charter boat cpatain, but look at her. Barely breathing, the gristle all gone. And leaving her body behind would give the cops one more complication, a little extra twist on the ball.

What were they going to do anyway, match up his dick prints? Run a make on his jism?

Irv had made her a happy lady, driven her a little crazy there at the end. He watched those closed lids, knew her eyes were flickering around behind them. He curled his finger against the trigger and sent her off to the land of dead old ladies.

6

Irving McMann built himself another vodka gimlet, to the brim of the squat glass. He carried it across to the sliding glass doors, sipping it down as he walked. The curtains were open. He gazed out across the third fairway. On the other side of the fairway was a narrow fringe of rough running along the seawall. Beyond that the channel out to the Atlantic. An early-morning squall in the distance out over the water.

Just a big water hazard was all the Atlantic Ocean was to most of the people at Coral Reef Club. Even the ones with yachts, what did they know about the ocean, about navigating? All the rich owners with their Vietnam vet captains, young guys who kept their boats going hot, straight, and normal while they were below wanking off or getting shit-faced. Irving's old man was one of those, so Irv knew what went on below while the captain stayed up on the tower listening to rock and roll, keeping his superior distance. Irving hated those guys, know-it-alls, with the "yes, sir, no, sir," military bearing. He hated them, and he hated the old red-faced farts like his old man who'd bought into chicken franchises at forty and now had the money machine pumping in high gear.

He hated them 'cause they were doing nothing with their lives, nothing of any creative purpose, but they gave him all kinds of shit about how he seemed to be fucking off all the time. Especially the goddamn captains, the guys his age. It was nothing specific they said; they wouldn't come out and insult Irv. They played their same ass-licking game with him they used on his father, always yes, sir, no, sir. But with Irv they had a hint of a smirk. He'd called them on it, caught them doing it to him. Even pointed it out to his old man. But his old man was always so fucking stoned, so grateful to have anybody around who could park his damned yacht without knocking down the dock that he just let it all go. Fucking burned Irving up. One of these days.

Irving gulped the gimlet. It was his third in the last hour. It was what, only nine o'clock? As usual neither of them could sleep after a job. They'd gotten back ashore about twelve last night, just been smoking dope, drinking, watching TV ever since.

It was That's No Way to Treat a Lady Week on Channel 8, so the two of them sat through *The Boston*

Strangler with Tony Curtis and a middle-aged Henry Fonda. Curtis kills all these women, and nobody has a clue about him; but he blows it by doing a robbery. Irving talked the whole way through it, saw it as a lesson to the two of them. Specialization was the only way these days. You get good at something, you stick to it, you learn it inside and out, refine the technique, become the fucking Nobel prizewinner at it. Milburn, moaning about his bloody eye the whole time, missing the point, hardly even bothered to watch it. And there it was, like a message from the gods, right to them.

Irving still smelled the fish stink on him, tasted the fucking minnow chum that she'd thrown at them. Rotting fish at every breath. What a scene. The gimlet hadn't covered it up. Listerine, Lavoris. He'd splashed Giorgio cologne all over himself, showered again, and more Giorgio. But the smell was still there. Like some kind of voodoo curse. You can kill me, but you'll smell like this forever.

And with Milburn whining and complaining all night, Irv was growing himself a category five headache.

"Let's go on down to Largo."

"The fucking doctor doesn't open till ten. What do you want, man? Sit out in the parking lot, let everybody have a good look at you with your goddamn bandage?"

Irv tossed back the rest of the gimlet, feeling the acid rise in his stomach as he swallowed. All in all, though, acid stomach and a headache were better than a slug in the chest, which it could've been if she'd been any kind of shooter. It sent him back to the wet bar just thinking about it. He'd cut it kind of close, maybe hammed it up a little too much at the end. No reason for it really, just felt like doing a scene.

"Don't yell at me, man," Milburn said, trying to muster a threatening tone. "You're the one should be down on his knees asking forgiveness. I'm going to lose this fucking eye for sure. Half blind, and for what? So you could play some movie scene, man, milk it for some kind of ego thing?"

Irving drew back his gimlet glass for a fastball down the gut, but Milburn flinched and looked so pathetic covering himself up on that checkered couch, there in his pink polo shirt and white pants, so much like a big, ugly girl in his stringy hair and bland white face that Irving didn't have the heart for it. Though the shit deserved it, if for nothing else, for that whine, whine, whine.

"You know you dig it, Milburn. You do. You're going in there and going to ask the doctor if you can wear a black eye patch. Tough guy, pirate eye patch. You're whining, but you love it. It's the first real thing that's happened in your measly life since I beat the shit out of you in prep school."

"Look," Milburn said. "It was a simple operation. We go out there, splat the old lady, dump the carcass, and get the fuck out of there. We sit down, figure it all out, agree on everything. We practically have it in writing, it's so definite. And we get out there and you fucking flip out and start some other goddamn scene. I mean, what's the point?

"I'm standing there not believing what I'm hearing, thinking maybe you've had a nervous breakdown or some shit. I mean, it's Jack Nicholson out there, flipping out like in that movie, going after his wife and kid in that hotel.''

''The Shining.''

''Yeah, that's it. It's like that. I think for a second I should shoot you, kill that fucking devil that's taken over inside of you. Man, like you were possessed.''

Irving took a hard look at Milburn over that.

''What are you talking about shooting, you fucking moron?''

''I'm just saying . . .'' Milburn shifted on the couch. ''I wouldn't do anything like that for real. Hell, no. But it's like you weren't normal.''

''You're goddamn right I'm not normal. If I was normal, I'd blow you away right now for saying what you just said.''

''It's like you become somebody else. It's like—I don't know. It's scary. You can't stay with the fucking plan.''

''The fucking plan, the fucking plan.'' Irving reached around and drew the curtains shut. Dramatic effect. Scare the big shit. ''What it is is a play.'' He wasn't so much angry anymore. Even a little relieved that Milburn had revealed his murder fantasy. Made it easier someday when he had to turn the gun on him, fill a slab with a slob.

''Some play,'' Milburn said. ''You shoot the fucking audience in the last act. I mean, who you doing this for? 'Cause if it's for me, this big production, forget it. I'm not applauding. You see me applauding? It doesn't win any Oscars from me. Do it the fuck like we talked about it. That's creative enough for me, believe it.''

Talking himself in deeper and deeper. Irving was

enjoying this. He liked talking about it. The postmortems. And he liked Milburn talking himself into a deep pit of shit. Make it real easy someday. Very little regret.

"I don't give a shit about you. I want to make you applaud, I'll slide a barrel up your butt."

"Who then? Who's it for? The hit? You doing it for the hit? She was real impressed, let me tell you. You scored big with that old lady, man. I mean it, she just loved the hell out of that routine."

"You're out of control."

"Listen to Mr. Mental Health."

"I'm an artist," said Irving, not giving a rat's ass anymore if Milburn laughed or not. He was up to here with Milburn anyway. "An artist looks at the script and goes it one better. The idea is to create, for its own sake. You play to the audience and you're dead. That just shows how stupid you are. An artist, it just rolls up out of him, like that, like you're just the channel, the conduit for the art. I don't plan this or that. It's spontaneous, but it's disciplined spontaneity. Premeditated spontaneity. Very Zen."

"Like I said, possessed."

"That's the reason you flunked out of college."

"The fuck it is." Milburn got off the couch, grimacing at the effort, rubbing at the edge of the bandage on his eye. "I flunked out 'cause of all the dope we were doing. Same as you."

"You were too stupid," Irving said, happy now, grinding his favorite asshole.

"Stupid," Milburn said. "Stupid, huh? What's your IQ? Mr. Jack Nicholson, Zen master. You know what it is, and I know what it is. What is it, above average?

Would you believe, ladies and gentlefolk, it is subnormal, a mere shadow of a brain, the very edge of handicapped, we're talking Down's syndrome here, way, way down."

"And you're the big Mensa hotshot with the hundred forty IQ and shit for brains."

"One hundred fifty-three. I'm the smart one in this group. You should be paying attention to me. You should be following my plan."

"You're a joke, Milburn. I heard this same speech, what, a hundred times? A hundred fucking times, and it never varies. You should be the leader; you should be rich like your daddy; you should be running this and that. Well, how come you're such a dirtbag then? How come you're not governor, or mayor, or even the head of the fucking garbage department? It's because you're such a fucking jerk, a wimp, and a goddamn whiner."

Milburn swallowed another Percodan from the bottle on the glass table, chased it with the rest of his St. Pauli's Girl. He sat down at the wet bar, threw a dart at the dart board. It hit the outer rim, hung for a second, and fell to the floor.

"All I'm saying is, it's a weird fucking thing to see when you start up with that Jack Nicholson shit."

"You love it. The whole thing. There we are, the ultimo Cubans. We had her fooled every way from Tuesday. I just wanted to see her face, man, when she finds out she'd been had. Tough old lady captain. Big billfish dyke. That's what it's all about, man, see their faces when you take off the mask and they see they been dancing with the devil.

"So don't give me your shit, man. If it wasn't for me

not following the fucking plan, we'd still be stoolies for Abe Philpot. You liked that? Flying around everywhere, tagging around behind Abe, looking mean? You want to go back to that? Waiting for fucking Abe's check every month to buy groceries? Man, if it wasn't for me coming up with our own plan, inventing things, we'd still be muscle for some two-bit real estate contractor, putting a barrel in some zoning official's ribs so Abe can build a couple of extra fucking stories on his condo. You want that? You want to get back to that kind of fucking, dim-witted life, being somebody's lackey? Man, I don't believe you sometimes. Mr. Plan Follower."

"I need to get down to the doctor, man." Milburn not whining now. The pain turning him serious. The sweat making a dark butterfly on the front of that pink shirt. He was probably right about that eye. He'd lose it. That old lady got the tip way in there, punctured the shit out of it.

Irving found the keys to the BMW. He felt fine, happy. Not so much the five thousand for the job. Shit, he'd given Ricki the bargain basement rate anyway. Five thousand, he got that every month from his old man. Smelled like fried chicken, every dollar of it.

But it was the idea of it, his profession. He was sailing now, a career in the fine arts. His name getting around where it mattered, people with money and some dirty little deal to do. People he'd met when he and Milburn had been Abe's goons were calling him up. New Jersey, Pennsylvania, all over the place. They remembered Irv, said they liked his style, his unfucking-predictabilities.

He felt good. Even getting fat Milburn on his feet and out the door. There were parts for a lifetime. Parts and parts and parts. He hadn't even scratched the goddamn surface.

7

The Puff, the Hard Puff, Wild Harry's Delight, the Muddler, Improved Nasty Charlie, the Horror, Bonebuster, Purple Shadow.

Thorn sat at his rolltop desk and looked up at the cork board where his collection of flies was displayed. It was quiet, still an hour till daybreak. He could finish maybe three Crazy Charlies before the roosters started in.

There was an old rooster and a young one that'd recently begun to debate over a brood of wild hens that lived in the mangrove woods that bordered his house. The chickens provided him with feathers for his flies, and the crowing coaxed him back to an earlier day when the Keys were more a cousin of South Georgia than

Miami's weekend playground and a tour stop on the Disney World circuit.

Captain Eddie would be showing up at dawn. Seven days a week he poled up to Thorn's dock, even at high tide, when there was water enough to use his engine, always wanting his half dozen assorted flies.

And after Eddie it would be Bill Martin, a retiree from Massachusetts, a professor of something or other who had discovered fly-fishing for bones and had acquired gradually the same reticence and sun-glazed stare of all bonefish addicts. And on like that all day, Thorn tying between their visits, never enough, always learning from them what was catching fish this week. And standing out on his coral dock, wondering with them why in the hell that little scrap of hokum brought those fish awake.

Crazy Charlie was the epoxy flat base fly he'd created in June. It skittered across the mud flats, trailing purple flasharoo, these Mylar strings that shook like tassels on a stripper's skirt. Silver beads from a key chain for eyes. A pinch of white squirrel fur for the body. Like a Martian roach. Glitter and flash, dressed for a twenty-first-century nightclub.

He had a desk full of animal fur, pelts, tails, whiskers, toenails. His friend Jerome Billings had a contract with the county to keep the dead animals off the highway. Thorn got his pick of the daily supply of highway cats and dogs, squirrels, raccoons, and rats. If the pelt were still fresh, Jerome would drop it by. Thorn gave him flies as payment, though he knew Jerome had never fished a day. Either Jerome sold them, or Thorn couldn't imagine, displayed them somewhere, used them in the bedroom? Scraping up squashed animals all day might have put a deep kink in there somewhere.

He laced the Crazy Charlie tight with the purple Mylar, tying a double turle knot and leaving a single thread, something to attach the last of the squirrel fur to. All glitter and flash, but a bonefish might smack that thing and rip off a hundred yards of line in about four seconds. All torque, that fish wouldn't waver or jump, just burn those reel bearings, one long frizz. The pole straining. Heart crawling up into the esophagus. Thorn had been there; he'd been there and been there. And now he was here.

He loosened the vise a notch and rotated the Crazy Charlie. That vise had cost him a couple of hundred. It was a custom job he'd designed with a machinist in Tavernier. It had a needle-nose vise, rubber-coated gripping surface, and a largemouth vise with a fine-tune setting so he could hold a hook without marring the finish. Beautiful little tool.

The vise was about the most expensive thing he owned. His house. A few tools. A trickle of cash to pay the lights, and more anytime he wanted to speed up production. A library card. The land was his. Taxes paid from the trust fund Dr. Bill had left. A little cash left for gas for his rusted-out '65 Cadillac Fleetwood, his Keys Cruiser.

It'd been Dr. Bill's final car and had just enough life left to make the journey down to Islamorada once a month for Mexican food. It was about that often that Thorn wanted a break from snapper, grouper, trout, lobster, his payments, or gifts, from the guides who knew who he was, where he was, and what he did better than anybody else in the Keys.

All of his two dozen regular customers could tie their own flies, often bringing one by so Thorn could admire. But Thorn could do something else, some bright tiny nightmare magic he could bring to that chenille, that pipe-cleaner body, the flourish of calf tail or rabbit fur or cat. His flies caught fish. And not one of them looked like anything real.

Let it drift down into the murky dull mud of a salt-water flat, down into the drab world of bonefish, that little wedge of clear epoxy with bead-chain eyes and a flare of calf tail, and drag that fantasy through the silt anywhere in the peripheral sight of a bone and it'd smack that thing and run that zinging line to Bimini.

Bones ate like paranoid schizophrenics. Scared of food half the time. Offer them a jumbo shrimp, flicking away in front of their noses, snap, they'd be gone into the fourth dimension. But flicker one of those garish little gremlins nearby and they just might gulp a ton of them. You never knew. Not even the best ever knew.

Far as Thorn could tell, it was a kind of voodoo. He didn't have any picture in mind, but he'd sit there at that old railroad desk, start pulling scraps of fur from pigeonholes, badger, possum, raccoon, horse, cow, dog. Get his clear nail polish ready, his bobbin, his scissors, his hackle pliers, holding, tying, looping, imagining. Three-eyed Louie came in a frenzy like that. No plan. But it emerged, three silver eyes across a bar in front, and for one whole June in 1979 it caught bones every day from Marathon to Card Sound. Then poof, it was over. The guides standing out on the dock, shaking their heads, grinning at the bounty, frowning at the ongoing search.

That was the great pleasure of this for Thorn. The

minor wacko variations. Permutations of eyes, head, body, tail. And always the barbless hook. There were a hundred thousand possible bonefish flies. Oh, hell, lots more than that. Nobody had found one that worked every time. Nobody ever would. The best bonefishermen in the world could go a week without having one on. They could pole across a hundred miles of flats, see a hundred tailing fish, lay a quiet line and a perfect lure right in their path, perfect presentation a hundred times, and that fish would rather starve.

Those guys were priests. They thought like priests. It meant whatever they thought they kept to themselves. When they did talk, they all talked alike, quiet as dust floating in church. And they had eyes burned hard and transparent by the sun off shallow water, from tracking ghosts with a ten-ton pull.

Thorn had been one of them for a decade. Back from his failed year at college, he'd started up. Nineteen and with about nineteen years of experience on the flats. Baptized out there. Knew how to be quiet and blend in. For ten years he tried to learn how to take money from strangers who knew how to do neither.

The lures, though, they were the real art. And as he moved through his twenties, he found it was tying flies, dreaming into life these surreal roaches, that sustained him.

At thirty he had quit guiding and started carving soap molds for his epoxy bodies, looking for the shape that slid across the bottom, glided and twitched with that rhythm he could picture but not describe.

Until Sarah had begun to change things, he'd been content with the hours of narrow focus. Willing to warm himself before these small, fiery creations. For years he'd stayed hidden away in the woods, the only action in his life happening deep inside. That had been enough. The silence. The reading. The food. The weather. The bonefish strikes. But now it wasn't. He was starting to feel a hunger. Lately he found his eyes drifting up from the desk, looking off.

God, Thorn couldn't believe it, but he'd even begun, at those moments, his eyes wandering out into the distance, to speak her name.

Thorn finished the Crazy Charlie. Set it beside the Flig and the Muddler he'd finished last night. Crazy Charlie—its knobby backbone was glossy purple. Iridescent trailers. Bug-eyed with a silver eyelet for a mouth. This one had a small disposition problem. Thorn noticed it now. One of its bead-chain eyes looked askance. Walleyed Charlie. It wasn't pleased, brought together like this.

Thorn broke the eye out of the epoxy body, touched the socket with another speck of clear nail polish, and reset the eye. There it was. A straight-ahead look. Smug, cocky even, but still vulnerable. Not an inch long, and nothing on it had ever met up with salt water before. But the thing would drift down to the marshy bottom and flicker into the dreams of the strongest, spookiest fish there was.

He stood and stretched, walked outside, and sat on his porch railing, watching the distant mangrove island lighten. His stilt-house was twenty feet from Blackwater Sound, a quiet bay rimmed with mangroves. His coral and limestone dock ran out a hundred feet into about two feet of water at high tide. Behind him the two sets of French doors he'd put in were opened, and a breeze stirred the musky air of his house. The smell of pelts, salt marshes, brackish air.

Dr. Bill had left him the house. When Thorn was still in high school, Dr. Bill had used it as a retreat. Just three miles south from their house, but still a getaway. Thorn had never even seen it till Dr. Bill died, and suddenly it was his.

It'd been full of carpentry tools, saws and the belt sanders he'd used to smooth off the edges of those molded, sculptured chairs. That was something else Thorn had never seen or known about till after the funeral. The furniture he'd grown up with had been country-simple, straight-backed oak chairs and round oak tables and plain oak breakfront.

Thorn had scoured his new house, searching for the sex magazines or leather harnesses, any secret that could've made Dr. Bill more than the tough, flat-sided man he seemed. It was just chairs.

Uncomfortable-looking things. Everyone who visited tried to avoid them. Without cushion or pad, they looked like the chairs in the corner of the classroom for the misbehaving kid. But once Thorn had coaxed a newcomer into one, they would sigh, go slack, close their eyes like they'd just eased into a warm bath. It was weird, because Dr. Bill had never been a rester, never been a coddler either. The chairs threw Dr. Bill out of focus.

Thorn kept a few of them, donated the rest to friends, the Salvation Army. "You sure you want to get rid of these? These aren't junk."

"Absolutely."

Now the one-room house was uncluttered. Plank

floors. No shades on the windows. He had an acre of buffer on both sides. He was about four hundred yards down a gravel road from U.S. 1. If anyone wanted a peep of him, they'd have to pole into the flats offshore.

He had a small collection of books, some poetry and sea stories left from childhood. He'd run two shelves for them above his bed and filled up the spaces between them with horse conchs, queen conchs, and cowries he'd salvaged from around the reefs twenty years before. There was a Frigidaire that Dr. Bill had kept stocked with Black Label, still chugging in one corner, and a sink next to it with a red checked skirt to cover the plumbing and Ajax and roach spray. Kate had given him an Oriental rug he laid out between the foot of his bed and the sunset porch. And there were two pole lamps with lampshades covered with nautical insignia, boat wheels, life preservers that an old girl friend had given him. The walls were pine paneling, Dade County pine, supposedly impervious to termites, though he'd been finding suspicious-looking wings in cobwebs the past few months.

There was a footlocker on one side of his bed where he kept his underwear and socks. And on the other side another footlocker, which was his nightstand and where he kept, wrapped in an oily rag, the blue Colt Python. Four-inch barrel, .357 magnum. The pistol he'd once dreamed of using on Dallas James.

8

Every load fired from it, every careful squeeze and bruised palm had been for Dallas James. He'd bought it late one night in the parking lot behind the Elks Club his junior year in high school. Hidden it from Kate and Dr. Bill, and had spent a year practicing with it in the woods. Hell of a wallop, made him flinch just to raise it toward the target. But wing somebody with that and he'd stay down, traumatize him out of action.

Thorn hadn't ever been proud of the Colt. Had never flaunted it in front of his buddies. It had always made him queasy to hold it, loaded, leather holster off. As if he were looking over the edge of a tall building. Legs drained. Heart wallowing. Afternoon after afternoon of his boyhood, he had forced himself to overcome that feeling in the woods south of his house.

He was only an average marksman, even with all those hours of shooting. He could never group more than four within a baseball-size circle, always wavered at least one round a few inches away. Passable, but nothing more.

Funny thing was, he'd left the Colt behind the day he hitched up to Miami to settle up finally with Dallas James. He hadn't even been tempted when the time came. All those afternoons in the woods fantasizing, that had just been to learn how hatred felt, to practice it, to learn to hold it up clear of the rest of the emotions. The .357 had been just a tool for doing that.

For the last few weeks he'd been meaning to make a present of the Colt to Sugarman or maybe take a boat ride out beyond the reef and feed it to the sea. But whenever he got ready to do it, he found he had no stomach for opening the trunk, touching it again after twenty years. He always discovered something important that needed doing.

When he finished the last Crazy Charlie, he went out onto his porch, leaned against the railing, and for a while he watched a heron standing in the shallows next to his dock. Its neck coiled, beak aimed at some shiny shadow. Finally, after minutes in that pose, it struck, nabbed a silver pinfish, and walked over to the mangroves in its stiff-legged gait.

Thorn walked down his stairs, humming, smiling as the words came back to him, phrase by phrase. "I Want to Hold Your Hand." Such a silly song, about such a silly feeling. He walked, humming the words, out the dock to the concrete picnic table on the point. He sat out there and looked east across the island to the sunrise sprouting through a wall of ragged clouds. Was this a rosy-fingered dawn? He'd never got that. Rosy-fingered? Never seen the fingers, but he'd kept looking. As Thorn watched, the clouds grew pink, their fringes darkened. He should ask Sarah about it. All that college. She'd know.

He stretched some creakiness out of his neck, stood, and touched his toes. Something to kick-start his heart. He'd been feeling it lately. The first nicks. Bruises taking too long to disappear, a burn in the knee joints in the morning. The squeaky wheels of the winged chariot gaining on him.

Sugarman's patrol car came crunching down his drive. Thorn waved him out to the dock. A part of the ritual of Saturdays. Sugarman, off from the barroom brawl shift, came over to wind down, shoot the shit, let the sun come up before going home. He was back in his off-duty things, cutoffs and a blue work shirt.

Sugarman went about six-three, leaner now than ten years ago. The only features he'd gotten from his black father were the black, coiled hair and the dark eyes. His skin was lighter than Thorn's tan. He had a straight, almost delicate nose and his mother's sharp cheek-bones. Long lashes. If Thorn had just seen this guy on the street, he would've guessed Sugarman put on a Lena Horne revue in some late night Key West bar.

"I brought the book back." He dropped the novel on the table and sat down with a sigh.

Thorn asked him how he'd liked it.

"Truth is, Thorn, I couldn't get into it. Got as far as him hitching down U.S. 1 on drugs."

"That's the first page."

"Yeah, well, I skipped around some, too. I'm sure it's a good book. I appreciate your loaning it to me and all. I don't know, I just didn't have any feel for the way it was going. The way it's written. It's like the sentences don't sound like anything I recognize."

"It's got Key West in it, fishing the flats, gunplay, all the stuff you like."

Sugarman shook his head sadly. "Jeannie read it. She flipped it open and started reading it out loud and what the hell. She came right to a place where two of them were going at it doggy style, and she asked me what kind of books you were trying to give me."

"Whoops."

"It's OK." Sugarman picked up the book and fanned himself with it. "You know Jeannie, hell, she's not against sex, but it's got to have a born-again thing in it. She read and read this book, and she said, 'Well, maybe it has some Bible references and maybe it doesn't.' "

Thorn laughed.

"Well, look at you," Sugarman said, reaching out and touching a finger to Thorn's bruised cheekbone. "I heard about this. Those wood rat meetings can get rough."

"Some nail whacker," said Thorn. "Giving Kate a hard time."

"You got to keep your left higher," Sugarman said.

"Kate's coaching me already." Thorn looked down at the darkened knuckles on his right hand. "So," he said, "what else is new on the Jeannie front? You getting that worked out?"

"I'll tell you, Thorn. It's just more horny ideas every day. This week it was all One Corinthians, Chapter Twelve." Sugarman drummed his fingers on the stone table, looked off at the bay. "About how there's parts of the body we think of as inferior, but God wants us to honor them, which she takes to mean my pecker. And I'm saying there's nothing inferior about my pecker, and she says that's exactly right, and she won't be satisfied until she's spent half the night down there, between my legs, doing everything she can think of to honor my pecker, talking to it, for chrissakes."

Trying to set a serious look on his face, Thorn said, "What's she say to it?"

"I don't know," Sugarman said. Worn out thinking about it. "She's down there talking to it, I can't hear her. She might have been praying with it."

"Maybe you should just lean back, enjoy it for what it is. Stop making a deal out of it."

"Yeah, I know." Sugarman stood up, combed his fingers through his hair. "This new minister at the church, Robert Redford type, he's got them in Bible study groups, all talking about sex and marriage and the kind of stuff you never thought you'd hear in a church."

"California comes to Key Largo," Thorn said. "It'll be hottub baptisms before you know it."

"I guess it's OK," Sugarman said. "It's sure perked up our sex life." He picked up the book again, looked at the jacket photo. Fanned himself with the book.

Thorn said, "You know, there are those would doubt you. Who'd think you are fantasizing all this about

Jeannie being a born-again nympho to cover up an empty sex life?''

"You want to see my pecker? It's in shreds. She's like this for, what, five months almost? In heat and more heat.'' Sugarman took his eyes out of focus, seemed to be revisiting the recent past.

"Or maybe you could just tell her straight out it's too much for you. That you'd rather go bowling. Maybe that's the thing, get her out bowling.'' Thorn thought, Good God, bowling!

Sugarman gave Thorn a halfhearted smile. "I couldn't do that. It's a religious thing now. It'd be like I didn't believe in God or something. What was it two weeks ago? Still Corinthians, Fifteen or something, that week it was about celestial bodies and terrestrial bodies and how there is glory in both of them. Glory, glory. I was in pain. That week, bad pain.''

"Well,'' Thorn said. "I don't know, man, I'm having a problem working up a lot of sympathy here. Maybe she just loves you. Ever think of that? Just loves you a whole lot.''

He considered it and said, "Yeah, well. It's not that bad, I guess. She's always there, cooks good, interested in my work, who's been beating up their wife, who's been brawling at the Caribbean Club. All the gossip. I never knew, man, how much gossip there was before I took this job.''

"Well, quit complaining so much,'' Thorn said, feeling a grin take shape. "Glory?''

"She'd yell it out. I shouldn't be telling you this stuff. But she'd yell out, 'Glory, glory.' Bucking around, 'glory, glory.' ''

"Stop, stop."

"How about you? We never talk about you, man. What're you hiding these days?"

"You mean, do I invite ladies over here to read the Bible?"

"How'd it work out with that weight lifter? Darcy?"

"Yeah, Darcy," Thorn said, managing a smile. "Where you been? That was finished in June. I was too puny for her. She was always complaining about my pecs, my lats. Pinching me, checking for body fat, like that."

"Better your pecs than your pecker," Sugarman said. "Well, what about that other one? Sally?"

"Sarah," said Thorn. "Things are good there. I like her."

Sugarman craned his head forward, peered at Thorn, crooking an eyebrow. "Is this the fever? Is this what I been noticing in my old buddy? His head lifted a little higher."

"What're you, a love narc? Gonna bust me for excessive smiling?"

"Hey," he said. "I should've known. You're all lit up. Friend should notice something like that, not need to be told."

Thorn said, "I have a lot of energy these days. I feel good."

"You always had energy."

"No, but this is different. This is real energy. That other, that was sublimation," Thorn said. "Driven, but not driving."

"You want to talk about this, you got to use words I know."

"I feel good, is all I'm saying. She makes me feel good."

"Well, now that's good." Sugarman leaned forward, stroking his chin like he wore a goatee there. Peering into Thorn's face. "But the question is, bud, do you make her feel good?"

Thorn inhaled, held it, gave Sugarman a cagey smile. "I think I do. It seems I do."

"A new man, Thorn. That's how you strike me." He clapped Thorn on the back.

"She's been pressuring me a little," Thorn said. "Tell her things about my past."

"What past?" Sugarman said. "You got no past. You been on this rock all your life."

"Yeah, well. About the accident. All that," Thorn said. "And hey, I got a past, things I'm not proud of. Things I haven't even told you, buddy."

"Yeah?" Sugarman said, leaning forward on his elbows. "So? You going to tell me or what?"

Thorn watched his fingers drumming on the table. He said, "No, I guess not."

"That good, huh," Sugarman said, cocking an eyebrow.

"You hide anything from Jeannie?"

"If I had anything to hide, I sure as hell would. She'd stand up in church and confess to everybody what it was."

"I mean, if it was something you weren't sure how she'd take it. She might leave you, it was that bad. Or you were worried if you didn't tell her, you'd have to leave her, 'cause there'd always be this vacant area, this lie between you."

"You're doing it again, man. Talking that way."

"I've found somebody, that's all it is, and I don't want to lose her."

"And just in time."

Thorn asked him, in time for what?

"Thorn, it's serious danger out there. I've been very worried for you. It's like you date these days you need a full-body condom."

Thorn laughed. "A what!"

"Lubricated on the inside so you can slip into it. Nipple end, like an air tank. I mean, it's just an idea I had. Might be a little awkward and all, but you could forget herpes, AIDS, all those new VDs. Stay in there till you find somebody's clean, and then you crawl out. Not just your pecker. Hands, mouth, the whole body."

"Great, Sugar." Thorn looking off at Blackwater Sound, at the dazzle of sunlight there. A breeze whisking the edges off the hot morning.

"We get all these pamphlets at the department. AIDS, VD stuff. All these people exchanging bodily fluids. Things of that nature. It's just an idea. A full-body condom. I think it might go."

Thorn said, "Yeah, and for down here, for the mosquitoes. Instead of bug spray. Man, I'd buy a dozen." Thorn told himself, what the hell, he'd rather be talking about Sarah some more, but this was all right. "And let's see. Yeah, you'd have to have different colors, too. A black one for fancy dinners. Pink for going down to Key West."

Sugarman laughed, a tear squeezing out of one eye. Thorn was flushed, feeling a giddy swell in his chest. "Sort of like a wet suit, but without any openings."

"Like galoshes, but all the way up," Sugarman said.

Thorn said, "You put it on like a sock hat, roll it all the way down."

Sugarman spurring him on: "Yeah, yeah."

Thorn said, "They could double as handcuffs, roll a big guy up in a little one."

The radio in the patrol car squawked, and Sugarman wiped his eyes, let go of a long sigh. "That's me, sounds like."

While he talked on the radio, Thorn watched the last pink bleed away from the eastern sky. A small flock of egrets drifted low over the hardwood hammock, floated down on the grassy lawn near the shore. Sugarman was having a long conversation with his squawk box.

Out on the edge of the flats Captain Ernie was poling across the low tide. Thorn stood up, waved out to him. He jogged back upstairs for Ernie's flies. Feeling a smile taking a firm hold. He stood up there before going in for the flies, relishing it. Like the windows were all thrown open, airing the place out.

When he returned, Sugarman was waiting for him at the bottom of the stairs. His face had gone empty, eyes lightless.

"Something's happened."

"I can *see* that," Thorn said. "At home?"

"No," Sugarman said. He started over, voice official. "Kate have a charter yesterday, you know of?"

"I don't know. I think so, yeah. She mentioned it."

"Did she mention the name of the party?"

"Sugar."

"Does she keep a logbook?"

"Sugar?"

Sugarman said, "Radabob Island. Coast Guard found

the *Heart Pounder* run aground. Sunrise this morning. Brought her to Pennekamp Park. Sally Spencer's got the body at the funeral home."

Thorn said nothing.

"She's dead, Thorn." Sugarman's eyes were cloudy. Professional mask gone. Just old Sugar. It lasted another few seconds. "Shot."

Thorn looked over at Captain Ernie tying up at the dock, slow, arthritic. Kate's age.

"They're keeping the boat at Pennekamp. Body'll stay at the funeral home for the autopsy."

Sugarman looking off at the treetops, the coconut palms fanning the light. Thorn felt groggy, something seeping out of him, a kind of amnesia.

Rosy-fingered dawn. Maybe the fingers were shafts of light through perforations in the clouds. Or clouds in the shapes of fingers dyed red by the sunrise. It was such a simple thing. He'd ask Sarah about it. She'd know something like that.

Thorn fishtailed into the parking lot at Spencer's Funeral Home, missed by a foot the white Cadillac hearse parked out along U.S. 1. Sugarman following with his blue light on.

The Fleetwood's brakes shrieked, gravel dust flooding into the car. Thorn sat for a moment, staring at the front of the pink building, gripping the steering wheel. The motor was off but still dieseling.

Sugarman at his door said, "You don't have to make ID. Spare yourself, man."

Thorn got his wind back. He climbed out, pushed past Sugarman, and went inside. His first time there since Dr. Bill. The room as cold and dim as a mile-deep cave. The same loud air conditioners, the same dark rug, same smell of something coppery.

Sally Spencer was standing in the middle of the dark foyer. Tall, blond, a narrow, sunken face. In cutoffs and a white T-shirt. Standing in his way. Thorn fought off the anger, the panic.

"Where is she, Sally?"

"I'm sorry, Thorn, I truly am," she said. She seemed to be edging him to her office up front. The walls in there covered with plaques. Thorn shrugged past her, started back into the dark hallway.

A tarpon was mounted on the wall back there. Sally's first husband had been a taxidermist. The narrow, shadowy hallway back to the operating room was decorated with his work. Trout, dolphin. A sailfish.

Halfway down the hall Sugarman had his hand on Thorn's shoulder, tugging him to a halt. Thorn swung around. Sent Sugarman backward with an open-handed shove to his chest.

The door to the operating room had no outside handle, so Thorn had to pry it open with his fingertips. Then he was in there. In the brightness. One of Sally's twin girls, about five years old, playing on the terrazzo floor. Red and blue blocks, building a skyscraper underneath one of the operating tables.

Sally's helper, a young guy with swept-back blond hair, wearing shorts and a polo shirt, was standing beside one of the surgical tables, watching Thorn. A fat, bald corpse lay naked on the table, tubes running into the dead man's jugular and out again, connected to a clear cylinder on the wall. Blood gurgling into the cylinder, rising fast. And the cylinder beside it was pumping an orange fluid back into the fat man. A black bumper sticker fixed to the wall beside the pump said, MORTICIANS DO IT LAST.

Thorn steadied himself against the table.

The blond kid scowled and told Thorn he wasn't allowed back here.

From the doorway Sally said, "She's in here. This way."

Sally and Sugarman stood aside as Thorn stepped into the small refrigerated room. Kate was laid out on a chrome rack, still in her fishing clothes. A dark tear through the breast pocket of her khaki shirt. Another hole in the shoulder. Dark stains there surrounding the ragged holes. Her face painted white. Her belt undone, pants ripped at the button.

Thorn stared at her through the steam of his breath. Her expression. Consternation. A serious concern, but not angry. He'd seen this look all his life. Already the forgiveness blurring her frown. A blessing, not a curse, forming on her lips.

Kate's house was all windows, louvered shutters on all of them, but still bright. Furniture from nameless periods, everything comfortable, cotton, pastels. Wood floors, wood walls, beams exposed, a paddle fan stirring the warmth. There were no chairs, only couches in her living room. Four of them, simple squarish things, you could sit five without touching. Covering most of the living room wood floor was a heavy straw rug.

A philodendron vine was growing from a wine jug by one of the front windows, and the vine had made a complete circuit of the room and was starting to lap itself, running along the doorframes and above the window, rising up to twine around the ceiling beams in a couple of places and drooping over the hearth. As though it had spent its years searching for a way out to the sun.

Thorn stood in the middle of the room, Sugarman waiting behind him. It had been Sugarman's suggestion to come over here after the funeral home, to start the investigation. Thorn had come, but it seemed wrong to him now, to be standing there where her scent, maybe even her breath, still lingered.

There were framed photographs on one wall of the living room. Fishing trips mostly. Prizes, everybody dressed in khaki, all with long-billed hats, usually the men unshaven, the women beaming. Dockside weigh-ins, or out on the water, nine-pound sea trout held up by the mouth at fishing camps, a few from Alaska taken before Thorn, before Ricki. A primitive table where the Eskimo guides were cleaning walleyed pike while Dr. Bill and Kate and some friends laughed, drank, and smoked.

Some of Thorn, blond flattop, rawboned thin, holding up grouper he could still remember boating, and then later as a young man, his first season as a guide, looking serious, standing on the rear platform of his skiff with his pole in hand, all in khaki, long-billed hat.

Thorn watched as Sugarman made a quick inspection of the gallery. Thorn sat on the couch where he'd done his homework as a boy, the one that looked out across the seawall toward Carysfort light.

That was how his nights had been once, read a little Thoreau, do some algebra, and look up, shifting his body so he could see through the louvers the fragile pulse of that marker light, and let his mind roam, first out the twelve miles to the reef and then pushing farther, out past the shipping lanes into a world he pictured as gaudy and loud, chaotic. Bright colors and horns honking, exotic vegetables and market stalls, and water, clear and deep and shadowy, an ocean of fish, larger and more powerful than those he had hauled to light. Beyond the reef.

From that same couch Thorn had told Kate and Dr. Bill that he was getting the hell off that rock. Twenty, a year of guiding behind him. Ready for the gaudy world.

His time away had lasted three months, one semester at Johns Hopkins. It was the only school Thorn had heard of, where Dr. Bill had done his medical degree. One semester of listening to bearded grad students talk about Vietnam instead of whatever courses they were being paid to teach.

Three months of seeing Dallas James every time he shut his eyes, the blood spilling out of him, Thorn wondering if the burn in his gut was guilt or satisfaction. Three months of drinking at wharfside bars and listening to fishermen talk, a language whose words sounded familiar but whose rhythms were all different. Finally hitching home before exams.

Thorn had been sick of hearing about a war he hadn't even known existed. Worn out from staring all night at anatomy texts and coming to class in the morning to find the instructor had gone down to Washington to a protest march. Sick of the brittle weather, the smell of not enough air in the air, even disappointed with the waterfront, not the same Atlantic as he knew. This one dark and chilly, opaque as oil.

Sugarman asked him if he was ready to discuss this.

"Not really," Thorn said. "Not really."

Sugarman nodded, sat down on the couch opposite him. "I called Ricki from the funeral home," he said. "I told her. I hope you don't mind. I was doing it according to the book, next of kin."

Thorn swallowed, trying hard to come around. "So, how'd she sound?"

"You know, like Ricki."

"I know," Thorn said, "smartass." He brought his head up, straightened his back against the couch.

"Yeah," said Sugarman. "I got the impression she wasn't going to spend the afternoon crying."

"You remember how Ricki was. She's still that way."

"I remember her friends," Sugarman said. "I was in love with one of them. I can't even remember her name. Short girl. Had a tattoo on her forearm, a heart with a dagger sticking into it. I used to look at that."

"Brenda. Brenda something. I remember her. That's how Ricki was. Still got friends like that. Only worse."

"I used to stare at her, Brenda. What were they, punks?"

"I don't know. Late beats, maybe. Early hippies. Something. That stuff gets all twisted around by the time it gets to the Keys. Who knows? I think Ricki just considered herself butch, big mama for all the outcasts. Did it to drive Kate crazy, I think."

"Pretty girl like Ricki, with hoods like that." Sugarman wiped the sweat gleaming on his forehead. "You want to sit out on the porch? Might be cooler."

"In here's OK."

Sugarman glanced over at the wall of photographs again.

"Those were some days," Sugarman said. "You know back then a cop's life looked good to me. People didn't bother the cops about little stuff. A little bar brawl. Some broken furniture. Hell, don't worry old Morty. He's probably listening to a ball game or the gospel hour at the station and wouldn't come out till it's over anyway. Not like today, hell. With nine-one-one, every time a baby's howling with diaper rash, the neighbors call in a child abuse. Dog barking? Punch nine-one-one. You know I blame it on these push-button phones. It's too easy. Used to be to dial a nine or a zero took a commitment. Now you punch it, it's like any other number."

"I guess I'm ready, Sugar, get going with this."

Sugarman put his coffee down, looked pained at Thorn. Slipped his wedding ring off and slid it back on. "I'm sorry, buddy. I feel like I been run over. I'm not thinking real clear. Talking about Brenda, all that."

"It's OK, Sugar. I understand."

"Well," Sugarman said, starting over now, watching Thorn close. "Ricki said, she wanted to know was there going to be a funeral."

Thorn said, "She's already thinking about that?"

"I said probably, far as I knew."

"Kate never said what she wanted. Dr. Bill was cremated. Dumped at sea. I guess that's the thing. What else is there? That or dynamite a hole in the limestone behind the goddamn house."

A flock of ibis was grazing on the lawn, poking at palmetto bugs, silk spiders. Thorn stared at his hands.

He could still feel the jolt from shoving Sugarman. Second time in twenty years he'd used his hands that way. Sugarman and the nail whacker, all in one week.

He felt it rising in him. A hot surge. He wanted to wait, push it back down until a better time. This was still business. Questions. Answers.

Sugarman rose from the couch, sniffed. Put his sunglasses on. He cleared his throat and said, "I need to see that logbook. Wherever she might've kept records on her charters. Then I got to go take a look at the boat. There's a couple of things there got us puzzled."

"Like what?"

"It's just something. Nothing, really. Let's look around for that logbook."

Thorn said, "Don't keep hovering, Sugar, looking at me like that. I'm doing OK. It's OK."

There was a leather-bound logbook on her desk, but the last entry was two years earlier. Thorn browsed through the desk drawers, not stopping for the photos or matchbooks, the old report cards, diplomas, certificates for this and that. Later. He'd manage that next week.

Sugarman wandered through the kitchen, opening drawers, looking around the telephone for addresses, notes. He brought the Sierra Club calendar out to the living room.

"Your friend Sarah. What's her last name?"

"Ryan."

"Yeah," Sugarman said. He put the calendar on the desk in front of Thorn. July. "She spent a lot of time with Kate. Twice a month, says here."

"Hmmm."

"What? That surprise you?"

"Some," said Thorn. "I knew she was here once a month, but more than that, no."

Sugarman massaged his forehead. "Says here she was out with Kate last Sunday."

"Yeah, I saw her last weekend. And Thursday, she was down again for that wood rat meeting."

"Then there's this on Friday. 'YT.' Know what that is? Somebody's name?"

Thorn thought about it.

"Yellowtail," he said.

"I didn't know Kate chartered out for yellowtail."

"She and I, we yellowtailed some. But not charters. Not as far as I know."

"Does, uh, Sarah strike you as maybe a little left of center? Maybe outside the law a little?"

"How's that?"

"I don't know, Thorn. I'm not real good at this, to tell the truth. Bullshitting, wheedling things out of people. I can't get used to it."

"What's the story, Sugar? Go on, tell me."

Sugarman sat down on the couch across from Thorn, squared off to face him. "There's dope, marijuana, all over the *Heart Pounder.* Stems, leaves. Seeds. A half a pound scattered all over the deck. We're sitting on that so the DEA guys don't swarm all over this, but I don't think we can do that much longer."

Thorn was quiet.

"So, I see this calendar. Sarah down here twice a month, and I think maybe they're doing a little contraband. Going out to some mother ship. Like a hobby."

"Sugar, what in the hell are you talking about? Kate! Kate? And Sarah? She's a public defender, for godsakes."

"I'm just telling you what there is. How it appears at this moment. Sheriff'd have my ass if he knew I was even letting you in on this. He's only letting me have a piece of this 'cause I'm close to you."

"You can't believe this. Kate? Dope?"

"There's the remains of a bale. Plastic garbage bag, strapping tape holding it together."

"Come on."

"There's other things it could be," said Sugarman. "She could've been out there. Seen a bale floating by, picked it up, and the owner might've wanted it back. Or she's out there with somebody fishing, here comes a bale. Her charter hauls it out; she tells him no, they argue. Bang. It doesn't have to be she's running dope. But the fact is, Thorn, there's some high-quality pot scattered all over that boat."

"It's a plant then."

"It could be that." Sugar shook his head, went over to the couch facing the Atlantic.

"She had money," Thorn said. "What would she be doing running dope?"

"She talk to you about her money situation ever?"

"No."

"Well..."

"She owned Vacation Island. That place is worth millions. She and Dr. Bill had investments all over. What kind of shit is this?"

"OK, OK," Sugarman said. He shifted around on the couch, glanced back at the wall of photographs.

"I'm going to have to talk to Sarah. You know how to reach her?"

"Yeah," Thorn said. "I have a number for her."

Sugarman said, "Look, I hate this. I hate the whole thing. If Kate was killed by somebody in the drug business down here, we'll find out. If it was something else, we're going to find out. But we *will* find out. And, Thorn, we got to go where it leads us. I can't rule out something just because I don't want to think about Kate running grass. Christ, man. Last month I had to bust the Baptist minister. Drying out a bale in his backyard. The sucker found it fishing, just brought it on home. I mean, it gets so nobody thinks of the stuff as illegal. It's just this thing, like broccoli; only it's worth a bunch of money."

"I need a minute," Thorn said. "Give me a minute, Sugar." Feeling it coming now.

Thorn got up and walked down the main hall. His old bedroom. A view north into Hurricane Lagoon. He closed the door and lay on his old bed. He shut his eyes. Let it rise inside him, food up into his throat. A kind of panic. Dry at first. Almost an experimental sob. Then it came. Like an old friend back from a voyage. He covered his face with the pillow and let it take him.

Outside, the usual summer afternoon buildup off the Everglades was darkening the sky above Miami. Blue-black clouds. In Hurrican Lagoon a barracuda was feeding on the glassy minnows, the calm water boiling in spots as though someone had thrown a handful of buckshot into it. Then it was quiet.

10

Ricki Truman propped herself up with a pillow, watched Grayson. He was in the rattan chair, the throne kind, his eyes on the view out that third-story window. La Concha Hotel, treetops, the old Coca-Cola plant. When the wind was strong from the east, brushing back the trees, a slab of the Atlantic was there. Grayson watched the view, recovering from the view he'd just had.

She didn't like this, letting him watch her with another girl, but it was rent. Or it had started as rent, a monthly thing. She'd tried to keep it to just once a month, but lately Grayson was around every weekend, fixing things, always seeing if he could catch another session. She didn't like it, but she liked what it gave her, more than rent, a good tight clutch on Grayson's short hairs.

Maybe, just possibly, this was the last time. Kate's will should be settled soon. Grayson had said six to eight weeks was considered normal. Cases like this one, without any problems. Only when there was a large family, squabbling, dissension. That could last for years. Or like Howard Hughes, somebody so rich and known every hitchhiker thought he should be made a baron of some little corner of the kingdom. Kate never picked up hitchhikers. Unless you counted Thorn.

Ricki certainly didn't count him. For one thing, he wasn't blood family. And anyway, Christ, what would he want with money, land, any of it? He'd been wearing the same shorts, sandals, the same exact pair for fifteen years. No, Thorn was no problem.

Grayson brushed the pants of his banker suit. Only guy in Key West dressed like he was headed for Queen Elizabeth's for supper. People considered him a local eccentric for that, one more quirk of quirkdom. He didn't own a pair of shorts or a T-shirt, far as she knew. Tell the truth, Grayson was quirkier than anyone she knew. Sitting there watching her and a friend making out, never blinked, never played with himself. Ricki had never even seen a bulge.

But then, when they were finished, tired of faking it for this jerk, he'd just stay there, sitting, gazing out that window, mopping his face with a red bandanna he brought along. Some fantasy working overtime. Not a word spoken, never came across the room from that rattan chair by the window. But instead going way back into some kid's dream, or maybe some other lifetime, his eyes not looking sharp or crafty or quick anymore, but lazy, drifting. It was something to watch.

A couple of her girl friends actually requested return engagements. "That guy? The cute lawyer owns Sandpiper Bay Club? That Grayson? I heard about him, but I never knew what he looked like."

"Yeah, but don't let it get around. People might think I was some slut, doing it in front of a major loot and plunder developer."

Ricki put on the green kimono. A present from one of her girl friends' ex-husbands. When Ricki added it up, it was like half what she had came from her friends' divorces. Weird.

Kate, rich as she was, let Ricki waitress in Key West, just get by. Depending on divorce charity. It made Ricki furious every time she let the thoughts come.

All that money Dr. Bill had put away, all that cash coming from Vacation Island, and Kate living like a derelict. And there was Ricki having to take omelet orders from ignorant Canadians, zonked on bloody marys at nine in the morning. For what? What the hell did Kate have in mind? Character building? Ricki figured it was just one more eccentric trip, one more quirk in a world of quirks. Probably had all the money stuffed into mattresses. But that was all done with now, thank whatever Lord there was.

"How much you think it'll be?" Ricki sat on the edge of the water bed, sloshing it lightly with her hand. Grayson was back from heaven. Tie straight, pants smoothed.

Hammering from the house next door. Another bed-

and-breakfast hotel was going in there, another Conch moving north with a suitcase full of cash. A bunch of gay carpenters, trim and sunburned, a few feet outside her upstairs window, were moving around like spiders all over that dilapidated house.

"You ever get tired of thinking about being rich?"

Ricki said, "I'm thinking about buying an island somewhere."

He shook his head. "You live on an island already."

"I mean an island island. Cut off, no phones, no tourists. No planes in. Nobody selling T-shirts with the name of the island on it or some dead writer's picture."

"No food," said Grayson. "No batteries for vibrators."

There it was. His cute shot. She let it go.

A power saw screamed. More hammering. Ricki waited till it had passed for a moment.

"OK, so what happens next?"

"This is a bedtime story for you, isn't it? Got to hear it over and over. Recite it for me, Daddy."

"Screw you," Ricki said. "The first thing is, I'll get a call from the lawyer for the estate. Probably one of your buddies."

"I doubt that. My buddies don't practice south of Philadelphia."

Grayson stood, checked his fly, brushed some lint from a shoulder. "And anyway, I don't do Florida inheritance work. Strictly real estate."

"And you don't give a shit, anyway, at this point, huh? Even to help me know where I stand."

He was at the window, looking down on the work next door, at the scaffold, the young men changing the

Conch house from bright white to muted salmon. Restoring something that had never been there.

"Ricki, we've been over this and over it again. I don't know what anyone's bank account is. I have no idea what anyone has put into their will."

"I need three thousand bucks."

"What?" He turned from the window.

"I need three thousand right away, to pay for it."

"Hey, look," Grayson said.

"I'm serious. Those guys. You know who I mean."

"I don't want to talk about this. Any of it. It's your business. If you've got some business with two guys who you owe three thousand, then I suggest you pay them the three."

"My money won't be here till after probate or whatever. These guys don't wait six to eight weeks. I paid two up front, all I had in the bank. I had to borrow half of that. I thought they'd wait for the rest of it."

"I don't want to hear this."

"I need three thousand."

"This is your action. If you made a contract with two guys to render services and that service was rendered, then you have to pay them. The law is damn simple on that. If you stated in that contract that payment was contingent on future funds being released to you, six to eight weeks, then they should honor that understanding."

"I assumed they could wait. We never said anything about it."

"That's different."

"I need the money, Gray. This is Tuesday, the what?"

"Sixteenth, July."

"They said by the twentieth. That's Saturday, this Saturday."

"Jesus, Ricki. You spring this on me. I can't believe you." He strayed across the room. Hammers picking up a beat, staying with it. It sounded to Ricki like a TV headache commercial.

"What's three thousand to you?"

Grayson combed his hair in the rattan-framed mirror. All of it was his ex-furniture. Ricki always tried to rent from lawyers. You get the furnishings they bought on the way up. Their discards were better than anything Ricki could afford. But those days were almost done. Her ship was coming in now, almost in the harbor. Loaded to the gunwales.

"You going to just let these guys crawl over me?"

"Ricki, Ricki."

"You know I can pay you back."

"That's hardly the point."

"What's the fucking point then?" Ricki stood up, knotted the kimono tight.

"I can't help you."

"Oh, yeah," Ricki said. "I get it. You put the idea in my head to make all this happen. Slip me a couple of, what did you call them, possibly useful phone numbers? Get me all involved, do all the work. Put me out front with my hands very dirty, and now, soon as this little chunk of land falls into your lap, you leave me standing out here, fucked. Two guys wanting to collect their pay. Two guys, it makes me wonder how you have their phone number."

"Now, Ricki, let's get this real clear what happened. You wanted something to happen in your life, so everything would be easier for you.'' He put his comb in his vest pocket. Checked himself out one more time before turning to give her his full frontal. The pompous-lawyer voice starting to rise in him. "All I hear from the minute I meet you is how you can't afford the rent, you can't afford this and that. You shouldn't have to live like this, a girl with a mother owns what yours does. You badgered me with this tearjerker for the last two years.''

Ricki straightened the sheets on the bed. A reminder to him, make it very plain, help me remember what he'd just been staring at, where that fantasy of his caught flame.

"I need that three thou.''

"This song. Same song, I heard it a thousand times. You were wishing your mother was dead long before you moved in here. It was a matter of time with you. You told me five minutes after I met you how you had this mother you wished you didn't have. Sitting in here dreaming all day with the blinds down, you and your rubber penises and your dykey friends.

"Listen to me on this, Ricki. Brush off the cobwebs and get this very straight. Your mother was killed in a sour drug deal.''

"No one's going to buy that. I cannot believe those guys. Professionals. Shit. I'm going to lay out five thousand dollars for something like that, nobody'll ever believe a second? And so when they see through that, what's the motive?''

"Political recalcitrance is always a possibility.''

"English,'' Ricki said.

"She was a wood rat lover. She kept grocery stores

from being built. Kmarts and condos and high rises from going in.''

''That's the Everglades coalition; that's not her.''

''Tell the fucking carpenters, electricians, plumbers, all those guys going to the land use meetings, the zoning hearings. Who do they hear all the time shooting down the building? She had a few people didn't like her. Believe it.''

Ricki shook her head, not good enough. She was still right out there. Practically number one suspect.

''You owe me that three thousand. I did you a favor. The dirty work on this.''

''You did yourself a favor.''

''And this.'' She patted the water bed. ''You think this doesn't count?''

Grayson sat down in the chrome sling chair, her television chair. He'd gone cold quiet. Sat there for two minutes, running his eyes over her, over the room, back to her, sizing her up and down, his lips just short of a snarl. The Conch Train clattered and rang its bell from Elizabeth Street, two over. Ricki worked on a mouth manicure, a dry cuticle. The thing kept snagging on the kimono, earlier in Lillian's hair.

Grayson sighed, shook his head. ''You're living up here, what, with three lesbians? Largest collection of rubber products north of the Amazon. Playing games, this and that, things somewhere between outrageous and illegal. All this, you might call it, your collateral, like what you have to show when you put your word up against mine.

''See, I think your understanding is a little murky here. You think 'cause I'm a rich lawyer, I'm vulnerable, could get my reputation smirched and hurt business. Let me tell you something about rich lawyers, Ricki. First thing is, nobody gives a shit about what we do out of the courthouse. Long as we convince His Honor. Smirch away, if you think you can.

"And second thing is, rich lawyers get rich, generally, from making their version of the truth the one that people believe. You know, planting a whisper in the right ear and then standing back as the squad cars get rolling.

"So, what I'm saying is that if someone had it in mind to create some gossip, let some juicy things slip here and there, that same someone might be surprised at what sudden interest the law enforcement authorities might show in someone's recent grievous loss of a parent. OLD LADY KNOCKED OFF SO DAUGHTER CAN PURCHASE PLATINUM DILDO."

Grayson giving her a seventy-five-dollar-an-hour glare. The look must've won him a few cases. Ricki wasn't scared of him, but still, she had trouble making eye contact when he had the volume turned up like this.

"You try that, Ricki. Just follow your line of reasoning, patting the bed, all that coy shit. You try to use that, if even a squeak comes out of you sounds like blackmail, or I hear something on Duval Street about how some lawyer may be a weekend voyeur, hey, Ricki, your little world is poof, gone. Poof."

"These guys, Gray. I've got till Saturday." Pleading now. He had her. Or maybe not; she wasn't dead sure. But she'd try this anyway.

One of the construction guys next door had turned a radio way up, letting the neighborhood hear the Beatles doing "Yellow Submarine." The racket of hammers maybe falling in a little with the beat. "And our friends are all aboard!"

"I'll find my way out," he said. "And oh, by the way, I was awfully sorry to hear about your mother."

At the door he wasn't mad anymore, a dippy smile. A wink.

11

Irving McMann sat in a golf cart on the fourteenth green. Milburn in his own golf cart, glancing up at the stars printed in a clear sky.

"Fucking mosquitoes, Irv. I'm going in."

"Not yet."

Milburn mashed another one on his forehead, like he'd just solved a burning problem. Waved others away from his ears.

"We can talk inside, Irv, please. This business, talking out here, afraid the condo is bugged, this is melodramatic horseshit. We're in bugs up to our asses out here." Milburn laughed.

"Shut up." Irv took a slug from his flask.

"Give me some of that, at least."

Irv slipped the flask into a pocket flap in the cart.

Milburn swatted more mosquitoes, banging his ear and cursing.

"This bitch," said Irv. "First we give her the budget plate; then I agree to take half up front 'cause she's a friend or something of Grayson. I figured what the hell. But it's no way to do business, whining now that she doesn't have the other half yet."

"So you fucked up. Let's just wet her and write off the loss."

"Maybe we will," Irv said. "Or maybe not."

"Aw, shit, I'm going in. I can't take these fucking suckers."

Irv placed his shiny little .32 on the dash of his golf cart. "We're having a business conversation," he said. "You don't walk away from business conferences."

Milburn stopped thrashing at the mosquitoes, stared at Irv.

"Jesus H. Christ, Irv. Where do you get all this stuff? We're out here talking, and I'm donating blood to the environment and you tell me you're going to shoot me if I don't stay. And fuck if I don't believe you would and just roll me into a sand trap and that's it." Milburn slapped his neck, his arm, his neck again, fanned his hand around his head. "You with all your goddamn garlic, you could sit in the middle of the Everglades and nothing's going to take a taste of you. Maybe a dago mosquito."

"We have a decision to make," Irv said, raising the

.32 and sighting it at the sliver of moon. The case against Milburn moving into the final stages.

"I got my own blood all over my hand, my shirt, these black, greasy little fuckers." Milburn wriggled a finger under the corner of his eye patch and scratched at the bandage. "And this eye. It's fucking killing me."

"Take some more drugs."

"There aren't enough drugs in Florida to make this fucker quit."

"I told you, jerkhole, you should've had the thing out. The doctor's standing there practically promising you you'll die of infection if you don't. And you're whimpering for him just to do whatever he can short of taking it out. Man, it was fucking embarrassing."

"It'll fix itself. If I can stand the goddamn pain, I know it'll fix itself."

"If you can forget your fucking eye for a fucking minute," Irv said, "there's a major business possibility here. I see a small window of opportunity that's opened up, and we're either going to keep on with status quo or get in that goddamn window now."

"Tell me. Get it over. I just as soon you shoot me as take much more of this shit."

"That old lady, the boat lady."

Milburn brushed mosquitoes from his arm, twisted to scratch at his shoulder blade.

Irv said, sighting the .32 at the flag on the fourteenth hole, "This old lady. You wonder why an old lady like that is dead now? Huh? Like why her own little girl wants her button pressed? Inheritance? That's OK. Nothing unusual there. But what's Grayson got in this?

This is a guy from Ivy League country, business tycoon. This guy has bucks, so if some boat captain needs to be dead to make him happy, then somewhere there's a lot of money changing hands. This guy is not going to risk getting shit spattered on his suit unless there's a whole duffel bag of cash changing locations.''

Milburn moaned, slashing at more mosquitoes. Irving panned the pistol around slowly until it was staring at Milburn.

''Shut up, Milburn.''

''OK, I'm just shutting up and letting you say whatever it is that's so fucking important I got to bleed to death to hear it. I got to get malaria and hookworm and who knows what else so I can hear it out here. The great plan, the great next step. Go on.''

Irv nudged his golf cart forward, circled around Milburn once, twice. Came to a stop beside him. Their carts parked parallel, an inch or two apart.

Irv clasped his hands behind his head, leaned back to look up at the stars. He could feel Milburn shivering in the dark beside him. Had him on the run again, or on the waddle anyway. Not even much fun in it anymore.

''Know what I like about you, Milburn?''

''Yeah.'' Shiver, shiver.

''Yeah,'' said Irv. ''Not a goddamn thing.''

''Maybe we should dissolve.''

''*You* should dissolve,'' Irv said.

''OK, I will.'' Milburn budged his cart ahead, but Irv cut him off in less than a yard.

''Here's what I think we should do,'' Irv said, his hand on Milburn's steering wheel. ''I think we should cruise down to Key West Saturday. Take the Scarab. Pay some calls. Sniff the wind, wet our finger, and put it up in the air. Just see what it is some old lady boat person has to die about. See our bitch employer, check her assets, pay some visits. Do some undercover shit. Costumes. You know, run some goofs."

"What's the point, Irv? For a lousy three thousand. Who cares?"

"I'm not talking about three thousand," he said. "Mr. IQ, don't you listen ever? I said I'm thinking of crawling through this window of opportunity, get out of the liquidation business for a while, just check the want ads, see who's hiring. Move up to leading man, that sort of thing."

"OK, Irv," Milburn said, sweeping mosquitoes from his arms, his other hand brushing across his shoulders. "Whatever the fuck you want, man, it sounds good to me."

"Oh, I'm just so thrilled," cooed Irv, Scarlett O'Hara, southern fag. He floored his golf cart and spun around Milburn, around and around. "I just can't tell you how my heart spills over with pleasure knowing I have pleased my wonderful pal." Around and around.

Everybody else in Coral Gables, in practically all of Miami, was putting up bars, lacy steel grillwork over windows, caging in porches, keeping the family silver safe, and color TV sets. But Sarah's mother was still oblivious, front porch was still bare, windows still vulnerable. Her damn front door was even unlocked.

Sarah stepped into the foyer and could hear the TV going in the den. She raised her eyes to the ceiling and shook her head. They were watching it for the second time since Christmas that year. Second time she knew of. Sarah's mother and Father Monahan of the Church of the Little Flower, old friends, they got together to watch *It's a Wonderful Life* every time one of them spotted it in the *TV Guide*.

Sarah thinking, Oh, shit, not tonight.

It was quarter till ten, fifteen minutes left, so Jimmy Stewart knew by now he was alive, and now he realized how his sugarcoated little town would have looked if he'd never been alive, and he's hurrying home through the snow to hug his wife, kiss his children, make amends, accept whatever pains are still his due. And the town is all gathered in his living room, about to pay off his debt for him, and Sarah stepped into the den.

Father Monahan turned his head and glanced back at her, slick ribbons running down his cheeks. He nodded to her and smiled and opened his arms for a kiss, one hand holding his brandy snifter. She might have been a burglar, anybody, and Father Monahan probably would have done the same.

Her mother looked at the priest, then turned and saw Sarah standing there next to the dictionary stand and the Boston fern.

Her mother said, "Wait till the commercial." She had tear trails, too.

Sarah knew she should just walk. Give Father M's hand a squeeze and just go. Get out of that room before she strangled on her mother's perfume, go back to her apartment and think this out. Just as the malignant bank president appears in Jimmy Stewart's living room, the commercial breaks in. Some young lawyer with his shirt sleeves rolled up, asking them if they've ever been hurt through someone else's negligence. One of Sarah's colleagues, a fellow seeker of justice. Give these guys a little more time, and they'd come on the screen riding alligators or strapped to the fuselages of biplanes.

Sarah came around in front of their chairs and turned down the sound. Father Monahan wiped his eyes on the sleeve of his black coat while her mother blew her nose. Sarah stood there watching these two with the color TV light the only light in the room, the greens and blues playing on their faces. A ceramic bowl half full of popcorn on the table between them.

"How are you, Sarah? It's been months," the priest said.

"I'm not good," said Sarah.

Her mother craned to watch the TV around Sarah's body.

"What is it, child? You look terrible." Father Monahan put his brandy snifter on the side table and moved to pull himself up out of the recliner. Sarah held up her hands to keep him put. She didn't need that, a hug from the family priest. He caught himself and eased back in the chair.

"Mother," Sarah said. "Mother."

Her mother cut her eyes briefly to Sarah's, and she could see how angry her mother was at this interruption.

"Kate Truman was murdered," Sarah said.

"My God," Father Monahan said. "This is your friend?"

"Yes," she said, "more than a friend." Still looking at her mother.

"I knew something like this was going to happen,"

her mother said. "Didn't I warn you about something exactly like this?"

"I should go," Father Monahan said, and began to rise again. But Mrs. James put her hand on his arm and kept him there.

"The movie's not over," she said.

"If you'd like me to stay, Sarah," he said. "You need a good ear, or anything?"

Her mother said, "This Kate Truman is just an acquaintance of hers. A radical down in Key Largo, protesting things."

"She was a lot more than an acquaintance, Mother, you know that. And she was murdered. I got a call just now. I'm going down tomorrow, and I may have to be there for a while, I don't know. But I came over here tonight to tell you where I'd be and because I..."

"Because you're upset," Father Monahan said, and tried again to stand, but Sarah's mother put her hand on his shoulder, held him down.

"We'll talk about this," her mother said, "if we must, *after* the movie. In a few minutes."

Sarah said to Father Monahan, "I'm all right. It doesn't matter. I'll just go."

"No, no, I insist." Father Monahan pushed himself to his feet and moved to the TV and punched it off. He took Sarah's hand and peered through the dark into her face.

Sarah's mother aimed the remote gun at the set and switched it back on. The town was all talking at once in Jimmy Stewart's living room. Donna Reed and the children were all smiling; Jimmy Stewart was shaking his head, amazed at everything. Happy as no man on earth had ever been before.

She used the remote switch to turn down the sound, and said, "He knows about your going down there, about your fantasy. Dallas didn't have an accident. Dallas was kidnapped. Dallas was murdered. He's heard it, Sarah, and he has some thoughts on the subject." She turned to the priest. "I think you ought to tell her what you told me, Bryan."

"Now, now," Father Monahan said. "Sarah's had a shock. She's grieving."

"Father Monahan thinks you should see a counselor, a trained psychologist. Don't you, Bryan?"

He sighed.

Sarah's mother watched the TV intently as a hat full of money was set in front of Jimmy Stewart, more than enough to pay off his debts. What was the message here? Sarah wondered, as the three of them watched the movie end and the ten o'clock news update come on. Die and come back to cash in? If Sarah died right now, it would be just these two passing the hat for her. Some consolation that was.

"Father Monahan says this is neurotic, hanging on to Dallas like this, denial, trying to keep him alive, pretending someone murdered him. Living this fantasy life. He's seen this sort of thing before. Didn't you say that, Bryan?"

Father Monahan switched on a desk lamp, turned, and gave Sarah what he meant to be a sympathetic look. But Sarah saw now he was drunk. Face red, eyes not fastening tight to anything. Mouth open. It'd been happening more and more in the last year or two as the parish had grown increasingly Cuban and the pressure was growing to hold services in Spanish. His time was nearly up.

"Mother, what are you trying to do?"

Her mother kept her eyes on the news show, and said, "Am I going to have to die before you'll take any interest in me?"

"Oh, God," Sarah said.

"Now, now," said Father Monahan. "Now, now." Sarah caught the priest taking a wistful look at his brandy glass on the table.

"It wasn't Dallas that died," her mother said. "It was me, wasn't it? I was in that car. Your father, he's more alive than he ever was. And I'm sitting here and I'm the one that's dead."

Her mother wouldn't look at her. Sarah came over and stood in front of the TV, close enough to kick her mother's shins.

"I agree with Father Monahan," her mother said. "You need help. Professional help."

The priest sat back in the recliner, swilled the rest of his brandy. Stared down into the empty glass.

"Look," Sarah said. She turned and flattened the power button on the TV. "It's not a fantasy. It's not a delusion. I've met the guy who killed Daddy. I know him. I see him every time I'm down there. I have everything but a confession, and I'm very, very close to that."

Father Monahan was staring at her. Her mother watched the blank TV.

"He kidnapped Daddy, drove him down to Lake

Surprise, and killed him," she told the priest. "That night nineteen years ago."

"See what I told you," her mother said to the priest. "It's gotten worse. Worse and worse."

"Sarah." Father Monahan set his glass aside. "Would you come by? Come by and see me? I know you have your doubts about the church, its power in your life. But we could talk. Just normal adults, talking."

"He came here late one night," Sarah told Father Monahan. "Dragged my daddy off, and he killed him. He did that, and I saw him. And I know who it is."

Her mother said, "She punishes me with this obsession, going off down there. I don't know how I've stood it for so long."

"Sarah," Father Monahan said, "if we can help . . . spiritually or otherwise . . ."

Sarah picked at the seam of her work shirt sleeve. Standing there in front of these two, trying to get a grip on this little thread. Silence inflating the room, overinflating it. Sarah thinking. Yes, that's what it would take at this point, Jimmy Stewart's guardian angel, who led him on the tour of his hometown. That's what it would take, her own assigned angel to come into this and give her peace. To show her how shallow and dismal all these people's lives would have been if she had never lived.

But she knew that was wrong. If there'd been no Sarah, nothing would have turned out any differently. The world would be exactly as it was anyway. As corrupt, as forgetful. She was as anonymous as if she had never lived. She'd had exactly zero effect on anvone's life. Except. Except, God help her if it was true, she might have had some effect on Kate's.

"There are worldly ways I can help," the priest said. "Things a man in my position can do that no one else can. You would be surprised to know the men of power in this community who heed my counsel."

"Have another sip of brandy, Bryan," her mother said as Sarah was turning, walking across the floor, getting the hell out of there.

12

Thorn fell asleep near dawn and an hour later jerked awake, in the middle of some dream about being chased, or chasing, he couldn't remember. He was sweating, and his heart was in overdrive. And then he looked around, saw where he was, still at Kate's house, still in his old bedroom.

He drove back to his house, showered, dressed, caught up in a manic current. He was pacing the porch of the funeral home when Sally Spencer showed up at nine. She got down from her van, looking at him as if she weren't sure which side of sanity he was on.

"I'm OK," he said to her, raising his hands, showing her his palms. "I'm OK."

She unlocked the front door and led him to her office, put her purse into the desk drawer, and sat down. She was wearing a yellow dress, had her hair up today. They looked at each other for a minute or two. He could tell she saw something in his face she didn't trust.

"It's not my place, Thorn. It's a police thing now. Talk to Sugarman."

"Was she raped, Sally?"

"I told you, it's not my place to say anything."

"I saw her pants. She was raped, wasn't she, Sally?"

Sally thought about it for a moment more and nodded yes.

They sat that way, Thorn feeling the blood massing in his throat. Angry at her because there wasn't anyone else around. Because she'd chosen such a shitty business. Because she was a woman and women got raped.

They sat looking at each other. Thorn held on to the arms of the chair. It wasn't going to go away. He knew that. There had been Dallas, and now there was this. He could scream at Sally now, he could tear down all her plaques; but it was going to be there afterward, and after a long while it would still be there. Riding there below the surface.

Together they decided on cremation. Sally would drive the body to Miami today. Spend the day up there and bring home the remains tonight. She called them cremains. Thorn almost got angry again. Almost told her what he thought. Even if none of it was her fault, even if she was being sympathetic, open, kind. She shouldn't have called it cremains.

Thorn said no, he didn't want to see the body again.

Afterward he drove to the Caribbean Club, a bikers'

and construction workers' bar with a water view. He ordered a beer. Drank it while he looked out at the bay, at a couple of Windsurfers sailing across the bumpy water.

Thorn ordered another beer, and when the bartender brought it, the man said they'd heard about Kate; as a matter of fact, they'd all just been talking about her. Thorn didn't like how the guy's voice sounded. Or how he exchanged smirks with the guy sitting beside Thorn.

"Yeah?" said Thorn. "So?"

"So nothing," the pale bartender said.

"Hey," Thorn called as the bartender was walking away, "hey, how come nobody in here but me is wearing a shirt?"

" 'Cause it's the fucking Keys, man," said the guy beside him, a Hun with his metal SS helmet on the bar in front of him. His belly covering his belt. "Ain't you heard, white boy? Isn't no fucking law down here."

" 'Cept the law of the fucking jungle," his pal said, leaning forward, trying to look crazy mean at Thorn. He was a little guy with a squashed pit bull face. He was still wearing his black cycle helmet.

A skinny man with a ponytail and a vest exposing his bony chest drifted across from the pool table, cue stick ready.

"Yeah?" Thorn said. "Law of the jungle, huh?"

"Sure as shit is," said the Hun. He took his elbows off the bar, leaned toward Thorn, gassed him with his beer breath. Grinned, and called back to his buddies, "Let's have another goddamn toast! To whoever croaked the rat lady. If a fucking rat can't make it on its own, it should be extinct."

"To extinction!" his little pal said. "To the law of the fucking jungle."

Thorn took hold of his Budweiser by its long neck and backhanded the Hun with it across the eyes. Stepped quickly behind him and put his hand on the back of the little guy's helmet and spiked his face into the bar. The guy with the cue stick took a batter's stance, edging toward Thorn, choking way up on the cue. Thorn tossed the German helmet underhanded at him, and he swung at it, and Thorn stepped in, did a punter's quick kick into the guy's crotch. Got a reasonable hang time. The bartender had ducked out of sight.

Out in the lot Thorn thought briefly of dominoing their Harleys. But no, hell, he didn't want to get guys like that riled up. No telling what they'd do.

He drove slowly, south down U.S. 1, trying to hold back the quiver that had worked into his hands. Every exhalation a sigh. Saying "goddamn" to himself, stringing them together, a dozen goddamns.

That four-lane highway ran like a spine through the center of the island. There were spots where the island was so narrow you could stand in the center of the road and lob a rock to either the ocean or the Florida Bay. Hear it plop.

Right now it all looked wretched to Thorn. There were just a few survivors of the old days, wood-frame houses with tin roofs and cisterns and cupolas, stranded between the Pizza Huts and skin diving shops and the shell stores that had mounds of queen conchs piled out front. A haze from deep-fat fryers hung over the cluster of franchise restaurants. Even the steady sea breezes couldn't seem to wash the air of that smell.

There was no town in Key Largo, no grid of streets, no courthouse square, no park with statues. Not even any sidewalks. Just this hot four-lane strip of road with a rutted bicycle path running along its edge. Gas stations, mobile home parks, auto body shops, mom-and-pop motels, and bait stores with sailfish painted on their outside walls, billboard after billboard urging drivers forward through the tackiness to Key West.

There was still an occasional empty lot, an open space that gave a sudden panorama of the Florida Bay or Atlantic. A flash of fifteen shades of blue and green water, then more cinderblock buildings selling flood insurance and hamburgers.

The island widened in several areas to a few hundred yards, where neighborhoods of concrete-block stilt houses had been built. But there was no need for a Key Largo architectural preservation league, no historical society. What the hurricane of '35 hadn't scraped away, the bulldozers were working on.

Everywhere there were shadows where there had never been shadows before. The oldest thing still standing for a hundred miles around were the people. And all but a handful of them were new arrivals, retirees so used to the shopping centers and vast parking lots back home, in fact, so proud of their malls, so quick to describe to the Conchs what luxuries the rest of America was enjoying that defectors had been showing up everywhere.

Even some of Kate's oldest friends had begun to desert her. Kmarts, not wood rats. Tired after all these years of driving up to Miami to do any serious shopping. Tired of being pioneers. Thorn thought for that moment of turning the Cadillac north and driving till the car gave out. Living there, wherever it turned out to be. Better to live where hope was long gone than stay here and see it all unravel, stage by stage.

But he drove home, sat in the Cadillac for a while, then walked out to the end of his dock. Just stood there, breathing, not looking at anything. It was ten when Sarah finally arrived.

Thorn stayed out on the dock and watched her get out of her red Trans Am. Watched how she was walking, how she was dressed, how her hair was. Was this how drug smugglers looked? He couldn't tell anything. She had on brown corduroy jeans, a dark short-sleeved blouse, tennis shoes. Sunglasses. Her walk, her hair said nothing.

She came out on the dock, stood in front of him, and asked him how he was, and he said OK. He said he needed a drink.

"Think I should come along?"

After a while of looking at her, he replied that he did, he thought she should come along. He let her take his hand as they walked to her car.

Thorn told her to drive to Vacation Island. It was the resort Kate and Dr. Bill had bought a share of thirty years before. For years there had only been a few frame cottages. It had been a convenient place for the Truman family to dock their boat, a place to go on weekends to get out of the house. Sugarman's foster mother, a white woman Kate's age, had been one of the owners and had brought Sugarman every weekend to fish and boat and snorkel with the other children.

Sarah parked and waited while Thorn sat, looking out the windshield.

"Why here?" she asked.

"I need to do something," Thorn said.

Thorn led her around the island, pointing out where the cottages had once been, the boat ramp, the volleyball field, the croquet course. The long picnic tables and stone barbecue pit where the five or six families had gathered and cooked their fish and potatoes and had sung their songs.

One of the partners in Vacation Island had been a lawyer, and it'd been his idea to build a small motel off at one end, something that wouldn't be much trouble, would generate a little cash. A place for relatives to stay when they visited. Tax advantages.

The rest of it happened so gradually no one ever objected. Some mangroves uprooted here, a little fill added over there. Another building. Some clearing of shrub. Thorn would always remember one exquisite fall day, the first cool weather of the year, breaking into the seventies. He had walked past a furious volleyball game out to his skiff and had not seen a person he knew. The invasion complete, outnumbered at last.

Now Vacation Island was completely public. Boat slips, three bars, a four-story motel, two casual restaurants, one fancy, a snack bar, and a row of specialty boutiques. It had also become in the last few years, to Kate's dismay, a popular local trolling spot for singles.

He led Sarah behind a bikini boutique to a shed of weathered gray pine. The planks on its side warped, its corrugated tin roof rusted over. It was the last structure remaining from those days. Ten years before, when

Thorn had given up guiding tourists across the flats, he'd stored his skiff and battered Evinrude there.

Thorn found the key on his key ring. He opened the padlock and swung the heavy double doors open and stood looking into the shadowy room. The motor was mounted on a sawhorse in the middle of the shed. Thorn went across to it and set his hand on the cover.

"I got to get this going," he said to her.

Standing with the sunlight behind her, making a fine nimbus around her hair, she nodded that she understood.

First, he cleaned and oiled the tools he'd left behind in the workbench, and then he tore apart the thirty-horse motor. He scraped corrosion off the power heads with a putty knife. He sent Sarah out for replacement seals and gaskets. He disassembled the carburetor, soaked its parts in gasoline, and rebuilt it. All the rubber rings were rotted. It needed new points, plugs. When Sarah returned with the gaskets, he sent her out again for another list of parts. The cylinders were OK, a little scarred, but OK. He polished the rings.

Later Sarah stood in the doorway of the shed, watching him work, bringing him a fresh beer every half hour. He drained a trickle of black oil out of the lower unit, flushed it out. The gears were still rust-free, flywheel still moved.

Around six o'clock he wrestled the engine onto the skiff and hauled it on the trailer by hand to the docks. With Sarah and a few of the mates from the deep-sea yachts watching, Thorn poured a sip of gasoline into the carburetor and cranked the Evinrude. On the fifth crank it caught and belched blue smoke, and the propeller began to swim lazily through the water. A couple of the mates clapped.

"Good work, Thorn!" one of them called out.

Thorn stood up in the skiff, breathing fast, staring around him.

"You all right?" asked Sarah.

He said he was. But he could see from her face and in the eyes of the others that no one believed that. He looked down slowly at his right hand. It was clenched in the shape of a stiff claw, as though he were still gripping his wrench.

"Maybe a drink would help," he said. "Four drinks."

"It's been known to."

"Ten drinks," Thorn said.

They went to the Tiki Bar on the top floor of the motel. Sarah ordered iced tea. Budweiser for Thorn. She asked him for whatever facts he had, and he told her everything: the dope on board; the rape; the fact that Kate had been yellowtailing. He watched her for signs and saw nothing. Afterward she went silent, just sat there watching Thorn in his greasy clothes, accepting condolences from the bartender, waitresses, just drinking her iced tea.

At seven they went downstairs to the poolside Coconut Hut. Sitting across from each other under the umbrella, at a spool table. Thorn with bourbon now, Sarah still with tea. Biting her lip now and then, avoiding Thorn's occasional glance. A few tourists wandering about. Midweek, midsummer. Thorn was trying not to think about Sally Spencer, where she was, what she was doing.

As the sun set finally, Thorn switched to tequila at

the Margaritaville Express, a little shack bar on the edge of Vacation Island's paltry man-made beach. They sat at the bar, and Thorn watched two guys jet skiing out in the evening waters, spotlights brightening up an acre of the Atlantic.

At eight-thirty Sarah ordered conch fritters, ate silently. Thorn watched the evening crowd arrive. While Sarah ate, staring down into her plate, he swiveled his stool around and listened to two nurses from Michigan, who seemed drunker than he was. Talking for his benefit. Glancing up at him from their little picnic table.

"Blow jobs, blow jobs, blow jobs," the red-haired one said. "All I ever hear."

Her black-haired friend with tinted aviator glasses smiled at Thorn for the fifteenth time. "Guys don't care," she said, looking at her friend. "They think it's caviar, this big favor. God's knobby gift to girls."

"That one at the Pier House."

"Freddy."

"Yeah, yeah," said the redhead, sneaking another invitation at Thorn. Come down off your stool, big boy. Participate. "Blow job, blow job. He wanted to sit in his Porsche and have me do him, him looking at the sunset."

"Romantic guy."

"I drive four thousand miles to wedge my head underneath some steering wheel? While some guy who thinks his beat-up Porsche makes him a stud movie star watches the sunset? No way."

"Hears you're an RN and he thinks, Oh, boy, take my pulse, take my temperature. I think I've got a fever."

Sarah nudged Thorn's elbow.

"You ready?"

Thorn watched the jet skis flash in and out of that patch of light. Imagined what it would be like out there in the dark, lost, no reference point but that blind white stage.

"I am," he said. He climbed off the unsteady barstool.

Two guys in tennis shorts and Hawaiian shirts were standing beside the nurses' table. One of them short with a five o'clock beard, mean little eyes, his hair worn away in the back to a circle of scalp. The other one tall and heavy with a pirate's eye patch, long, greasy hair. They must have homed in on all that blow job talk. A last smile from the redhead for Thorn before she plunged in with this new one, Hawaiian shirt opened down to his black, curly chest.

Thorn said, "I know who did it."

"You're blotto, Thorn." She stirred her straw through the last of the iced tea.

Thorn watched the short, intense Hawaiian shirt slip his hand under the table to the redhead's knee, starting the slide up that smooth track.

Thorn looked at the bill and laid some money on top of it.

He said, "Guy at the elementary school. Other night, the lumberjack. Guy I shut up." Thorn smacked the bar with his open hand.

"God, Thorn." Sarah hitched her purse over her shoulder. "There's five hundred guys like that. Their wives. Their kids. All of them could've harbored a heavyweight grudge against Kate. That guy was nothing special."

The two Hawaiian shirts were watching Thorn. Their nurses walking off to the bathroom. These guys not sure whether Thorn was just another drunk or had entertainment potential.

Thorn looked around at the picnic tables, couples with their pink drinks, their pitchers of beer, Christmas lights strung from coconut palms. All of it suddenly in brutal focus. All these people dropping their french fries on the ground where Dr. Bill had taught the kids how to clean fish, where Kate had taught them the names of the constellations, the second verses to the songs.

It was when they began to drive the twenty miles back up to Key Largo from Lower Matecumbe Key in Sarah's Trans Am that Thorn's eyes finally began to blur. He let his head slump against the headrest, closed his eyes, but felt the guttural vibration of the muffler, the twitch of the wheel from Sarah's nervous late-night driving, every keen snap of night bug against the windshield.

Back at his stilt house Sarah parked on the grass as near the stairs as she could get. She helped Thorn untangle from the cramped car, muscled him up the stairs. Opened the door for him and gave him a light push into the room.

Thorn said, "You staying? I'd like it if you did."

"I'm staying," she said from far away. "I'll be there in a minute."

Thorn undressed in the dark, feeling the wobble and sway of the whole day of drinking, the house riding a moderate chop. He tried to brush his teeth, to reconnect with the ritual, but couldn't get the cap off the toothpaste.

He heard Sarah out on the porch. He carried the

toothpaste to thc doorway and saw her sitting in Dr. Bill's chair, small convulsions shaking her.

Thorn stumbled out onto the porch, got his bearings, squinting toward the shivering bay. He moved beside the chair and looked down at her, her face buried in her hands. He wanted to reach out and put a hand on her shoulder, bring her back. But she seemed already to have sailed too far away.

13

Irv was glad the black-haired goddess had left the bar. He'd been having trouble concentrating on the nurse he was with. And the sunburned stud queenie was talking to, this blond guy tossing back shots of tequila, looking like a cross between Jimmy Buffet and who was that fucking tennis robot, Bjorn Borg? This guy had kept giving Irv the eye, to the point where Irv had been hatching a scheme to maybe hijack the two of them out in the parking lot. Run off with the goddess for a few hours of fun, find a swamp for the blond dork.

Irv thought black-haired queenie looked a lot like that ice skater in the Olympics a few years ago, very white skin, very black hair, blue eyes that were sleepy, a little hooded maybe. And good sharp cheekbones, a nice long neck. Something to hold on to.

Anyway, Irv was developing the parking lot scene when his new nurse friend gave him a little tweak under the table, gave his balls a little pinch and twist. And bang, he was back with her, to hell with queenie and the drunk blond guy.

And now the nurses had headed off to the bathroom, Irv supposed to wedge in their diaphragms, and he and Milburn had just been sitting there getting more snockered ever since.

"They dumped us, man," Milburn said. "And that redhead, with those Hindenburgs."

"Hey, don't worry," said Irv. "She should be here in five more minutes. I see her nipples now."

The nurses finally returned, leery now, like they'd been debating the issue of picking up these two. Irv, seeing it, switched gears to sincere, getting sincere into his voice. It took ten minutes, but he and Milburn maneuvered them down to the docks.

Good little boys, showing the visitors the sights. Gentlemen, suggesting a moonlit ride in their sleek craft. Glances exchanged all around. Irv playing a great role, modern liberated man, respecter of women. Harmless and courtly. Milburn smiling like a eunuch.

Irv thinking Cary Grant, Rock Hudson, charm charm. He finally worked them on board. Milburn cast off; Irv fired up the Mercs.

Right away the redhead shouted, "How much horsepower does this thing have?" Trying to stay with it, act like this was the kind of insanity she was used to, guys like him, boats like this.

Irv just smiled at her and flattened out the throttle, sent the other one lurching against Milburn. His date, so he should like it, right? But he yells at Irv to slow down.

This black-haired one, women's lib sunglasses, Irv didn't like how she'd checked him out, quibbled at dockside about where they were going, how long. He about told her to get fucked right there. Offering her a boat ride on a Scarab with two four-hundred-horse Mercs, and she's bitching about whether or not it's going to be worth her time. Right there he assigned her to Milburn. Up until then he'd been chatting them both up and hadn't made up his mind which one was his.

Milburn yelled at him again to slow the fuck down. He did; he notched it back a little, aimed for the marker on Mosquito Bank His redhead curled her arm through his and rubbed the side of her breast against his biceps. He glanced at her and dropped his hand to the front of her shorts, let it dangle there for a second and then tapped on her pussy with his little finger.

"You sure you're ready for me?" he asked her, wind ripping at his voice. She smiled at him and shivered, yes, hugged his arm a little tighter.

Milburn had moved up onto Irv's other side. Left his date leaning against the leather bumper at the back of the cockpit.

"Let's head back."

"We'll go back when I'm finished showing these ladies my boat."

"Now, Irv. Penny's not feeling good, and I'm starting to feel it, too."

He powered on toward the light at Mosquito Bank,

rubbing against her shorts now with the chopping side of his hand. He thought he could feel it cooking in there.

Milburn went back with the lib complainer. They were talking, Milburn with his arm around her shoulders. Cute couple, just what Milburn needed, some woman who hated men. Perfect. As for Irv, this honey was just right, somebody who'd spit shine his prick and be happy for the privilege.

At the marker light Irv killed the engines. While he was getting a bottle of champagne from the little cuddy cabin refrig, the three of them started whispering at the back. The woman with balls seemed to be pleading her case to her friend.

Irv brought the champagne and plastic stemmed glasses up and set them out on the console. He drank a fast one and poured himself another.

"Irv," said the redhead, coming over, "we best be getting back. Penny's sick. I'm a little chilled, too, actually."

"Fuck sick," he said. "We're out here, the water and the moon and the stars. Warm summer night. Some girls would kill for a chance like this. We're talking paradise here. Look at those stars." Irv caught her shooting a worried look at her friend. "I said look at the fucking stars."

She was staring at him, her life getting a little weirder than she'd wanted.

"Cut the shit, Irv," said Milburn. "Let's get on back."

"Let's swim," said Irv. He reached under the console and drew out the boat .44. "Let's skinny-dip, ladies."

"Fuck, Irv. Don't get in one of these."

"Come on, ladies. A little swim. I want to see what kind of shape the two of you fine ladies are in. We want to see a little race. Like over to the marker light. First one there, gets . . . whatever you'd like. A ride back, a warm towel." Irv aimed the automatic at one, then the other. Took the starch right out of the libber. Dick fell right off, balls came loose.

"What is this, Irv?" The redhead took a step toward him.

Milburn said, "He means it. He gets like this."

"OK, OK, Jesus Christ." The redhead started to undress. Her friend stood there, glaring at Irv. "I don't mind, Penny, letting him have a look. And it *is* a nice night." A real making-the-best kind of girl. "You guys coming in?"

"Sure thing, babe, soon as you finish the race. Come on, princess," he said to the other one. "We're going to see a race. Over to the light. Show us your stuff." He drew the hammer back with his left palm, old cowboy dramatic stunt. John Wayne about to shoot a silver dollar out of his sidekick's hand. Slow and careful. Terrific ass-grabbing stuff.

"Go down the ladder," Milburn said when both of them were naked. Not enough damn light for a real good look. But they both were built. Firm, good legs. The redhead with one giant tit and one normal one. That was news.

They got in the water. Seemed like the black-haired one might have been whimpering a little. They swam along side by side, breaststroke toward the light. Seven miles from shore.

"Come on, Irv. This is shit. What if they get back and make a big stink?"

"Say what? They don't know our names. They don't know shit about boats. Nobody at that place got a look at us. If they had a dockmaster at the marina, I might worry about it. But who're they gonna say we are?" He watched the two of them stroking along. Milburn shook his head and went back to sit down on the stern seat.

"Anyway, even if we didn't get laid," Irv said, "we got a good look at this Vacation Island."

"So *what*?"

"So, now we know something. This lady we smacked. She's not just some little fish guide. See, I told you it pays to catch the obituaries after a job. How you gonna find out about who you took out unless you read the papers? And can you believe that place? Vacation Island. That's big money. Can you picture owning a place like that?"

"Get serious, man."

"I mean it. All the chicks you'd have running around. Restaurants, anything you wanted to eat, you just tell your fucking chef to cook it up. Man, like your own little world. You could be like some fucking czar; you didn't like how things were, you just fire people, hire some ass kissers, and get it just right. It appeals to me, Milburn. I don't know why, but I like it. A place to call my own."

"So how you going to get it away from this Ricki?" Trying to sound bored, but Irv could hear it: The fat sack saw a free tit in there for him somewhere.

"Oh, I don't know. I think we have to go down there, Key West, like I said. Get cozy with her. Use my fucking famous charm. Turn up the kilowatts."

Irv started up the big engines. He threw the spotlight on the girls. They were to the light by then. He idled over toward them. The redhead was holding on to the girders of the marker light, probably cutting herself to shit on barnacles. He got to within ten feet of them before he smacked the throttle down, pushing the tilt switch at the same time so he'd leave them splashing in one incredible rooster tail.

"I saved you, man!" Irv screamed back at Milburn. "That bitch was looking to add to her *cojones* collection." They raced north along the reef line, back to Coral Reef Club.

14

What breeze there was only ruffled the tops of Thorn's trees, as sultry and useless as attic air. He and Sugarman sat out on Thorn's porch. Sarah was inside, dressing.

Thorn's hangover was in full bloom. He was behind his darkest fishing glasses, his eyes tender and keeping time with his heart. He was wearing a pair of cutoff blue jeans, tan boat shoes, and an orange T-shirt that said KEY WEST, THE LAST RESORT.

Sugarman had been silent since opening the door on Thorn and Sarah, tangled in the sheets asleep, the sun well up.

"So tell me," said Thorn. He took another sip from

the can of Coke, tried to keep his head upright as he did it. "What do you have?"

"You tell me first, Thorn."

"What?"

Sugarman said, "You're not going to be one of those. Going around knocking on doors late at night. Reading nobody their rights. Lone-wolf justice."

Thorn lifted his eyes, looked at him.

"That how I strike you?"

"Yeah, it is."

"I'm a pacifist, man," Thorn said.

"It's how you got those split knuckles," Sugarman said, "being extremely peaceful with some guy."

Thorn said all right, all right.

"OK, here's how it is. The DEA guys are in it now. They spent yesterday doing the boat, digging chum out of the deck, sniffing it with computers to see which ocean it's from. Fine-tooth stuff. They had the slugs in and out of the lab already. Punched it all into the National Crime Information computer, and bang, it says, 'Sorry, boys, start over. This amounts to zero.'"

"This is the information that's supposed to keep me from kicking doors in?"

"Hold on a minute," Sugarman said. "We know it was two guys. They chartered her for the night; they take it out to the reef, scuffle with Kate; the chum flies; then the guns go off; then the marijuana gets sprinkled. It's archaeology. Layers. All of it right there in layers.

"Ned McLean was on Pickles Reef, pulling up hog snappers, around eleven Monday night. He heard the shooting, but he stayed put 'cause he thought it was a drug deal falling apart. His radio was on the blink, so he didn't tell anybody about this till yesterday. Stayed out there all night he was so scared, didn't want to start the engine.

"Then Larry Mayfield at Tremble's Marina called up and placed Kate at his docks fueling up at five o'clock. She told him she had two Cuban gentlemen for the evening. Bought six bags of chum.

"And we got us a big fellow and a little fellow. From the footprints. We got two pairs of new shoes. Some black thread that got snagged on the cabin door. And we got a fishing rod with a bloody tip."

Thorn was silent, pinching the bridge of his nose.

"Looks to us like Kate got in a lick or two. The rod's in the lab up in Miami."

Thorn shook his head, looking at Sugarman, trying to fend off the scene that was forming in his mind.

"The DEA is following the drug angle. It's what makes their world spin. It doesn't matter what I say about Kate, she's running pot as far as they're concerned. She's dead 'cause she didn't have her union card. They say the dope was scattered as a signature. Let this be a lesson to you others. Simple. File the whole case under 'Clumsy Amateurs.'"

He heard something wrong with Sugarman's voice. The way he got when somebody'd whispered "nigger" in the same room with him.

Sugarman said, "But it's not drugs. It could be backlash from her environmental stuff, or it's something we don't know anything about yet. But you're sure and I'm sure it's not drugs."

Thorn met Sugarman's eyes, and he could see how heavy they'd become. Clouded and yellow.

Sugarman said, "I had the boat pulled. Larry Mayfield's cleaning it up, patching a couple of places. He'll take it around to Kate's. So you don't need to worry about that."

"There's something else, though, isn't there?"

"Not about Kate." Sugarman glanced at the French doors. The toilet flushed inside.

"Sarah?"

"No, it's Jeannie again." Sugarman took a breath. "I don't want to go into it."

Thorn said nothing. He tried to slide a breath past the throb in his throat. It wasn't the hangover anymore. It was Kate taking a stab with that rod. Gutsy, resourceful. Dead.

"I know it's not the time, man, but I got to tell you." Sugarman glanced at the French doors. He said, "She spent last night with the preacher. The dude I told you about. Robert Redford with a Bible. She's standing in the door on her way out with her suitcase, telling me I'm not sexual enough for her. She's got to have this honkie."

Sugarman turned his face to Blackwater Sound.

"She says she wants to stay there some nights, stay at home some nights. Says she loves us both, but in different ways. I don't know, Thorn. I think I'm sexual. I think I'm damned passionate."

Thorn nodded.

"I don't know what the hell to say to her. I actually thought of calling that TV lady last night, the one with the accent. That's how bad it got." Sugarman laughed wearily. Thorn made a smile. Looked away at the horizon.

When the door opened and Sarah stepped outside in white shorts and a white blouse, Thorn turned and thought he heard faint music. His hangover playing dumb tricks. He tried to tone down his smile. Knowing he wasn't doing it, not keeping anything secret from anyone.

Sugarman stood up, nodded hello to her, and Thorn introduced them. Sugarman put out his hand, and she shook it like a man.

"So, am I still a drug runner today?" she asked. "Should I start looking for a bail bondsman?"

Sugarman said, "Thorn, you turkey."

"So I told her, yeah. Why shouldn't I? You don't believe it anyway. She look like a cannabis cutie to you?"

Sugarman was shaking his head sadly, making a quiet groan. Sloppy procedure, counting too heavily on the likes of Thorn.

"I'll be happy to answer your questions," she said.

They passed a glance around the table.

"What can I say, Sugar?" said Thorn as he reached out and touched Sarah's arm. "I get warts when I lie to people. Big, ugly warts. Size of bottle caps."

Sugarman stayed around five more minutes, listening to Thorn explain to Sarah what the police had at the moment. Sugarman sneaking looks at her.

When he'd gone, Sarah stood up, said, "I need to take you somewhere. You need to see something."

"This *does* have something to do with you."

"I don't know," she said. "I hope not. I sure hope not."

They took her Trans Am south, almost to Plantation

Key. Thorn watched her hands on the small wheel, watched her shift cleanly, keeping it at the speed limit but weaving around Winnebagoes, the slower local traffic, never getting hung up anywhere. She drovc as if she were used to driving much faster, no wasted motion, all four hundred horses knowing who had the whip.

He told her she was a good driver.

She didn't answer.

"I meant it as a compliment."

"It's just a sensitive subject."

Thorn was quiet, looking at her profile, the air conditioner stirring her hair.

She said, "Driving is important to me."

Thorn wondering how he'd strayed into such a minefield.

Sarah watched the road, said, "My father died from bad driving."

"You never said anything."

"It was a long time ago."

Thorn rested his hand on her shoulder. "Doesn't matter how long ago it was. Those things last. I know."

"Yeah, I believe you do," she said.

She turned into a gravel drive on the bayside, just beyond mile marker ninety-two. There had once been a small fishing camp back there, on maybe fifteen acres. He knew the fishing cottages were gone, but he hadn't paid any attention to the property.

Sarah got out and walked ahead to a rusty chain drooping across the road. She found the key on a large ring of keys in her purse and opened the padlock. Dropped the chain off in the weeds.

They drove down the shaded road around a tight bend, bushes brushing the car. Thorn recalled now. It had been a condo development, or had been planned as one.

"Sunny Hammocks," he said.

Sarah looked across at him. "That's right," she said.

There were five two-story buildings in the shade of giant banyans, unfinished concrete-block buildings. Only one had a roof. The others with three-quarters walls. Vines ran the walls; weeds grew five feet high at their bases. A small rubber tree grew out of the gutter of the one with a roof. Broken windows. A pile of boards covered by a purple blooming vine.

Sarah wound through the narrow road, down a sloping asphalt section that was deeply pitted, weeds breaking through. There was a tennis court and a swimming pool thirty yards or so from the beach. The beach was covered with plastic bottles, scraps of rope, buoys. She parked alongside the pool, and they got out.

The pool was brimming with a green soup. Frogs and lizards fled as Thorn and Sarah crossed the wooden decking around the pool. Fallen branches, coconuts, and giant seedpods from the palms. Huge fronds scattered everywhere, black and rotting. The Jacuzzi was clotted with the porridge. As they approached the beach, a great blue heron squawked at them and untangled into flight.

"Do you remember Kate giving you a key a year or so ago?"

Thorn fumbled around in his head.

"She gave you a key and told you it was important, not to lose it."

He said, "Yeah, I remember. I got it." In his fly-tying desk. The tool drawer. He pictured it, a gold flat key beside the needle-nose pliers, clippers, razor knives.

"Good." She led him down the lawn toward the beach to two chairs, green Adirondack chairs of thirty years ago. They sat. Thorn looked out at Tarpon Basin through those dark glasses. It looked almost cool out there, the trick of Polaroids. Sarah watched him.

"That key," she said. "It was my idea. Kate wanted to give you something, and I showed her how."

He relaxed in the chair, had a fast memory of trout fishing with popping corks out in the basin. Out there drifting across grassy beds. Back when there'd still been trout out there, when there'd been grassy beds. Before it all turned sterile and bare from too much silt stirred up, dredging up new land for new islanders.

"That key is what's known as a tender of gift. It means a gift was given, an act completed. That's very important, or it could be, if Ricki gets it in her mind to fight this. She won't win, but she might try."

Thorn stared at her.

"Won't win what?"

"This place," she said. "Sunny Hammocks, and half a dozen others like it up and down the Keys."

"This ghost town? Kate owned this?"

"She owned it. You own it now. She wrote you in on all the mortgages. With right of survivorship. It's a gift to you. Not an inheritance. Technically she made you a gift of this place the day she gave you that key to her safe-deposit box. There was no reason to explain it all to you then."

"She bought this place and let it get like this?"

Sarah frowned.

"She bought it *in order* to let it get like this," said Sarah. "This is her legacy and gift. It's a natural hammock, and there are mahogany trees back there the developers were planning to cut for more building. And I know it makes everybody laugh, but there are wood rats back here, too."

"I'm not laughing," he said.

"She put every cent she could into places like this. From her savings, the insurance from Dr. Bill, his annuity, all the cash flow from Vacation Island, rents mainly and long-term leases. All that money to keep these developments from being built any farther.

"One of these places would get in trouble, miss a couple of payments. Or the Sierra Club, Audubon Society would get the investors so bogged down in suits and court cases the owners would get tired or nervous waiting, making the payments, till building can get going again, and Kate would step up, make them an offer, either buy it outright or buy into it and keep increasing her share until she had it. All sub rosa, of course. She's fighting these places publicly with the wildlife groups, and undercover she's trying to buy them out. Soon as she owned a place, the hammers stopped."

Thorn was leaning forward, looking at her. His headache rekindling.

"My job was hiding Kate from view. We used blind endorsements, parent corporations, anonymous trusteeships, mock subscribers, anything I could come up with to keep it legal and keep Kate's involvement concealed. It took awhile sometimes, but eventually any of these places she set her sights on, she'd find a way to get the other owners so impatient or pissed or worn down that they sold to her.

"But it all still requires cash flow. All of them have property taxes; some of them still have mortgages. And it's Vacation Island that's the money pump. It has to work at absolute efficiency to keep these places ghost towns."

Thorn cleared his throat, looked down at his lap. He said, "You caught this one a little late. Land's been cleared, buildings built. I mean, it doesn't seem like this qualifies as *saving* a place."

Sarah watched him for a moment and said, "I didn't know, but I didn't expect this reaction. I thought you living like you do, close to nature, you'd just see this automatically. I thought you'd see it."

"I'm looking." Thorn feeling heavy in his chair. "I'm trying to see it." Taking his time, looking back at the buildings, the vines. "It just looks like a sore. Healing over wrong."

"Well, it's your sore now. You want to start up with these places again, sell time shares, get half of Minnesota flushing their toilets into the bay, you can do it. There'll be lots of people happy to help you.

"And Vacation Island. That's yours, too. So you could just yank the plug on the money machine and this whole thing would be up for grabs."

"What's Ricki get? She's blood kin. I'm just this orphan they took in."

"I updated the will just this spring, so I can say with some certainty that Kate considered you more than some orphan. Ricki's getting exactly twenty-five thousand dollars."

"But there's something else, isn't there? There's more to all this."

It took her a moment, but she nodded that there was.

"Well?"

"I'm thinking." She took a deep breath and laid her head against the chair back as if to catch these late-morning rays, put a little color in the cheeks. Thorn took her in, her throat, the twin points of her collarbone, the rise of her breath, the lace of her bra through her gauzy shirt.

She turned her head slowly to face him, still resting it against the chair. Thorn played his eyes across her face, settled on her mouth. There was something familiar about it, some other mouth he had known, not for very long, but well. He couldn't place it. But it bothered him. That she should remind him of anyone else seemed wrong.

"You sure don't make it easy, Thorn." She drew in a full breath and tried a smile. She glanced back at the tumbledown buildings. "But I guess I'm going to trust you on this one."

15

Sarah drove north to where State Road 905 split off from U.S. 1. Leaving behind the strip shopping centers, the real estate offices, the new banks housed in double-wide trailers. Nothing man-made along 905. Everglades on one side and on the ocean side a dense thicket of vines, mangroves, palmetto. It was the area where Thorn had gone to practice with the Colt years ago, hacking into the snarl of brush with a machete. And now it was known mainly as the last existing home for the Key Largo wood rat.

Thorn listened to her quote estimates of the impact of Port Allamanda. Twenty thousand pounds of solid waste output per day, a million gallons of water use a month.

The numbers coming to her quickly, stacking them up in front of Thorn.

At the head of a long straightaway Thorn saw the alligator crossing sign. It had been one of Kate's first causes. Ten, fifteen years ago she'd lobbied to have it put there. But gradually it had become obvious that tourists considered the sign just one more motel towel. Somebody would have it unbolted and back home on the bedroom wall before the summer was done.

Thorn listened to Sarah go on with her numbers. He leaned forward a little for a better look at her mouth. It'd started to worry him, not just that he couldn't remember it but that it was associated with something vaguely unpleasant.

"You listening to me, to any of this?"

"Twenty thousand pounds of solid waste," Thorn said. "That's a load of shit."

She didn't smile.

"If you're going to help, you should know a few things."

"Would you marry me?"

"Thorn!"

"Yes?"

"No. No, I won't." Not looking at him, nothing soft or regretful in her voice. Turning down another helping of beans.

"But you want to think about it? I can tell. You're going to give it some quality thought before answering."

Taking a deep breath, she slowed the car and turned right, off into a narrow drive.

She drove in silence a hundred yards down that jeep

trail, the dense shrub scraping at the car doors. Potholes. Fallen limbs across the path.

"This is Amos Clay's," she said. "Kate said you know him."

"That's it? That's all I get?" Thorn said. "I say those words and you flinch and keep on driving. That's it?"

She hit the brakes, and Thorn caught himself, thumping his hands against the dash.

Sarah slid the shifter into neutral and tapped the shift knob with her fingernail, thinking it all over, watching her finger as she tapped.

She said, "I have a life, a whole world you don't know anything about."

"You mean men. Men."

"A lot of things, Thorn. I like you, I think of us as very close friends. Friends who can confide in each other."

"Friends who can confide in each other." Thorn watched her tapping out her Morse code. Her eyes still lowered.

She said, "I like to talk to you. I like you to talk to me."

"You have other lovers?"

"I see other men." She looked up, let him have a taste of her sharp blue eyes.

"But you like to talk to me. For me to talk to you," Thorn said. "I'm trying to get this straight. I'm trying to hear what you're telling me."

"Thorn, Thorn, Thorn. I don't know what to do with you." She took his hand and held it in both of hers. She shook her head and brought his hand to her mouth, kissed the back of it. Thorn watched her kissing it, her eyes closed now.

"I'm going too fast," Thorn said. "I'm scaring you, going this fast. You think I'm just saying this 'cause Kate was killed, 'cause I'm in shock, 'cause I've got a hangover." He knew his voice sounded frantic, uneven. He swallowed, gave her hand a squeeze.

"No, Thorn. You don't scare me," she said. "I scare me." She put his hand back in his lap. "I'm trying very hard to be honest with you. I don't want to have to hurt you."

"So," Thorn said, trying to shift into an upbeat voice, "what's Amos Clay have to do with this?"

They sat silently for a few minutes in Amos Clay's drive, and then Sarah cleared her throat and began to explain it to him. Amos Clay's 430 acres was the proposed site for Port Allamanda. The tract hadn't been purchased yet by the Grayson Group. They were getting all the environmental impact rulings settled first, all the public hearings, all the variances. The investors were leery, not ready to sink millions into the project and have it held up somewhere in court once it got started.

So when Kate had learned this, she'd sat down with Amos Clay and had made a deal with him. This old lobsterman who'd bought that worthless isolated land a little at a time for thirty years, Amos Clay, was ready to cash in. And his old friend Kate Truman had wrangled an agreement out of him, a right of first refusal. Before he could sell the tract to the Grayson Group, he had to give her a shot at it.

"The contract expires August first," Sarah said. "Either we complete the deal by then, or Grayson and his people get the land."

"How much does he want?"

"A million cash."

Thorn laughed.

"What? You think that's high?" Sarah said. "It's a steal. This is the last major tract of waterfront this size between Homestead and Key West. Everything else is off the auction block. Either it's state park or it's been designated by the state as in an area of critical concern, not for sale. Amos's land's probably worth ten million, maybe more. But Amos has it in his mind to be a millionaire. One million's all he wants."

Sarah gazed down the path. Broken chunks of limestone in their way. An egret picking at a patch of dirt.

"Oh," Thorn said. "Now I'm getting it. I'm a little slow. Somebody knew what Kate was up to. What the both of you were up to."

"Maybe, maybe not," Sarah said, still looking at the egret. "That wouldn't be a good thing if they did. A lot of people would be very pissed off. It'd be more serious than making speeches about wood rats. If Kate owns this, there's no project, nothing. And you know—don't you?—we're talking about millions of dollars here. Huge profits. Lots of jobs, lots of spillover business for Key Largo."

She put the car in gear, and Thorn sat back. His hangover was loosening its grip. He breathed in the brackish air, feeling it fill a new hollow inside him.

"Maybe I do, maybe I don't."

"Sure you do, Amos. We were up in Shark River, in your old seventeen-foot skiff, and you'd been filling up the fish box all morning with snapper and redfish and we went up the river a hundred yards and I caught a six-pound bass. Liked to give you a heart attack finding freshwater fish so close to a saltwater fish.'' Thorn talking Florida cracker, or trying to.

''I never fished with you.''

''I'm Kate's boy.''

''Where's Kate at?''

''She's on a trip,'' said Sarah.

''Where to?''

''Up north.''

''Well, I know *that*,'' he said. ''Ain't nowhere else to go but north.''

''She may be away for a while,'' said Sarah. ''That's why we stopped by. I wanted to make sure you knew we're planning to close our deal the thirty-first of this month.''

Amos mulled that over. He was sitting in his rocker, one of Dr. Bill's chairs, an early model before Dr. Bill'd begun to mold the wood like sculpture. Amos's coral house still smelled the way it had twenty years before, when Thorn had come over for visits with Kate or Dr. Bill, to take Amos fishing in the backcountry. It was thick with the odor of moldering laundry, mildew, and whiskey.

The thing that had changed in those years was the floor. It now sagged so badly that anything that wasn't fastened down had begun to slide toward the middle. Rotten floorboards probably. A deep trough ran through the whole house, and from where Thorn sat, he could see drinking glasses, beer cans, and silverware that had slid into the sag. The lamp beside Amos's chair was leaning dangerously toward the middle of the house. Some of the pine planks had splintered from the strain, and tumbleweeds of dust were caught in the prongs of frayed wood.

"I told you I wanted it in cash now. Don't think I'll take any goddamn check or anything else."

"It'll be cash," Sarah said.

Amos turned on Thorn, his gray stubble catching the noon light. On his cheeks and forehead there were dark pigment spots like dried spatters of blood.

"Who's this you brought along?"

Sarah rolled her eyes, beseeched the ceiling.

"You know me, Amos. I'm Thorn. Kate's boy. Dr. Bill's."

"I don't know any Thorn."

"We went fishing together. We caught us a mess of fish. You were the best backcountry guide anywhere around here."

"That don't mean nothing. Don't try to butter me up. Nothing from back then matters worth a damn to me. I'm headed out of here before somebody hangs a sign on me. And starts charging Yankees a nickel apiece to see the last Conch in captivity."

"Amos? Have you spoken to anyone about our contract?" Sarah couldn't hide her impatience. She was bent forward toward Amos, her face ruddy in that dim light.

"Hell, no. She told me not to. Don't get me riled. Making me out to be some goddamn nitwit. I know what's right? *You* know what's right?" He swallowed some more of his drink. It looked like whiskey in the tea glass.

"It's important, Amos," Thorn said. "You mustn't tell anybody about Kate, or about Sarah."

"I can handle this, Thorn. Please." Sarah was on her feet, leaning away from the downhill pull of that sag. "I'm preparing all the papers, Amos. And I wanted to set up a specific closing time. I was hoping the afternoon on Wednesday, the thirty-first, would be OK with you.''

''I got other buyers,'' he said. ''I'm giving Kate a chance at it, but it don't matter none to me. I'm going to be a millionaire either way it works out. I always knowed I'd be one. Don't ask me how, but I knowed it since I was little I'd be a goddamn millionaire. John D. Himself. Yes, sir, it was a time everybody laughed and laughed when I bought more of this land. But they're dead serious now. Dead serious.''

''We've got to settle on a time first, Amos,'' Sarah said.

''I heard you.'' He swallowed some of his whiskey and gave Sarah a cagey stare. ''The thirty-first,'' he said, jutting his chin out, in control, the millionaire.

''That's right,'' said Sarah, ''good, the thirty-first then.'' She hitched her bag over her shoulder.

Thorn rose.

''And I won't deal with nobody but Kate.''

Thorn watched Sarah field that. She smiled at Amos, stepping over to him, and patted him on his shoulder.

''Amos,'' she said. ''Kate's been trying to get Thorn here in on things. Get him more involved so he doesn't wind up a mean old housebound coot like you. She was hoping you'd deal with Thorn on this. Go ahead, just like normal, same price, same terms. But it'd be Thorn signing the papers and handing over the cash.''

Amos looked down at Sarah's hand on his shoulder. He sniffed. Squinted at Thorn.

''I knowed who you were, boy. I knowed the minute you walked in here. I remember that afternoon clear as a photograph. And it weren't any six-pound bass. That's just like you. It was four and a half. I can still recall the important things. If it's got fish in it, it's still up here." He tapped his temple.

Thorn smiled at him and stepped across the floor's divide to shake his hand.

Amos glared at Thorn's extended hand and shook his head fast and hard.

"I ain't shaking your damn hand till it's full of money. You come back here in two weeks with my million American dollars and I'll be shaking both your hands. Now get on out of here, the both of you."

As they were driving back down 905, Sarah said, "Do you trust him?"

"No."

"Me either," Sarah said. "He's not a bad man. Just highly porous."

Thorn could feel Sarah glancing at him. But he kept his face ahead, watching the rough asphalt pass beneath them.

"You mad at me, for telling you how I feel?" she asked.

"I wouldn't call it mad."

"What is it? Tell me."

"Where does the cash come from, Sarah?"

Her foot came off the accelerator briefly. As she eased it back on, she said, "That's another story."

"I want to hear it."

"It's too long to go into now," she said.

"Were you bringing in dope?"

"Thorn, don't be an ass."

He turned and stared at that mouth, tried hard to place it.

She dropped him off at Kate's. Thorn, keeping his voice neutral, told her she was welcome to stay there.

She said she guessed she'd go back to Miami. She was way behind at work. He watched her drive away; then he went inside the house, found Kate's car keys. He took the VW south to the Waldorf Shopping Plaza. As he drove, he thought he could still smell the sickening honey aroma of dead wood rat.

He drove south to Key Largo's only shopping center—a dime store, two gift shops, and a run-down grocery. A bookstore specializing in fishing magazines and shell books. He cut through the parking lot and drove back into the neighborhood behind, along a winding street past half-million-dollar houses on deep canals. Most of them deserted for the summer. A treeless neighborhood. Stark yards covered with pea-size rocks imported from North Carolina. Back in these new neighborhoods there was no grass to cut, nothing to fuss over during their season here and nothing to worry about after they shut up the house and headed back to Ohio. Glaring white houses. Each one positioned so it had a blue slice of the Atlantic for its own.

He parked the VW outside the Quonset hut that was the office for Jerome Billings, Jr. and Sr., owners of Bash-a-Bug, Key Largo's oldest pest control service.

16

There was a sign on the door that said KNOCK FIRST, so Thorn pounded three times and waited. Three more times. He bent over and peered through the dusty window. Jerome senior was leaning back in his chair, his bare feet up on the desk. A chrome hubcap near his feet where a cigar smoldered.

Thorn dragged the rusty door open and stepped inside.

"Hey, Thorn," Jerome called above the chug of the air conditioner. He waved Thorn into a chair and put aside the pistol magazine he was reading. "They find the sorry bastard yet?"

"Not yet," Thorn said, still standing by the door.

It was hotter in there than outside, and Thorn told him so.

Jerome said, "The gotblamed thing feels like it's stuck on reverse cycle."

"Be cooler without it," Thorn said, straining to speak above the rattle and huff of the machine.

"It just takes it awhile to catch up on days like this. I'm used to it."

Thorn asked him where Jerome junior was.

"Out in the bird," he said. "Poor fucker."

"What's wrong?"

"Oh, they're needle-dripping him. They cut him open, took out a goiter the size of a house. Kid's a goner."

"Oh, shit."

"He's gone deaf, too. Got to get up next to him and holler like the devil."

"Jesus, Jerome. They just find this out?"

"Two, three weeks back. Started off bleeding from the shorts. Never a good sign, bleeding from the shorts." He picked up his magazine again, found his place, and said, "Used to be, living down here, eating fresh fish, good clean air, people lived to be older than rocks. But gone are the days, Thorn. All the shit coming down lately, it's as bad as living in Miama."

Thorn opened the door, let the sun and air into the room. He said, "People say it was, but I sure don't remember it ever being a paradise."

"There was a time," Jerome said, "it was a shitload closer than it is now."

Thorn went outside and walked across the asphalt airstrip to the army surplus DC-3 the county used for mosquito spraying. Jerome had been flying it since high school, and there'd been a time when he and Thorn had taken a few aerial-busting rides together.

He climbed up the ladder and leaned through the cockpit window. Jerome was working under the instrument panel, a tangle of wires hanging down across his chest.

Thorn stretched in farther and yelled out Jerome's name.

Jerome lurched up, whacked his head against the back side of the panel, and squeezed out from under it.

"Good Jesus, Thorn!" Jerome twisted around and sat in the pilot's seat.

"Sorry, man."

"My goddamn daddy tell you to do that?"

Thorn said he had.

"Fucker's going deaf himself, and damn him if he don't think it's me can't hear. Whispers like he's in church half the time. He's driving me fucking crazy."

Jerome junior readjusted his black wig, checking it in the glass of a gauge.

"And this goddamn thing. Feels like I got my head stuck in a bucket of tar."

"Your daddy lying about the cancer, too, I hope?"

"No," Jerome said. "He's right on that one." Jerome shot a thumb back at the steel tank showing behind him. "Thousand gallons of Malathion. Try flying inside a cloud of that shit for ten years." He reached into his shirt, dug out his cigarettes. He offered Thorn one, and Thorn shook his head. "Worse thing about having cancer is you got to drive up to Miama. I'd rather have them just cut my intestines than drive on those highways up there. Between the New Yorkers and the assholes with old-timers' disease, man, the way they drive, should send 'em all back where they come from. Shut the goddamn state border and lock it tight.''

Thorn watched him light the cigarette, flick the match out his window.

''I heard about Captain Kate,'' he said. ''Soon as I heard, I told Jerome senior she must've come across somebody's sweet little coke deal. That what it was?''

''Don't know yet,'' Thorn said. He took a sip of air from outside the cabin. ''She wasn't making a lot of friends trying to stop Allamanda the way she was either.''

''I was with her all the way on that, man. But don't bring it up around himself in there. That old man wants to sell the airstrip to a condo company. What the hell would I do around this place if I couldn't fly that plane? Wait tables? Make beds at the Holiday Inn? No, but him in there, he'd sell this place to Castro if he could. The dumb shit bought it when it wasn't worth nothing, and now he thinks he's a real estate genius.''

Jerome pressed at his wig. Ribbons of sweat coming from its edges.

''You know, about Captain Kate, I got to say, man, much as I don't like to, but she was hauling in *a lot* of fish lately. Lot more than looked healthy.''

''What in the hell does that mean?''

Jerome sucked on the cigarette and eyed Thorn.

''I don't know, buddy. I just saw her about every time I made a pass along her quadrant, her cockpit with four, five ice chests. Boat riding kind of low in the water. I thought *four* ice chests? Now that's a lot of fish. *One* ice chest is a lot of fish for me. So, naturally, I just thought . . ."

He flicked his cigarette out the pilot's window, smoke coming out his nose and mouth, raising his eyebrows at Thorn.

"I came to ask a favor of you," Thorn said.

"You don't have to say nothing to me, Thorny. I wouldn't say a word to nobody. Hell, I smoke some of that shit myself now and then."

"I came to ask a favor, Jerome," Thorn said, keeping his voice empty.

"OK, OK. I thought you should know, is all."

Thorn said, "I want to borrow the VW, Junior. I'll trade you Kate's VW for a couple of days."

Jerome gave him a look.

"The bash-mobile?"

"Yeah," Thorn said.

Jerome climbed out of the cockpit and led Thorn behind the Quonset hut where the car was parked. It was a bright pink Volkswagen with round black mouse ears coming off the roof, a long corkscrew tail welded to the trunk. And black whiskers fixed to the hood. Someone had tried to paint two buckteeth in black and white below the whiskers.

"I want to take it down to Key West."

Jerome said, "The motor'll get you there and back. But the damn ears are on the blink."

Jerome showed Thorn the small electric motor mounted on the ceiling inside. He thumped the metal box, and the ears began to wiggle furiously. He hit it again, and they stopped.

Thorn said that would be all right.

"People borrow this from time to time," Jerome said. "I never ask what they want it for."

"Good."

"But if it helps any," he said. "A good thing to tell somebody comes to the door is that you're out to spray for cement-eating scorpions. That scares the shit out of them six ways from Sunday. *Scorpionida concreticus* is what I say."

Thorn nodded. He gave Jerome the keys to Kate's VW.

"Oh, the hat," Jerome said. He dug around underneath the passenger seat and came up with a green baseball hat. A black cloth replica of a scorpion, its tail curled to strike, was sewn on top of the cap, its front pinchers hanging over the bill.

He handed the cap to Thorn.

"The Bash-a-Bug shirt's there on the back seat. In case you want to give the whole thing a little class. And the sprayer is in the trunk.

Thorn thanked him.

He drove the VW back out to the highway. Cut across the median to Sammy's Liquors. Before he got out, he had to smack the motor for the ears. He could hear them up there, waving frantically. It took another smack to kill them.

As he walked into the liquor store, the last of his hangover flared up. His stomach grumbling, wondering what the hell was up, coming into a place like this.

Sammy came down from his mirrored cubicle as soon as Thorn entered. Another guy Thorn had known at Coral Shores High. Back then Sammy used to amuse his gang with a pickpocket routine. Bump you from the rear, fish out your wallet, and then, while his buddies stood guard around him, he'd read out your love notes in his thespian voice or open your Trojans or anything personal you had in there while you tried to climb over his buddies to shut him up. Funny guy.

Sammy stood in front of Thorn, drooping his head a little.

"Sorry to hear, man," he said. "They found the fuckers yet?"

"Not yet," Thorn said. He pretended to be interested in a pyramid of vodka bottles. The four o'clock construction crews were arriving. A couple of them lining up at the cash register with their six-packs.

"I heard it was Cubans. A drug deal, that she walked into the middle of something." Sammy got a confidential tone, put his hand on Thorn's back, and maneuvered him into the corner with the cognac.

"Might've been that," said Thorn. "Listen, Sammy . . ."

Sammy called out hello to a couple of new customers. He straightened his guayabera and gave Thorn what appeared to be his complete attention.

"I heard some talk," Thorn said, "that you were planning on putting a new store up at Port Allamanda."

Sammy narrowed his eyes, caught himself, and tried to soften the look into a grin. "I've given it some consideration."

"I wanted you to know," Thorn said. "I'm taking over for Kate. Port Allamanda's dead on the drawing board."

Sammy laughed. He picked up a feather duster that was lying on a case of wine and began to dust the tops of bottles. He said, "Thorn, you're one hard-to-figure son of a bitch."

"It's dead," Thorn said. "I got a deal working, and when it's finished, Port Allamanda's gone. History."

"Wood rats, Thorn? You worried about wood rats?"

"This isn't speeches, Sammy. This is right down in the dirt. A cash transaction. Hand quicker than the eye. This is going to be final, no appeals from anybody, no bulldozers, nothing."

"You shouldn't shit people, Thorn. You shouldn't walk into people's place of work and give them a raft of shit. I don't care if your mother was killed or what, it doesn't make it OK, walking around doing your loony shit."

"It'll be dead inside two weeks," Thorn said. "I wanted you to know so you could start changing your retirement plans." Thorn made a show of patting for his wallet. He walked back to the front door, stood aside as another construction crew came into the store.

Sammy stared at him, holding that feather duster at his side.

Thorn sat out in the lot in the bash-mobile a few minutes, watching Sammy in there. Watching him go on with his hailfellow world.

Maybe it wasn't a billboard along U.S. 1, maybe not as effective as hiring a skywriter to put it up there on a cloudless noon. Still, in Key Largo, if you wanted coverage, you didn't need to call a press conference.

Thorn made it to Key West by six-thirty. The sun in his eyes for the last fifty miles. He managed not to think the whole trip, did that by driving like a maniac, cutting in and out of the passing lanes. Flashing his lights, honking. Letting those ears go crazy.

He came over the bridge onto Key West, turned left, and went around by the beach, the motor for the ears grinding away. He found a place to park outside Ricki's house. It was on Southard Street just a couple of blocks off the main drag. A Haitian art gallery across the street. A health food store and restaurant on the corner.

Thorn got out of the car. Bongo music was playing loud from somewhere nearby. He smelled fried plantains. The twilight was tinting the old wood houses on the block a vague pink.

As he was climbing the stairs to her house, the front door opened and she was there. Coming out in a T-shirt and white shorts, sandals laced up her ankles. Her step stuttered for a second when she saw him, but she caught herself and came on down the stairs with her usual bulldog look. She had Kate's boxy face and Dr. Bill's wide mouth and dark, weary eyes. She was so close to pretty that you had to take a second look to see she wasn't. It was the eyes, something sickly there, a lack of luster, tarnished by bile.

"You come all this way to see me?" She moved up next to him, making him taste her rum breath. "Somehow I'm not moved to tears."

"Yeah," he said. "I wanted to tell you something."

"I got a phone," Ricki said. "Next time phone me. The less you're around, the happier I get."

"I wanted to see your face when you heard this."

Ricki made a smartass frown. "Sugarman called me, bozo. Kate got herself dead."

Thorn said, "Not that. Something better. Something that's gonna eat you up."

Ricki hmmphed and began walking, heading toward town. Thorn followed, caught up with her in a few steps. They passed by a bearded man in overalls, barefoot, slumping on the front steps of the Haitian art gallery. He drew himself up when they passed and shuffled after them.

"Leave me alone, Thorn," Ricki said. "Go on back up there and leave me alone. You're out of your element down here."

Thorn said, "I know why you had her killed."

She stopped and turned on him.

"Are you crazy! Have you finally totally freaked out?"

The bum was beside them now, grinning at Thorn, his eyes zooming in and out. He kept wetting his lips, rubbing his finger against his thumb.

Thorn looked at him. Shook his head.

Ricki set off again, and Thorn and the bum followed.

Thorn said, "And I also talked to the lawyer for Kate's estate."

She stopped and put her hands on her hips, pretending to fume, but Thorn could see a spark of excitement in her eyes.

Ricki stepped over to the bum. She said, "Dr. Leery, go find me a lizard. I want a lizard right away."

"OK, OK," he said, full of delight. Smiling at Thorn. "You want one, too? You want one, too?"

Thorn told him no, he was fine the way he was.

They were in front of a scuba shop, the street empty, the last light dwindling. To the west, downtown, Thorn could hear the faint bass beat of a jukebox. Dr. Leery was scrabbling about in someone's lawn a few doors up.

"Say it, Thorn, if you have anything to say."

"I know why you had her killed," he said.

Ricki shook her head in disbelief, staring at Thorn.

"Tell me, then. You came all this way, so tell me."

"It's not for hate, and it's not for the money," he said. "That's what you think at first. But it's not that. It's because you think you can't keep living as long as this other person is alive. You'd rather die. You think you're going to be happy for the first time in your life when this person is dead. The voices'll stop, the insomnia. However it gnaws at you."

"What game is this, Thorn? What kind of weird game?"

"Kate left all of it to me. All but twenty-five thousand dollars. Vacation Island, the house, property, all of it. You get twenty-five thousand."

She closed her eyes briefly. When they came open again, they were narrowed and mean and fixed on him.

"Twenty-five thousand." Thorn gave her back her look. He said, "Before it happens, you think you'd rather die than keep living with this other person alive out there. But then, when they're gone, it's all just how it was. And that makes it even worse." He bore in on her eyes. "That started happening to you yet? Started feeling any of that?" He saw something alive in there. A worry. Her eyes shifting back and forth between his.

"I'm late for work," she said in a small voice.

"I haven't decided yet what to do about you," he

said. "I know what you've done, Ricki. I didn't know when I came down here. But I know it now."

"You never were very smart, Thorn. And you sure haven't gotten any smarter lately."

She tried to burn him with a last look, then walked away.

Thorn watched her go. She had Dr. Bill's smooth gait, without bounce or sway. Dead serious. How you might walk through hip-deep water.

Thorn ate in a diner near the southernmost point in America. He ordered the southernmost burger with extra tomatoes. His hunger was back, and he devoured that one and ordered another when the waitress brought him his beer.

"You been away from food for a while, honey?" she asked him as she set his Budweiser before him.

"I have," he said. "For quite a while."

He picked up a leftover morning paper from the chair beside him and tried to interest himself in the miseries there. Everywhere there were eruptions, plagues, radical rearrangements. Better, worse. It was hard to tell that. But the stories were all about that one thing, how much it hurt for things to be suddenly different.

After eating, he left his car near the diner and walked five blocks to Sandpiper Bay Club. He had passed it on his way into town, and now he wanted a closer view of it.

Until a year or two before it had been the Sands Piano Bar. A restaurant and bar, a place where grit always covered the floor, tracked in by the beach crowd. At night a piano playing quietly in one corner of the room. It was always a place tourists had skipped because the bathrooms smelled and there was no air conditioning.

That place had been bulldozed. Now it was Sandpiper Bay Club, a condominium, five stories high. A gate out front with a security checkpoint. Some serious men in uniforms in the booth, seemed ready to do whatever was necessary.

Thorn walked the perimeter of Sandpiper Bay. He stayed on the sidewalk across the street from it to get a view over the twelve-foot wall. Lights were coming on. Up on the penthouse terrace there seemed to be a party. The place was pink, trimmed in white, and spotlights shone on royal palms planted beside the building. Like all the new buildings in Key West, it tried to convince you it belonged here, that it wasn't concrete block, that it had the same graceful airiness and gingerbread charm of the authentic Conch houses. It looked like a goiter to Thorn.

He found a jetty that hadn't gone private and sat out there in the strong southeaster. He took off his boat shoes and let his toes touch the water. Voices blew in from a sailboat anchored a mile out.

After a while two drunk couples discovered the spot. They were having an argument. They stood about ten feet away and took turns being articulate. It seemed to be about a friend of theirs who had turned gay. To one couple it was a devastating tragedy; to the other two their friend seemed unchanged by it. Was it possible, someone asked, for anyone every truly to change? Or weren't all changes in personality just the outer layers, a kind of molting? Nothing fundamental. They were talking loud and seemed to be impressed by their conversation, by its philosophical merit. They kept glancing at Thorn as if they were about to poll him about it. He rose and left them there, out in the hard wind, shreds of their conversation following him for a block.

When he got back to the bash-mobile, he let the passenger seat all the way back, wadded Jerome's work shirt into a pillow, and closed his eyes. He could hear the tide washing against the seawall at the southernmost point. He fixed his mind on that, picturing Ricki's face when he'd lied to her that he knew she'd killed Kate.

He saw again that day's hundred miles of bridges and Winnebagos and rental cars, Jerome in his wig, Sammy in his guayabera, Amos Clay. Thorn lay still and felt the hot wind coming into the car. A wind that rose from the deserts in Africa, flooded across thousands of miles of oceans. Bringing with it the scent of parched grasses, the bleat of extinct animals. Trade winds that carried to Key West the topsoil of another land, delivering it to Thorn's windshield, to his tongue.

Thorn kept his eyes closed. Southernmost insomnia.

17

Irving McMann marched the length of his ten-foot closet. Milburn watched him from the closet doorway, rubbing the raw skin around his flesh-colored eye patch.

"Come on, man. Let's just do tourists."

"*You* do tourists," Irv said. "That's how much imagination you got."

"All there is in Key West is tourists, Conchs, and fags. I'd rather do tourists."

"I knew I remembered this thing," said Irv as he reached in among the tight-packed clothes and withdrew a hanger with leather shorts pinned to it. "I bought it in Provincetown, this great queer store. Man, it's just right."

Irv slipped it on over his red bikini underwear. He

turned and modeled it for Milburn, jutting out a hip and pressing his chin to his shoulder. Fluttering lashes.

"I'm not going anywhere with you like that."

"I'm just starting, man."

"I'm not dressing up," Milburn said, there with his hairy gut hanging over the edge of a pair of tennis shorts. Tennis shorts! What a joke. Milburn swatting at a tennis ball, trying to get from here to there. They called him Earthquake at the Health and Racket Club.

Milburn said, "What's the idea anyway? You think this girl's going to come up with the money faster for some leather freak? Either she has the three thou or we wet her. It doesn't call for any big drama club thing."

"You see, Milburn. This is exactly the difference between us. You're thinking in a straight line: The broad owes us, so we collect, one, two, three. This linear shit, man, that's what's crippled you up. I'm over here jumping, like quantum leaps, a jump here, a jump miles further ahead." Irv loosened the spiked bulldog collar around his neck. He tried different angles with the leather Greek sailor's cap, found one he liked, cocked over to the side, almost touching his ear. Just right. Fruity but frightening.

"This Ricki person. She's gonna be a rich lady. She's gonna need some serious financial counseling as I see it. Like from this kinky Merrill Lynch guy, specializes in resort management."

"Man, you're batshit. Total certifiable batshit. Nobody, I don't care how flaky the broad is, nobody is going to hand over a resort island to some stranger buys his clothes at the pet store. You're slipping beyond the edge here."

"OK, Joyce Brothers, what do you recommend?"

"I say we go down there, get our three thousand dollars, or smack the broad. Either way, doesn't matter shit to me. Dress like boat captains or something halfway normal, hit a few bars, hang out at the nude beach tomorrow, catch the Sunday crowd, tan our hard-ons, and come on home. Nice relaxing trip. Nothing kinky. Cut the Hollywood bullshit."

"Yeah, OK, buddy. Whatever you say." Irv hatching an idea, taking off his collar, the hat, the leather vest. "You may have a thought there. I just may see a point to that."

Milburn staring at him now, a little nervous he was getting his way. Seemed to be sorry for a moment. Then shaking his head firmly and snorting. Like it's about time Irv paid more attention to his point of view.

The loran flickered in the dark, Sarah steering jerkily, overcompensating as she went off course by a few degrees and then overcompensating back the other way. Wonderful little gadget that loran, a computerized compass. It told her just where she was, but hell if that made her feel better.

At least she was away from shore. That had worried her most, running aground on the flats just offshore. Kate had shown her how it was done, aiming at the Carysfort light, keeping the dock light dead astern. But there wasn't much margin for error, and Sarah had plowed the bow into the edges of the channel twice, saving herself only because she was going so slowly.

The meet was at 2:00 A.M. as usual. Tonight the coordinates were 14201 and 30718. Not coordinates;

what had Kate called them? Time delays, lines of position. Places where the radio signals crossed. Every place on earth had a loran coordinate, every place on earth woven through with a tight fabric of radio signals. Impossible to be truly lost, as long as you could afford that seven-hundred-dollar little computer. But there was a hell of difference between knowing exactly where you were and knowing exactly where you wanted to be.

It was six and a half miles from Garden Cove to the Elbow and then about twenty more miles out, keeping the course by lining up the glowing center line with the boat position line. Like a video game, giving the whole thing a sense of unreality. Moving into what she knew was deeper and bluer water, out to about twenty-four hundred feet, four hundred fathoms. Four hundred fathoms. Impossibly deep. About half a mile above the earth's surface, kept aloft by the powerful, capricious Gulf Stream.

She had given herself an hour fudge factor. Leaving at ten-thirty, she could make the trip, if made without a hitch, in two and a half hours at fifteen knots. She would arrive and wait, starting up only to correct for the drift. No way to anchor at that depth, of course. It would take a half hour to load. That put her back at around five, if she chose to come straight back. But she wouldn't. She would stop at Carysfort Reef, throw over some chum, and set out a couple of lines. Fishing for mutton snapper, hog snapper, whatever. Smile for the cameras. And then come back in under cover of daylight.

That part was Kate's idea. The DEA had never had much luck locating mother ships unloading, so its strategy lately was to take up positions close to shore, watching for boats coming ashore at night. Boats without running lights at three in the morning.

So, under cover of daylight had become the new way. It was that Edgar Allan Poe story about the letter. Leave it out in the open, where no one would ever find it. There was nothing at all suspicious about a fishing boat working the reef all morning, unloading its catch at its own dock.

Sarah took a swallow of the gin she'd brought along in her father's leather-covered flask. She put the flask on the control panel beside the Colt .357. The gun was more symbolic than anything else. If Kate had been killed because of their smuggling operation, a revolver wasn't going to save Sarah's life at this point.

She had no way of knowing if something had gone wrong with this deal. She wasn't in regular contact with her old client, Jorge Palacio. She just received the loran numbers every other week in a small envelope mailed from Miami. When the time for the meet came, sometimes Jorge was on board, sometimes not. She'd just have to wait till the fifty-foot shrimp boat showed. If the deal had fallen apart, she'd know it then.

Jorge Palacio had been her client a year or two back. It had been a routine case. Sarah couldn't even recall which of Jorge's rights had been violated during his arrest. She did remember Jorge had seemed different from the usual run of traffickers it was her job to defend. Never a smirk, a glint of mockery at the wimpy American justice system. He had shaken his head in amazement when Sarah informed him he was free to go. Given her a number where he could always be reached if there were ever any way to repay her. Sarah had filed it.

But now it might be that some Colombian warlord

had taken exception to Jorge's method of repayment, this misappropriation of product. And then it was possible that Kate had been killed because of it. And it was very possible, in that case, that Jorge was also dead. But now, with the deadline on Port Allamanda two weeks off, Sarah had to go ahead, find out, make the trip. No time to develop another contact. That Colt the only comfort she had.

She could have stayed home, of course. But Sarah didn't walk out of movies, no matter how bad, how boring, how brutal. And anyway, she owed it to Kate to finish this thing, even if it did throw her way off her real mission. There was time to get back to that. Thorn wasn't going anywhere.

She needed to think it all out anyway. Things had gotten muddled now; the quest was tainted with these other feelings. She'd had plenty of practice at keeping her feelings separate from the workings of justice. You like the guy, hate the guy, it doesn't matter; your job is to find the glitch in the case against him that opens his cell door. Sarah had thought she was beyond sentimentality. But then there she was, over at this guy's house, bantering with him, going long periods with him without even remembering who he was, what he'd done, why she was there.

She had some friends in Miami she might have brought along tonight for protection. Lunch friends mainly. Good for ironic burnout jokes about work, clients, the impossible paper work. Good for a beer and a salad and back to work. There were a couple of guys she'd been dating, one especially from the state attorney's office, a guy she'd half opened up to once. But the guy had gotten nervous, hearing her voice change. He had some other things in mind.

Big help he could be anyway. She could just picture it. Hello, Stanley, want to take a little midnight cruise? Friday night, Saturday morning. Some light lifting, wind in the face, good profit margin. Some zippy South Florida thrills.

So there she was, alone. Kate was probably already smoke and ash, carried away by the steady easterlies. And Sarah, taking the air, guzzling gin, was preparing herself to be next.

Sarah didn't know, was it a good sign the shrimper was half an hour early? She watched its lights moving toward her. Sky very clear, a sickle moon, light swells. Sarah tried different things with the Colt while the shrimper drew close. Tuck it away in the waistband of her shorts, cover it with her shirttail, expose it, butt protruding. In the small of her back, TV cop style. She settled on display. They should know it was there, that it was going to cost them something to try to hurt her. At least make them move faster to kill her.

She watched as the boat slid up nearby. Some mother ship. To Sarah the term had always implied something formidable. This was just ten feet longer than the *Heart Pounder*, but with lots more beam and deep in the water. Usually with a crew of three. One would stay at the wheel while the other two swung down a cargo net with the bales. Two netfuls was her load. Fifty bales. And then one of them would come aboard sliding the bales around, settling most of them inside the cabin and the rest in ice chests out in the cockpit.

If Jorge were aboard, there would be some fast conversation; otherwise, it was just hurried work and move along, a quick handing over of a gym bag as the second netful was being lowered. Sarah stood, holding on to the starboard rail, watching the shadowy men appear on the shrimper.

She was alert to any slight variation of pattern. No way she was going to cooperate with that, nothing outside the routine, say, a voice she didn't recognize, a guy trying to board her before the first net load was lowered. The *Heart Pounder* was idling, ready to fly, but she'd still have to let go of the ropes they would throw over to tie her alongside. That would be the critical moment, the moment of exposure if she had to cast off to escape. She wished she knew some slipknot she could use to tie their lines to her cleats.

The captain of the shrimper reversed his engines, sidling up to her starboard. A dark figure appeared on the mother ship's port side. He cast her a line. She caught it, but an end lashed her in the eye.

Blinking back the tears, she tied the line to her stern cleat. She watched the shadowy man on the shrimper as she made her way to the bow. He tossed her the other line, and she made it fast as well. She looped it around the cleat and drew it tight, not cheating on the knot, connected now to this other ship, no matter what. No way to make a run for it. It had been silly ever to consider there was a way out of this, short of not coming. Silly to think the pistol meant anything to people determined to murder her.

She stood and turned back down the gunwale to the cockpit, hanging on to the chrome railing. Not even looking now. Absolutely aware of the boat, her peripheral vision and hearing tuned way, way up, but still not looking over there. All very normal, all very dignified. She tried to imagine Kate in her last moment, what stance she must have taken, what anxiety she had permitted herself when she saw what was coming.

As Sarah stepped back down into the cockpit, the screech of metal broke her balance. She stumbled back against the cabin door. Fumbled for the pistol in her waistband. Had a moment of freeze-frame terror as she accidentally cocked the hammer. She pulled the pistol free and stepped back into the cabin.

The crane groaned, cable screaming, as the net lowered over the open cockpit. A man was riding down with the cargo. That was new. She let her finger curl inside the trigger guard.

Sarah drew deeper into the cockpit, raising the Colt, half aiming it, half holding back in case this was just a small variation on standard procedure, something she hadn't seen, but still normal.

"Captain?" Man's voice, Latin undercurrent.

"I'm here."

"Who is it there?" Now *he* was on guard. It took so little to pull this thing way off course, into gunfire. The trust, even on a good night, was papery.

"Sarah. It's Sarah."

"Good evening, counselor." It was Jorge. Jorge riding down on the screeching cable.

But she was still nervous. Things change, Sarah was thinking. Jorge can change. From the warm, grateful man, courteous, sometimes even courtly, to something else. Sarah had been tricked so often by other Jorges, guys who at the jailhouse were docile, fawning, but who could turn sinister and bitter, lashing out at her without warning. After all, Jorge was succeeding in a business filled with paranoids carrying automatic weapons. It was foolish to be lulled by a warm voice.

"You are alone tonight?"

"Yes," Sarah said, still from the doorway. The revolver now out of his line of sight.

"Your friend? She is ill?" Jorge advanced slowly toward her, the netful of shiny black bales swaying behind him.

"No," said Sarah. "She was murdered." Clobber him with it, see if he flinches.

He stopped. He glanced quickly back at the shrimper. She could see him clearly now, from the shaded lights of the shrimper. Wary, a tightening of his stance.

"Murdered," he said. Weighing it, what it meant for him.

One of the others called harshly in Spanish from the shrimper, and Jorge turned and called back.

"There are boats in the area," Jorge told her. "We have been watching them all night."

"Following you?"

"Perhaps," he said.

"I need to know," said Sarah. "Have things fallen apart? Am I in trouble?"

"I hear of nothing," he said.

"Would you know, for certain, if someone did not want you doing business with me?"

"When was the woman killed?"

"Monday. Monday night."

"By this time I would know. No," he said, "I can tell you, no one cares about such a small quantity of marijuana. It could be of no importance to anyone."

Sarah felt her grip on the pistol relax, muscles hurting now from the pressure.

"Your friend was murdered for some other purpose," he said. "This amount. It is nothing to anyone." He turned and patted the net. "Now, we must work. There are boats tonight."

Sarah said, "One more load, Jorge. That's all I need. Tuesday night, this time. Right? The thirtieth?"

"*Sí*, and as much as you want, counselor. We are having a very good harvest. You want more, there is more for you."

Sarah actually caught a fish. She didn't know what to do with it, how even to get it off her hook. It was a pretty one, blue stripes running down its yellow body. In the early Saturday morning sunlight. It had fought hard as she reeled it in, turning on its side and thrashing. She had grimaced during the whole ordeal, and now that it was on board, she felt ashamed.

She knew she was only doing this for some invisible audience, which probably was not out there at all. Someone beyond the horizon who had her in his binoculars, someone who knew from her grimace that she was no fisherman.

She had put on Kate's khaki jacket and her long-billed cap, and as the sun rose, she had located Kate's sunglasses. Now she sat with this fish on her lap, looking out at the calm sea through Kate's eyes, inside her clothes. Eighty degrees already, but she was chilled. A shiver from the audacity of it, sitting out there in the rising light, loaded with enough marijuana to stone Miami for a month.

Her catch was in the fish box now, bleeding, panting. It fluttered, and Sarah squirmed in her seat. She rebaited the hook, choosing a shrimp that was already dead, and cast it out toward the dark reef. The line sailed out in a nice arc, and she closed the bail, picturing the bait sinking slowly into that bright world of fish and coral, doing it all as Kate had trained her. All for show, hoping her hoax would not require another fish to be sacrificed.

A boat had been nosing around for fifteen minutes, just far enough away so she could not make out more than its color. Red. Coast Guard was gray and blue, so it didn't arouse more than mild concern. But she watched it. Turning east, coming toward her, then back out, a turn south and then back north. She thought it might be trolling or some other type of fishing. All that was beyond her.

The boat stayed put for a while, due east, the sun rising just behind it, making it impossible for her to study it. She reeled in one of the lines. For a fast getaway. Her shrimp was gone. She set the rod in the rocket launcher behind the fighting chair and then reeled the other line in almost to the edge of the boat. She permitted herself a glance to the east. The crimson boat wasn't there.

She could smell the dope. The sweet herb was in the air. Like an Italian kitchen at suppertime. Surely the Drug Enforcement K-9 Corps back on shore were howling in their pens, raising their heads, trying to dig under their fences. Fifty bales wrapped in all that plastic, inside the styrofoam ice chests, and still its strong, dizzy scent was everywhere.

She sat back in the chair and checked the time. Seven-thirty. The Sabrosa Seafood truck would arrive at Kate's at eleven. Kate had always liked to arrive just before eleven so there was no gap between docking and unloading. Just part of her neatness. Boat captains had to be neat. Neat was survival. When the madness of marlin broken aboard, everything had to be orderly, in place.

The boat was beside the *Heart Pounder* only seconds after she'd heard it approaching. Its huge wake rocked her, and she saw one of the big ice chests full of dope shifting, readying for a long slide somewhere.

It was one of those ocean racers, possibly a Cigarette, one of those flashy, frivolous boats the guys in her office were always ogling as they roared past a bayside lunch restaurant. It was the boat of choice for cocaine smugglers and the Bimini-for-brunch crowd. That group of adolescents whose afternoon fun was running down porpoises out in the Stream, Bahamas and back to Miami for supper.

This one was red, and there were two of them on board. A short one in a tan uniform and a big one with a flesh-colored eye patch wearing the same uniform. They just stood there, staring at her as their bow banged her stern. She felt her pulse soar. Her chest tightened. They were taking too long, she thought. They seemed uncertain.

"Prepare to be boarded," the short one called.

"No way," she called back without thinking.

He opened his wallet and flashed a silvery card. "DEA, vice president's task force."

"I'm fishing," she said. She knew it was lame, but here she was, caught between roles. Which Sarah was she? "You have any kind of warrant?" There, that was better.

"We don't use warrants." He withdrew a large automatic from beneath his control console.

"You're not coming aboard my vessel without some probable cause," She was up now, inching back toward the cabin, the consolation of the Colt.

"We are coming aboard." But he didn't move. The big one with the eye patch was whispering to him. Maybe they were new at this, unsure, hadn't met such resistance before. She might be still within some rights she didn't know about. She wasn't even sure of the rules of boarding at sea anyway. But bluffing was the first skill of jurisprudence.

"I'm calling the Coast Guard to see if there are DEA in the area." Sarah moved into the cabin, keeping a watch on them. Raising the VHS microphone up so they could see her. Not turning it on. Waiting. Talking, mumbling. Waiting. Watching these two all the while. Mouthing some more into the microphone. Saying finally, "Over and out." It rang false as she spoke the words.

"There are no agents in the area," she called to these two. "I am within my legal rights to prevent you from boarding."

The short one, dark, curly hair, mirrored glasses, edged the racing boat closer to the *Heart Pounder*, craning forward, peering at Sarah. He said something over his shoulder to the fat one. The fat one braced himself against the rear seat. The wake it left splashed onto Sarah's rear deck, awoke her fish, one last thrash against the walls of the fish box, drowning in air.

Sarah sat down in the fighting chair, watching them go. Their boat's name, in gold script, *Perfect Execution*.

"You dumb shit." Irv pinched Milburn's tit and twisted hard, steering the Scarab with his left hand for a moment.

Milburn said, "I thought it was a goddamn ghost."

"I told you," said Irv. "You think when I shoot somebody, she gets up and goes fishing a week later."

"It was the boat, man. The same fucking boat. And it was a lady, looked just like the other."

"Man, you need an IQ transplant."

They were cruising at forty knots. Skimming the flat seas, cutting close to boats fishing the reef. Getting some mean looks, some up-yours fingers. Past the marker light where they had abandoned those nurses from Michigan.

"Well, it looked like her. Same clothes, same height."

"But about seventy-five years younger."

"Man, I'm still freaked."

"That old lady's history. We got us a date with an heiress. Let's get there." Irv mashed the throttle lever, trying to squeeze an extra knot out of those big Mercs.

18

Thorn ate breakfast at the same diner, had the same waitress, a woman Kate's age with a tall black confection of hair. He ordered three soft-boiled eggs and grits and a large coffee. The woman smiled at him but didn't seem to remember him.

He watched the diner fill up with Saturday locals. A couple of hippies still hanging in there in buckskin vests and granny glasses. Two tables of scruffy, red-eyed construction workers on their way to pick up some overtime. And a body builder in bright cologne.

After eating, he used the bathroom in the diner and headed back to the bash-mobile. It was a cloudy day, something ugly forming out over Cuba. Thorn took off his Last Resort T-shirt and slipped into the wrinkled Bash-a-Bug shirt. It was the same blinding pink as the car. On the back of it was a print of a cockroach, a booted foot coming down onto it.

He looked at his face in the rearview mirror, rubbed a few grains from the corners of his eyes. The face he saw there wasn't his own. The guy in the mirror seemed to know what the hell he was up to.

There were two uniformed two-hundred-pounders at the front gate of Sandpiper Bay Club. They were trying to perfect their smiles as Thorn pulled up to the gate.

One with a clipboard came over to the car. Thorn reached up and thumped the box on the ceiling, and the ears began to wag.

"Help you?" the guard said at the window, but not leaning down, taking a peek at the ears.

"Grayson wanted me to do a walk-through inspection."

The man stepped back, checked his clipboard. Turned and spoke to his partner. His partner checked another clipboard inside the guardhouse and shook his head at the first guard.

A silver Mercedes passed through the adjacent gate. The old man driving it took a second look at the VW, giving Thorn the evil eye.

Thorn said, "It's a little early to call Grayson, or I'd suggest you do that. He's the one ordered this. Originally I told him I couldn't get down here till next week, but after I thought about it, I thought every minute counted, so I came."

"If you're not on my list, you don't get in."

"This is a very sensitive issue," Thorn said. "The

department of health has given us strict orders not to reveal the nature of this scare. But I can tell you this much, I wouldn't be here on a Saturday if these bugs were just endangering the building."

The other one came out of the guardhouse, frisked Thorn with his eyes, stared at those ears grinding away up there.

"Little ants," Thorn said. "Almost invisible. They walk single file. Maybe you've seen some?" He watched them to see how he was doing. He had their undivided. "Up at Disease Control in Atlanta, they're making some linkups between these little guys and a couple of cancers; if I said their names, you'd recognize them." That lit up something in both their faces. "They eat infected food, crawl over your coffee cup, and there you go. Exchange of bodily solids."

"Little ants?" the second one asked.

"Size of coffee grounds," Thorn said. "Harmless-looking. And they won't bite you, sting you, nothing like that. It's swallowing them that's the trouble."

"We got something like that in there." He motioned to their cubicle. Standing there looking lost.

"I'll start here then," Thorn said. "Hey, you guys haven't had trouble with swollen glands, have you?"

They raised the gate, and Thorn parked in the first spot he came to. He opened the trunk and took out the spray can and a long, thin chrome rod he found lying there. Just the thing for probing for coffee ground ants.

It took him ten minutes, but Thorn found no trace of them in the security station.

"I swear I saw some little ants like that last week on Jackson's coffee cup," one of the guards said.

As he was leaving, Thorn said, "Could've been just pissants; there's a lot of those around, too."

He carried the sprayer back to the car and put it away. He glanced back at the guards. They were standing in the drive outside their office, one of them sneaking a feel of his throat.

Thorn walked through a breezeway to the pool and patio. Found an elevator and took it as far as it went. Fourth floor. He walked along the balcony, looking out at the Atlantic. It was as gray and choppy as the sky.

He walked from one end of the building to the other before he spotted what he was after. A stairway up to the next level. The heavy door was held ajar by a cushion of wind. Thorn climbed up through the wind to the fifth floor.

The view from up there was about fifty thousand dollars better. He could see water at the other end of the island. The ships steaming around the edges of the reef, the La Concha Hotel in the distance. And the other new high rises walling the city. In the heart of the town were the quiet treelined neighborhoods, tin roofs, second-story verandas, lacy white trim, those old Conch houses in the shade of the condos.

Just beyond where the balcony ended was the penthouse's wide picture window, mirrored against the sun. It had a panoramic view of the sea and the property below. The double doors to the penthouse were dark oak. There was a brass knocker in the shape of a ten-gallon Stetson.

Grayson answered the second round of knocking. He wasn't amused by Thorn's shirt, his chrome prod.

He was shirtless, a gold chain against his slick chest,

wearing faded jeans with ironed creases, a bandanna at his throat, and nothing else. Yippee ki-yay.

He seemed younger than he had that night at Key Largo Elementary doing his speech for the rowdies. Somewhere just past thirty. Probably not old enough to work up a good case of sentimentality about anything.

"Bugman," Thorn said.

"What?"

"Bugman," Thorn said. "Bash-a-bug."

"You're in the wrong place, bugman."

"Actually I didn't come to exterminate anything," Thorn said. "I wanted to talk. We have a friend in common."

Grayson glanced up at the darkening sky, back at Thorn.

"Get it over with," he said.

"His name's Amos Clay."

Thorn watched him process that. Grayson slanted his head and ran a make on Thorn. He seemed to come up blank.

"Amos Clay," he said. "So go on."

"Not out here," Thorn said. "I'm not gonna mug you. We're on the same side. It's just that I stumbled onto some information I thought you might find useful."

Grayson hesitated another moment, then stepped back and motioned Thorn inside.

Thorn stepped up into the room and waited as Grayson bolted the door. Thorn stared at thc place. A rough white stucco coated the walls, and an adobe fireplace was molded into one corner. There was a bleached longhorn skull on exhibit on the mantel. Dark stiff leather furniture, the leather worked with intricate designs. A cactus collection in clay pots.

In one corner of the room there was a tumbleweed the size of a stove. And on the picture window that Thorn had seen from the balcony there was a transparent Old West scene superimposed on Sandpiper Bay Club and the distant Atlantic. A band of Apaches were attacking some circled wagons. The settlers were hiding behind spoke wheels, firing rifles at the savages on their rearing horses. Outside, through the window, a cyclone of laughing gulls whirled. Someone on the beach was tossing bread up to them.

"Homesick for Texas?" Thorn said.

"I'm from Philadelphia."

Thorn sat in one of the stiff-backed leather chairs. Grayson standing, thumbs hooked in his belt loops.

"You mentioned a person's name," Grayson said.

Thorn said, "I wanted you to know. I thought you were the person who should hear this. I've heard you talk at meetings."

"Who are you?"

Thorn shifted in the Mexican chair. He crossed his legs.

"I'm somebody," he said, "who works inside people's houses and hears things I shouldn't."

"You've mentioned a name," Grayson said. "I'm interested in this name."

"I want to see Port Allamanda go ahead as much as anybody," Thorn said. "Know why?"

Grayson frowned.

Thorn, winging it still, said, "You get a whole lot of Yankees driving Lincolns, living out in the mangroves, first thing they're going to want is to pay somebody to come smush their palmetto bugs. They had roaches in Minnesota, but they didn't have these mother ships. These things, you try to kill them, they fly in your face. You try to squash one with your foot, it's like stepping on a piece of chocolate caramel. You get it stuck on your shoe, the floor. A real gooey mess, I'm telling you."

"Hey, I got all day. Saturdays I invite bugmen in and listen to their life stories." Grayson's face was taking on some color. He leaned toward Thorn, still keeping a distance. "Take your time, don't leave out anything. Know what I'm saying?"

"This person's name I mentioned, Mr. Clay," Thorn said. "Until lately I understand he'd been planning to sign over his bug ranch to a woman name of Kate Truman. Is that another name you know?"

"I do," said Grayson.

"Well, now she's dead, which I guess you heard about. I just heard myself yesterday, standing in the kitchen at Amos Clay's broken-down old house. And that's where I was when I heard this other thing I thought you should know about."

Grayson peered at him as if there were fog in the room.

"There's another person stepping in now. A guy, let's call him a relative of the deceased. How I hear it is this guy wants to run the bug plantation, raise mosquitoes. A real Bambi lover, this guy, worse than Kate Truman. Let the deer and the antelope play kind of guy."

"Oh, boy," Grayson said. He squinted at Thorn. "Who *are* you?"

"I'm a bugman. I hear things. I don't like to gossip, but some things I hear, they make me mad."

"Well, you shouldn't keep things bottled up if they make you mad," said Grayson. "Get ulcers that way. Know what I mean?"

"I do," Thorn said. "Some things, it's hard to go on living holding them inside. Not being able to talk to people about them."

Grayson said, "These days it's getting hard to find a good listener. It's how the pope stays rich."

"But people have needs," Thorn said. "Some people, they'll just talk and talk for free, and you can't shut them up."

Grayson pulled at a flake of skin on his lip, studying Thorn for a few beats of the heart; then he marched into the other room and brought back some fresh-looking bills. He held them by his side.

Thorn relaxed now, feeling he could sell this smart guy poison ivy for toilet paper, said, "I'm standing there in the kitchen, spraying Amos Clay's roaches, and I hear this guy in the other room say he's going to take up where Kate Truman left off, go ahead and buy this property. Guy by the name of Thorn. I hear the whole thing's going down near the end of the month, late in the afternoon the thirty-first."

"Look," Grayson said as he handed Thorn the money, "you wouldn't be shitting me, would you? Playing some kind of stupid game. You're not some wood rat lover, are you?"

Thorn said, "You kidding? I get paid to kill things like that. The more Yankees there are, the more I like it."

Grayson stared out his cowboy window, at a freighter rounding the reef line. "You know, I get a little paranoid. After a while you think nobody's on your side. I get made out as some kind of evil shit every day of the week. I'm this guy who's coming in here plundering your land, killing your animals."

"You don't look evil," Thorn said. Then he smiled and said, "But looking at vermin every day like I do, you maybe can't trust my judgment."

Grayson smiled uncertainly and said, "I hear nothing from these people but how I'm single-handedly wrecking the Keys. They're down here, soaking up all this sunshine all their life, smelling the breeze, making their rum drinks, and when somebody comes in and sees what they got and says, 'Hey, this is nice, I like this, I know some other people who'd like it, too,' they get their little armies together and get out there and say they love this wood rat or that butterfly and now nobody else can live here because this butterfly is all of a sudden more important than people. They're in the room nailing the door shut.

"If it weren't for men like me, this state would still be paying its way with roadside freak shows. Sure I made a buck on this and that. But you tell me something. When was the last time one of those people got out a machete and took a stroll through that land they're in such a hurry to protect? When was the last time they went out there in that swamp and played with a butterfly? They don't give a shit about any butterflies or mice. They're just as selfish as the next guy. This Kate Truman. She was the worst. In those meetings ranting about Port Allamanda and how bad it's going to be and she's cashing her checks every month on Vacation Island. Tell me that's not hypocritical.''

''July thirty-first,'' said Thorn. ''Fiveish.''

''Hey, bugman.'' Grayson stepped back as Thorn stood. ''You know what I'm saying, don't you? There's some intelligent people down here anyway, with an idea of what progress is.''

''I'm just an exterminator,'' Thorn said. ''If it's bigger than a spider, I don't understand it.''

''Thorn, huh?''

''Nice-looking guy, about my height. Most people up there know him. You might want to talk to him or something.''

''He have another name?''

''Not that I know of.''

''Tell me something.'' Grayson moved to the door and drew back the dead bolt. ''How do you keep your dignity wearing a stupid shirt like that?''

Grayson smiling away. Thorn smiled back.

''It isn't easy,'' he said.

Thorn prowled around Sandpiper Bay Club for a while longer, walking along the white dredged-up beach, trying to picture where the old Sands Piano Bar had been in relation to all that cement. He walked out the finger pier and looked back up at the hulk. Listening to the halyards clink.

The thunderhead had slid off to the northwest, headed for Naples and Fort Myers. Thorn watched a white-haired gentleman in red pants putt on the Astroturf green. He had his grip all wrong, holding on to it as if it were a mop. Dr. Bill had taken Thorn along caddying for him one summer way back, and he'd picked up a few things. This old man glanced over at Thorn, and Thorn could see the guy wasn't in a coachable mood.

Thorn walked past the pool, where the skin cancer crowd had begun to assemble. Over in the marina a large red Scarab was docking. Thorn leaned against the pier railing and watched the two guys in the racer tie up and come ashore. One was a big guy with a flesh-colored eye patch, the little one with dark, curly hair, puffing his chest out as he walked. Both very familiar.

They found a place at the outdoor bar, and Thorn watched as they drank down a couple of fast beers. That brought it back to him. The night of his drunk. The two guys with the nurses.

He hiked over there, keeping a distance from the bar, feeling a strange tightening of the throat. He walked along the dock, shooting looks at the two of them. The Scarab had drawn a crowd of kids. Thorn came up behind them and surveyed the boat. Very sleek. Muscular thing. Kind of boat Thorn had no use for because there was no use to it except to shear the tops off waves at fifty, fly across the Gulf Stream to the Bahamas, in the air at least half the time.

And he didn't like the smartass name they'd given her, *Perfect Execution*. He assumed it referred to someone's handling of money, stocks, bonds, some wonderful pirouette of capitalism that had scored enough cash to coast through a lifetime.

Thorn felt the wad of bills in his pants pocket. He thought maybe in the next lifetime being a bugman wouldn't be a bad way. Hell of a profit margin.

As Thorn was walking back around the pool, watching

the two from the boat, he saw Grayson on his way out the front gate. Dressed in tennis togs now, striding across one of the parking lots, head down. His attention focused on the pavement, as if he were scouting for the shimmer of loose change.

19

Ricki had borrowed three grand from her boss, showing him the clipping about Kate's death and giving him a story about having to pay for the burial, getting a little choky sound in her voice. Telling him she was going to be a rich lady soon and he'd get his money back then with interest. Then she'd told Lillian, her sometime lover, that if Lilly could come up with four grand, Ricki would turn it into ten in six months. So, bang like that, Lillian emptied her money market account, been building it for eight years waitressing and doing some topless dancing. True love.

When she got back to the apartment, she took a shower, trying to scrub Thorn out of her brain. She had a couple of belts of rum and was working on a third when she heard them come in downstairs. Making an asshole scene, laughing and giggling with Lillian.

They came into her room without knocking, walked around taking an inventory, not saying a word, not even looking at her. And she let them do it. Still knocked on her ass by Thorn's acting so cocksure. He seemed different. Something going on in his eyes she'd not seen before.

Ricki walked over and took her ceramic pink flamingo out of Irv's hand and put it back on the bookshelf. Though this was thc first time she'd met these two, she'd talked to Irv, knew what a prick he liked to be.

Trying for a businesslike tone, she said, "What I want to know at this point is, do you guys do accidents? Make it look like something else?"

Irv said, "Do we do accidents?"

"Our specialty is accidental death and dismemberment," said Milburn.

"I don't know about you two," she said.

Irv said, "This bimbo is being the hard bargainer. She's standing there, holding the wad of cash she owes us, in her chink robe, trying to play tough."

"I didn't like how you did the other one. The grass all over the place. That was dumb. How do I know you can do an accidental one worth a shit?"

"Call the Better Business Bureau, honey," said Irv. He edged toward her, as if he were picturing a quick snatch of that money.

"You ever hear of café coronaries?" Milburn asked her. "How Mama Cass died, scarfing down a ham sandwich? It gets caught in the airways, Heimlich maneuver stuff.''

Ricki nodded, not sure of this guy. A slight tremble cropping up in the hand holding all that cash.

''Well, we do boudoir coronaries,'' Milburn said. ''Falling out of the leather trapeze. Strangling on a dildo. Electrocution by vibrator. That kind of thing.''

Ricki stared at him. Looked for help to Irv, double-checked Milburn. ''He's kidding,'' she said.

''He's a kidder,'' Irv said.

Milburn settled into that straw throne chair. Coronation time in the kingdom of assholes, Ricki thought.

They were dressed very weirdly. Uniform things with patches on the sleeves. In small print the patches said, DON'T FUCK WITH AMERICA. Like Nazi Boy Scouts.

Irv said, ''Honey, thing is, your credit rating is gone to shit with us. We're not in this business for the applause. You want to fly first class this time, you're going to pay for first class.''

''I got your three,'' she said. ''And I got four more.''

''Four more,'' Irv said. ''You hear that, Jack Benny? She's got four more.''

Irv sat down on the edge of her water bed. She was standing by the window, noontime sun lighting up her dark eyes, glossing her short black hair.

Irv said, ''Honey. Normally, people in our profession never meet with our customers.''

''That's right,'' said Milburn. ''But we made an immaculate conception in your case.''

Irv staring at Milburn, like who *is* this guy!

Irv said, ''We looked you up, honey, 'cause number one, we're our own collection service, and you owed us some money. And number two, we wanted to get to meet you, a girl who had morals we can relate to.''

"Yeah?'' Ricki sat down at her dressing table. Her knees weren't taking this very well.

"It takes a special kind of girl to tack a halo on her own mother. Takes the kind of girl who knows what she wants and goes after it.'' Irv paused, cleared his throat for effect, and switched over to his consultant's voice, down to business with the good Death. "Now, is what you're telling us that there's somebody else standing in front of you in the gravy train? And you want us to finish this up, clean this guy out? Let the money flow?''

"That's right. That's the situation,'' she said.

"Who's the lucky guy this time, your daddy?''

"Adopted brother,'' Ricki said.

"Jesus F. Christ, is she something or what?'' Irv said to Milburn, clapping his hands and doing a little wiggle in the hips. "Well, like I said. We wanted to meet you anyway, cause we had an idea we could help you out in another way. Like with some of the assets that will be coming your way.''

"What assets?'' She had picked up a hair brush, was holding it now like a hammer. Like maybe she'd brush these two guys to death.

"Well, we had occasion to have a few drinks at a place up in Matecumbe.''

Ricki said quietly, "Vacation Island.''

"Ri-ii-ight. Very go-oo-od.'' Irv nodded at her and nodded at Milburn. "Vacation Island. Now that's what we would consider proper payment. For killing a guy who's related to a woman we already killed.

"See, I don't know if you're perceiving this thing all

that clearly. You kill one person, and nobody knows exactly what the deal is, 'cause this person could be into all kinds of bad shit. But you kill a second person shortly thereafter, a person who in this case is even related to the first, well, now you've established a pattern. Patterns, honey, we don't like patterns. Bad for business.

"So, if I say that yes, we'll do this, we'll yank the plug on some guy you name for us, so you can be a rich rich lady, then I'm saying it with the understanding that I can take a nice long vacation myself after the deed is done.

"Vacation Island," Irv said. "Vacation Island."

"Well, forget it then," Ricki said. "Take your three and split." She started counting the money on the dressing table.

"Honeybuns, honeybuns." Sounding grieved. "Think about this. You're not in a great position here. There's people around who don't care about you, who would just as soon you were an earthworm farm."

"Who?"

"Us, honeybuns. Me and my friend. Us."

"Forget it. Forget the whole thing. I'm finished with all this."

"Nobody's finished with nothing," said Milburn. "Hey, man. Let's just wet this broad and take our cash and our bonus and get on with it."

"See? See what I'm telling you? My associate wants to go have lunch. He wants to pinch out your flame and go have lunch. You see what you're up against here?"

"OK," Ricki said, her voice misty. "I don't give a shit. You can have Vacation Island. It sucks anyway. I just want the money. You do this guy, and you got it.

But it has to be an accident. None of this dildo stuff. A real live accidental death."

"Everybody's a joker," said Irv. "Everybody's up for an Oscar."

"His name is Thorn," Ricki said. "I drew you a map, how to find his house."

A half hour after they left Ricki's, Milburn was still going on about how they should have killed her, and Irv, concentrating on finding a decent restaurant on Duval Street, let him talk. He finally found a place beside a dime store. On the other side of it was a shop selling bikinis and T-shirts. Across the street was the Hemingway bar, its big doors open and inside looking dark and empty. Parachutes draped from the ceiling, Jimmy Buffet on the jukebox, moaning about what a drunk he'd become.

Irv hated Key West. It wasn't all the gay guys checking him and Milburn out, and it wasn't all the tourists with their funny hats and matching clothes. It was the smell. The funk of vegetables rotting in the sun. Food becoming something else.

You'd think with all that gingerbread on the storefronts, all that fresh paint, all that incense coming out of the little purple boutiques and the hammers going nonstop up and down Duval, they'd take more care with their garbage. Irv pictured a festering carcass down in the bowels of the city. Only city he'd smelled worse than this was New Orleans, the French Quarter. Another queer town.

"This guy," said Milburn, as Irv was combing his

hair in the window of the dime store, "this guy isn't going to be real happy to see us."

"Yeah."

"He told us, I remember it, 'Don't ever show yourself within ten miles of me.' "

"I remember. A nice guy. Sweetheart."

"I feel dorky in this uniform. We don't look like any boat captains I ever saw."

"Hey," said Irv, putting his comb back in his pocket, making Milburn squeeze out of the way as he headed for the restaurant. "Hey, man. You dressed us like this."

"I feel like a part of the vegetable kingdom," Milburn said.

Irv stared at him. What was with this guy?

"Here's the scene, Mr. Tomato. We're going to see him. Lay it out for him. We know something's coming down the pipe, something big. We can smell it on the way, and we want a small piece of it. We don't tell him about Vacation Island or any of that. We just go in there and act like we are there to give further assistance, but we're not in anybody's farm league anymore. You, you just stand there and try not to fart. I'll handle it."

"I say we go to the nude beach and get out of these things, forget Grayson, forget anything coming down any pipeline. You already got Vacation Island. You're pushing our luck we go in there. This guy is very unfriendly on the phone. I have no desire to become business partners with this person."

"I have no desire to become business partners with this person." Irv doing his sissy imitation. "Listen to you, man. Listen to your stupid self."

Irv swung the doors of the restaurant open and nearly whacked two thin young men who were walking past. One of them gave him the fluttering eye. Irv smacked his lips at the guy, blew him a kiss. La-di-da.

Shaking his head and groaning, Milburn dragged himself after Irv. As they were being seated, Irv reached around and touched the flat automatic holstered under his shirt. Mean little SIG/Sauer nine-millimeter printing its silhouette into his lumbar region. He tucked his khaki shirt in tight around it.

They had a beer at a bar that opened onto Duval. Sitting at a little table almost on the street. Irv watched all the bartenders fussing with ferns, polishing the brass light fixtures. While Milburn complained about his eye, couple of guys at a table nearby, dressed as Kmart managers, were having a late lunch, a conversation about somebody stealing stock from the warehouse. Everywhere you looked, people ripping off what they could.

Milburn ordered fried chicken, and Irv scowled at him.

"I like fried chicken," Milburn said.

"And you, sir?" The waiter was wearing jeans and an undershirt.

"Give me a barf bag," he said. And while the waiter watched him, Irv just sat there, taking the waiter's scorn or whatever he was sending out. Finally the waiter left.

"Can't you ever be nice?" Milburn asked him.

"What is it with you ordering fried chicken?"

"I *like* fried chicken. Just because Irv senior is fried chicken czar doesn't mean I can't ever eat the stuff."

That was it. Milburn was dead.

"Hey, enjoy it," Irv said. "Eat every greasy morsel. Slide it down into that grease pit of a body. It could be the last fucking food you ever eat."

"Jesus, Irv. I thought you'd be happy for once. Vacation Island. Think about it, man. You and me, running a whole big resort." Milburn raked his fork across the white tablecloth, a little kid, excited. Trying to whip Irv up. "I see myself as losing some weight. You know, getting down to my fighting weight, one-eighty or something. Get into one of those little bikini suits, start doing weights. Slay the women. Just stay out in the sun all day and fucking slay the women."

"Sure, Milburn. Sure. Dream on." Dead man.

"And like get out of this business. I don't like it anymore. It's not fun." Lowering his voice. "It was fun, but it isn't anymore. I'm having bad dreams. I like the idea of getting into something legit. You know. Like we had our fun, and now we're getting older and more serious. Mid-life crisis and all that shit. I'm ready for it, whip myself into shape, and sleep good again. I don't see any reason we couldn't be happy running a place like that. We can do it. Shit, the two of us? We're a fucking team, man."

Irv had just shoved Grayson's door open and walked in. Milburn behind him talking about being polite. Polite. What'd he think, they were missionaries? Inside the door they just stood there, Irv soaking up the ambiance. Place gave good ambiance.

Should have known Grayson would have a fag secretary. Blond guy looked like he'd just gotten off a

Swedish cruise ship. Blue eyes. Handsome sucker, and he wasn't having any of it from them either. Grayson was in, doing important business on the phone, and he wasn't seeing anybody didn't have an appointment. Not even old friends, not even old friends who'd come a long way. Not even old friends who had a wad of money.

Irv stood back away from the secretary and looked at the waiting room. It was in a one-story Conch house, with wood floors and couches and rocking chairs and paintings of seascapes and scenes from New England. Palms in clay pots. Somebody's parlor. This secretary didn't even sit behind a desk. He was there in a white wicker chair, reading a paperback, wearing tennis clothes. But on the glass-topped table beside him there was an appointment book, so Irv knew he wasn't shitting them. He was the gatekeeper all right.

Saturday morning, just jerking off a few leftover clients before he was off to the tennis club. It didn't sit well with Irv, kind of snob shit that ragged his ass.

"Hey, Adonis," Irv said, pretending to study a painting of sea gulls on the beach at Martha's Vineyard, "tell me something. You ever been shot? I mean with a pistol. Smith and Wesson, like that?" He heard Milburn making noises behind him.

"You two better leave now," Rolfe said, or Ingmar or whatever the fuck he was.

"I got this crazy urge. Call me nutty, but I just feel like opening up a new asshole for somebody. Does this mean I'm a sociopath? Is this what this means? I get down here, all this Hemingway stuff everywhere, and I feel like killing something and hanging it on my wall."

The kid was on his feet now. The guy had forearms. And calves. Probably a hell of a backhand.

Irv walked over to one of the potted palms, opened up the fly on those stupid khaki shorts, and took a leak.

The kid had the phone up to his face and was punching in the numbers. Irv zipped up and drew out the automatic.

"Put it back to sleep," he said. "We want to see our man, Grayson, is all we want. But we want that one thing very bad."

"Back here," said the blond. Businesslike now, like he'd had this experience before. You really wanted to see Grayson, you had to pull your gun.

He led them down a hallway lined with photographs. Ground-breaking ceremonies, ribbon cuttings. Same young stud in every one. Dark-haired, trim little guy with a haircut from Princeton or Yale or somewhere like that. Irv decided he would like this guy, like doing business with a person with a good haircut like that. Not some stringy, greasy-haired college dropout like Milburn.

The secretary said, "I'm sorry, Philip. Guy's got a gun."

"It's Philip, is it?" Irv cooed.

The four of them stood around and stared at each other. Finally Milburn sat in one of the green leather chairs, and that seemed to break the spell.

"If you're who I think you are, I am pissed off. I am very pissed off anyway. But if you are who I think."

"We're the guys you have your friends call up. That's who we are. We're the kind of people, things usually get messy when we're pissed off."

"Randy, go sit in the den," Grayson said.

"Randy stays," Irv said. "Right here. I don't want him to call up his doubles partners or anything like that."

Grayson was in tennis togs, too. His were more colorful, though. Dark green shirt, yellow wristband. Off-white shorts. Thick, hairy legs. He went about five-nine. Kind of guy you expect to see delivering the six o'clock news. Hell of a haircut.

He sat down behind his desk. It was a long teak thing, modern, completely bare. Not even a phone. Behind him there was a computer terminal, screen, printer. And the place was full of palms, the same kind Irv had watered in the other room. Five or six of them. Air smelled of fresh dirt.

"You stupid sons of bitches," Grayson said. Elbows on his desk, grinding the thumb of one hand into the palm of the other. "Put that stupid gun away."

Irv slid it into the front pocket of those pants.

"Now what do you want here?"

"Nothing much," Irv said.

"The bitch didn't pay you, I suppose."

"She paid us," said Irv.

Grayson seemed surprised.

"OK, then what?"

"It's about this deal. This lady, what's her name, Truman?"

"Kate Truman," Grayson said, closing his eyes briefly and exhaling through his nose. The topic was a direct hit.

"My associate and I are phasing out of the liquidation business. Too much bad karma associated with it. Take lifetimes to purify all we done already. We're on the lookout for other opportunities. Work with less of a hemoglobin factor. You see what I'm saying?''

Grayson said, ''I think I do.''

''And we were putting two with two the other day, and it kept coming up with your name. Like this woman, Kate Truman, and how she had to get buried on account of something that's to your advantage. Of course, the daughter just wants the inheritance. But we were real curious about how it was a cost-effective thing for a man like you. I mean, we figured this girl didn't just get our phone number from the yellow pages, and when we asked her about it, she said well, yes, it was you.

''So, it seemed like a natural coincidence. Synchronicity and all that. Us looking for a new career and you expanding your horizons all at the same time.''

Grayson had propped his chin on his right fist. *The Thinker*, giving Irv the full magnetism of his attention. Guy must have girls oozing under the doors at night. He sat up and pulled a red bandanna, of all the crazy things, out of his tennis shorts and wiped the sheen off his forehead. Some kind of cowboy nut probably, a saddle sniffer.

''Before I say anything else, let me make this clear. I think you two are scum. You're worthless asshole trash, and you're going to wind up as pet food.''

''He doesn't like us,'' Milburn said. ''Boo-hoo.''

Had to hand it to that Milburn.

''But I think I can use you. I think I can take advantage of your greed and stupidity and make an arrangement here that might be of mutual benefit.

That's my idea of good business. Where everybody walks away happy."

"Everybody screws everybody else at the same time. Daisy-chain economics," Milburn said. Man, the guy was really working, huffing along, trying to pull even. But no, Irv had already decided about Milburn.

"I was just on the phone," Grayson said. "With a friend of mine. A man from up in your neck of the woods in Key Largo. A nice old gentleman who is maybe slightly confused from not having enough blood running through his brain anymore."

"He must've been talking to my daddy," Irv said to Milburn.

"This gentleman is going to be a wealthy man soon. One way or the other he is soon to receive a million dollars. A million cash dollars."

Irv smiled. Yeah, he'd known there was something like that happening. He looked over at Milburn. The guy had a tit in his mouth he was so happy.

"In fact, I know the time and date that a transaction is to occur in which a million dollars in cash will be arriving at a particular address. I don't want this transaction to be completed. It is important to me, very important that such a deal is not completed. In fact, it's so important that I'm willing to deal with scum like you two to see that it does not reach fruition."

"All right so far," Irv said. Trying not to sound the way he felt.

"If the person or persons delivering the cash have to be hurt during this arrangement, then so be it. If one or more people have to be sacrificed, that's acceptable to me. But the old gentleman I mentioned. He is absolutely not to be touched. Absolutely off limits. The two of you intercept this cash and disappear. Buy a ranch and raise pigs. Do anything. But don't ever appear in my line of sight again. Ever.''

Irv was thinking maybe he'd find out which it was, Yale, Princeton, Harvard, this guy went to. What courses he took that made him such a hardass. It wasn't too late; Irv could go back to school, turn himself into this person.

Or no, maybe take his cash and go out to Hollywood, take some of those acting classes he'd always heard about. Buy himself an agent, get a part opposite Jack Nicholson. No, not Nicholson. Much as he liked the guy, Jack would upstage him. No, some broad. How about Julie Andrews? Yeah. Clickety clickety. Let the cash from Vacation Island fill up his bank account while he used the million for his movie career.

Irv stood up. ''This sounds suitable.'' He walked over to Milburn, stood behind his chair. Put his left hand on Milburn's shoulder. ''I think I can work with you, Grayson, even though you're clearly a shitty judge of character.''

Irv reached into his trouser pocket, drew out the nine-millimeter, took off the safety, and snugged the barrel against Milburn's neck. Before Milburn could even wriggle, Irv aimed straight down into his body and fired twice. Just more hammers nailing more nails in more buildings. An inspired moment.

Milburn didn't move for a few seconds; then he made a little shiver, a wheeze. Some other noise that could've been him trying to say Irv's name. His head dropped forward, jerked, and the sack of shit tumbled onto the rug.

The secretary kid jumped up, knocked his chair over.

"Sit down, Randy." Irv aimed at his face.

Milburn twitched on the rug, a dog having a dream.

"Sit," Grayson said. He glanced back over his shoulder out his window. Irv moved over there quickly to check the view. Just backyards. Everybody mowing and a stereo playing some rock and roll. Sixties acid rock. Key West, twenty years out of it, and holding.

Irv felt something new. Killing Milburn, it wasn't like the others. There was this feeling, queasy and hot rising inside his gut. Nothing like that before. It was a revelation. All those others had been strangers. He'd known them five minutes tops, basically strangers, and when they were lying there, seeping out onto rugs and decks, they were still strangers, and the thrill had been cold and white.

But this one was complicated. He felt the usual race in his heart, but there was this new acid zing of regret as Milburn collapsed forward onto the pale blue rug. A brand-new emotion. It was this whole new thing opening up to him, this full-bodied thing. This thing had been there all along, and now he'd discovered it, a continent of unexplored pleasures, killing acquaintances, family. Irv beamed.

"What the fuck are you thinking about!" Grayson's face pumped full of blood.

"I just made myself a half million dollars," Irv said.

"Good God."

"Hey, and what it is is you need to see it in person. You want to be Casey Stengel, you got to stand up close and watch the guys hit the home runs. Where you can hear the crack of the bat. Otherwise, man, you might think what I do is not worth the price. Hitting it out of the ball park, man, this's what you just saw. Hitting the long ball.

"And hey, let me warn you two. I didn't see the exit holes for those slugs. I think they're still in there traveling through all that blubber. I'd stand back away from this heap for a while, I was you."

"You need help, man," said Randy. The kid had lost his tan. His asshole probably wouldn't ever come unpuckered.

"What I need is a time, a date, and a place where a mutually beneficial transaction is to take place. That's all I need." Irv stepped across Milburn, avoiding the blood spreading through the carpet. All that IQ spilling out. Man, Irv was sailing, literally come loose from the earth.

20

Ricki lay down on the water bed, still in her Leonard's Lobster House clothes, white shorts and a T-shirt that said KISS OUR CRUSTACEANS. Tired but wired. It'd been busy for a Sunday night. Lots of Miami assholes, dawdling over their Key lime pie, trying to milk one more night out of their weekend. Getting drunk for the three-hour drive home. Ricki got most of her orders wrong, lost a credit card, and spilled minestrone soup on a woman from Oregon. Her hands had trembled so bad all day it was a wonder she'd held on to anything.

The bathroom light was glaring in her eyes, but she was too tired to get up and turn it off. She twisted around for a comfortable position, but the damn water bed kept shifting with her. It was good for some things, bouncing your hips back up, giving you a little thrust, even if you didn't have it in you to thrust back. But not so good when what you needed was a foxhole.

She sniffed her fingertips. Garlic and fish. She listened to the rattle of palm fronds at her window. Closed her eyes and pictured Tahiti, Eleuthera, Martinique, a smoky bar from a fifties movie. Black-and-white, about expatriated Americans. Sidney Greenstreet, Jane Russell, lots of bamboo furniture and louvered shutters, marble columns, and lazy paddle fans. All shot at night, about love and sin and danger. Usually this worked, made her mind go hazy, brought on sleep.

Ricki pulled herself up and poured some spiced rum into a plastic glass she kept beside her bed. She sat on the edge of the water bed and lugged half of it down. No. No. No. It wasn't guilt. She didn't feel a ripple of that, not a twinge, not a hint. Let Thorn mourn. Kate had been his mother, not hers. There was no doubt about it now. The will spelled it out. Thorn ate at the table; Ricki got what fell on the floor.

She stood up, took the rum over to the chrome sling chair in front of her little black-and-white TV, and switched it on. Abbott and Costello, test pattern, some nature show about African drought. She turned it off. Sipped more rum as she walked over to the front window. A good breeze off the water tonight. Of course, in Key West everything was off the water. She could see a narrow patch of it from the window, glazed with moonlight. Atlantic or Gulf of Mexico, she could never tell.

She lay down again on the water bed, balancing her

glass of rum on her stomach. Let Thorn mourn her while he still could. This puny kid, two years older than she was, who'd already had a good, solid grip on Kate by the time she was born. She'd never had a chance. Let Thorn mourn. Fuck if she would.

Someone was in the house, coming upstairs. Probably Lillian home from the Pier House, wanting to shoot the shit, or maybe wanting a tussle in the water bed. Not tonight. Ricki was beat, worn to shit. And still frazzled by Thorn and those two goons in uniforms.

She had it on her lips, "not tonight," as the door opened. But it was Randy. The blond stud that clerked for Grayson. Well, maybe she did feel like a quick frolic after all. I mean, come on, look at the guy.

She smiled at him, though it did strike her as mildly impolite that he hadn't knocked. Impolite or sexy, she wasn't sure.

She told him to come in, asked him how he'd been.

He just stood in the doorway.

He said, "He wants to see you."

"OK, that's cool." Ricki set her rum on the bedside table. "You tell him I'll come in about ten. Whenever I manage to untangle from the sheets."

"He wants to see you now," Randy said. Guy had no sense of humor. She remembered it now, why she didn't like him. One of those gays who liked men in direct proportion to how much they hated women.

"I'm too tired, Randy. Tell him I'll be in first thing."

"Get up," he said, shutting the door behind him. "Right now."

* * *

Grayson's yacht was a fifty-two-foot Hatteras. Bar was stocked with nonalcoholic beer and wine. The damn stuff tasted like Kool-Aid, and who could stand the taste of that stuff without the buzz? But Grayson didn't seem to notice, drinking one phony beer after the other. Ricki sat on the couch, and Grayson, wearing dark slacks and a navy Windbreaker, stood beside the bar. His eyes skimmed over hers, not locking on anything like they usually did. That, as much as anything, made her scared.

Randy had the yacht going flat out.

"Martinique?" Ricki asked. "Eleuthera?"

"Like that," Grayson said. "More exotic, though."

"Come on, man. Just tell me if you're mad at me or what."

"I'm not mad. I don't get mad at you, Ricki. I save mad for when I need a little extra boost, for when the competition gets stiff. Mad gets the adrenal gland humping. But I'm not mad with you, Ricki. It's not necessary."

"What did I do?"

Grayson smiled. Not a pretty sight.

"What did you do? What did you do? How to answer a question like that."

"I paid those guys. I got some money from a friend and paid those guys, if that's what this is all about. You were worried I hadn't paid them."

"I know you paid them."

"You do?"

"Yes. Can you guess how I know?"

"They came over afterwards, yesterday. To see you."

"I'm impressed, Ricki. You impress me with your deductive reasoning." All this without meeting her eyes.

Grayson paced the thick blue carpet, staring at his spotless Top-Siders. Ricki didn't like how fast they were going, how straight. She kept waiting for Randy to circle back.

"I understand you enlisted their aid again. That you instructed them to subtract another relative of yours from the list of the living."

"I knew you wouldn't like it," she said. "But they're going to do an accident. Like he was so torn up by Kate's dying that maybe he lost control of his car, something like that."

"Hey, babe, you're missing the point. The point is that you asked these gentlemen to remove a person I want to stay alive for a little longer."

"Thorn?" Ricki said. "Why?"

"You see?" said Grayson. "You're acting without the complete picture. You're sending people off to kill other people without the big view. But worse than that, Ricki, if somebody else from your family gets dead, I don't care how stupid or lazy the cops down here are, they're going to get a very big hard-on if something like that happens."

Ricki said, "It's my business. You don't have anything to say about my business. I helped you make out pretty good, and I got left with practically nothing. Twenty-five thousand fucking dollars."

Grayson opened another of those phony beers. Poured it into a fresh frozen mug. It foamed up like the real thing. Ricki watched him sip it, the head leaving him a momentary mustache. Not that she wanted one, but the jerk hadn't even offered her anything.

"Unfortunately, your business and my business have

become intertwined. If you're ever in some sheriff's interrogation room, all of a sudden I'm feeling very uneasy.''

''Come on, Gray, you think I'm going to give the police your name? You think I would put you in any danger?''

''No,'' he said. ''No, I don't think you will.''

''Well, good,'' she said. But she wasn't sure if it was good at all, the way he'd said it.

''I want you to see something, Ricki. Meet somebody.''

He held his arm up, beckoning her into the forecabins.

Ricki took a breath, stood up, and let him lead her down the stairs and into the narrow hallway. He stopped at the first cabin door, unlocked the door, and swung it open.

''This. This is what you were dealing with.''

Ricki looked into the cabin and saw Milburn, lying on his back on a tarp in the middle of the floor.

She sucked in a breath and turned away.

When they were back upstairs in the salon, Grayson paced the rug in front of her.

''I don't like loose ends, Ricki. And you are an appalling loose end.''

''You're taking me out here to shoot me.''

''No. Of course not.''

''Yes, you are. You're taking me out here and you're going to shoot me and throw me to the goddamn sharks. Along with that body. Jesus Christ.''

''Ricki, Ricki.'' Like he was offended. ''I wouldn't do something like that. You obviously don't know me very well.''

"Well, good," she said, relieved but still wanting to sound peeved.

"That's not my style." Grayson leaned against the bar, cocking his mouth into another smile. About as real as that beer. "All that talk about an island. You know, Ricki. It made an impression on me. I have a soft spot for islands, too."

Ricki stared at him. The bastard was getting off on this.

"I think I've found the perfect island for you. Deserted. Tropical. Nobody to disturb your meditations, your pursuit of higher consciousness. No tourist trains or high rises. Great water view. Excellent location to work on your latest mantra." Grayson was trying awful hard to sell her on that smile.

"There's only one thing about this island, Ricki. A minor drawback, actually, but it would be dishonest of me not to mention it." Grayson put his mug down on the butcher-block counter. "It's only an island about twelve hours a day."

Now he looked at her, square on, flat and lightless eyes.

Randy cut the engines and came down into the cabin. Ricki caught his eye and gave him a starving, helpless look.

"We're here," he told Grayson, his voice hard.

"OK. Take her out on the deck, put her onshore, and cut her." He was rummaging through a drawer behind the bar.

"Come on, Gray." Ricki stood and came across to him. Her voice was catching in her throat. "I'm no threat to you. I'll disappear."

Grayson held out a thin fillet knife to Randy.

"No way," said Randy. "This is sick. All of it. You, those guys, all of it."

"Do it, Randy. Do it now." Ricki stood back, looked for her cue, watching the knife catch the dim cabin light. She saw the reflection of this stiff little group in the cabin window.

Randy shook his head and turned away from Grayson.

Grayson glared after Randy as he walked out to the cockpit and climbed the chrome ladder back to the upper deck.

"All right," said Grayson, his eyes still on the path Randy had taken. "Come on." He gripped Ricki's upper arm and half carried her out to the aft deck.

It was like a seizure when it hit her, something giving her a strength she didn't have. Just outside the cabin door she wrenched her arm from Grayson's hold, thrashed her arms for a second, made a lunge for the knife. But Grayson had danced back from her. She moved quickly to the transom and screamed for Randy to help her.

She could see him up there, moonlight spilling over the tower. Ricki screamed his name, her voice tearing in her throat, but he didn't turn to look. She called out to him again, bleakly this time, "For godsakes, Randy. Do what's right."

She saw Grayson edging closer to her, the knife in his left hand. She bowed her head, tried to recall a prayer from all those years with Kate and Dr. Bill, but only a mealtime grace came to her: "For what we are about to receive, the Lord make us truly thankful."

When she woke, her jaw was very sore. She managed to sit up on the soft sand. Grayson had stripped her to her underwear. Gentleman to the end. She winced as she drew her throbbing left foot up to her lap like she might try a little midnight yoga. The gash he'd made ran the length of her sole. Maybe it was his idea of a final kindness, letting the blood leak into that rising water, calling the scavenger sharks.

The lights of his Hatteras were about a half mile off to the north now. She could hear voices out there, Grayson and Randy having it out. When the three gunshots came, a surge of energy woke in her, and she craned forward, focusing every nerve, every fiber of hope on those lights.

Five more minutes passed before the yacht's big diesels came alive. She watched as the Hatteras swung around and headed back in toward her. It must have been making ten knots when it passed fifty yards from her island. Without the strength to call out, Ricki watched it pass. A sob strangling in her throat.

Her island was about ten feet long, five feet wide. Ricki scooted forward across the damp sand and brought her bleeding foot to the edge of the water. The tide was running fast to the north, piling up some foam near her foot.

As the tide rose, Ricki kept herself propped up, stiffened her neck to keep her head from lolling. A gull or some kind of white bird landed on the sand a few yards from her. When Ricki was a kid, Kate had always been after her to learn the differences between birds. But hell, she'd always had more important things to do than learn the goddamn names of birds. The water tickled at her foot as Ricki tried as hard as she could to remember what those things had been.

* * *

On Sunday Thorn took his time driving home. He was relaxed. He stayed behind a Buick from Wyoming the whole way, developing a relationship with the two kids in the back seat. Communicating with them with the mouse ears.

He'd spent the afternoon on Saturday walking around Key West behind the two guys in the Scarab. He'd gotten very interested in them because they had drunk down those beers and gone straight away to Grayson's penthouse.

Thorn saying to himself, well, well, well. After they tried there, they walked back into the neighborhoods, seemed to be lost for a while, and eventually wound up at Ricki's two-story house. Thorn not saying anything to himself then. His heart sounding in his ears.

They stayed in her house for about an hour, Thorn sitting on the sidewalk down from Dr. Leery. Dr. Leery wasn't happy about it. At about eleven they came out, smiling, talking loud to each other, and walked down Duval and had lunch. From there to Grayson's office. Only the short one came out an hour later, and Thorn followed him to the beach at the Pier House, where the guy stared at topless women all afternoon.

At sunset the guy went over to Mallory Square and stood around with about fifty others watching the sun slip behind a mass of black clouds. He chatted up a tall, heavyset woman there who had a flame-swallowing act. After sunset the guy took her back to Captain Tony's bar, where the two of them drank till about ten-thirty. Thorn followed them back to Sandpiper Bay Club then and watched as the guy had a hell of a time getting through security.

At that point Thorn had gone out on the public pier across the way from Sandpiper Bay's marina and had watched them as they climbed aboard the Scarab and disappeared into the darkness. He'd gone back to his parking spot then and let the seat back in the southernmost bash-mobile and had a good, dreamless night.

At two on Sunday he was back in Key Largo. Jerome senior was in the office, watching a baseball game on the tube. He handed Thorn the keys to Kate's VW without taking his eyes off the set, watching the replay of a stolen base.

"Junior said to tell you he wanted to borrow your cruiser this week. Figures he'll survive I-95 in a Cadillac better than in one of the VWs." Jerome glanced over at Thorn for a second while the beer commercial played. "Why the hell you think he'd want to survive a crash in the condition he's in?"

"Just stalling," Thorn said. "Any way we can."

Thorn stopped by the funeral home. He saw Sally Spencer with a family in one of the viewing rooms and went into her office to wait. The cardboard box was on the corner of her desk, a white gummed label on its lid with Kate's name typed on it. He stood there for a moment looking at it, hearing someone weeping in the next room.

Out the office window Tarpon Basin flashed like a panful of diamonds. Thorn hefted the box, his eyes still on the water outside. He squinted at a passing skiff, a black silhouette against all that brightness.

* * *

That afternoon he stayed at his desk, trying to fashion one fly after another. But his hands were numb. Clumsy and uninspired, he kept on, trying to work through it, draw some magic up. But it never came. And all afternoon, as his regular customers showed up for their flies, he sold off more and more from his personal collection.

At sundown he showered and made himself a large glass of bourbon. He put on his one cowboy shirt and a pair of jeans and stood at the bathroom mirror, combing his wet hair, knowing it was time to get out the Colt. Wipe it off, give it a good cleaning, load it. He combed his hair some more. Got every hair where he wanted it, then ran the comb through again.

He walked to the bed and sat on the edge of it. He swallowed some more Maker's Mark and put the glass on the floor. He took the novel he'd been reading and the hurricane lantern off the footlocker and set them on the floor beside his drink. There was rust on the snaps of the trunk, but they still came open easily. He pulled the lid open and took the oily rag out of the footlocker.

There were a couple of dead roaches in the trunk, a box of magnum shells. The cleaning kit. But the Colt was gone.

Thorn dropped the rag back in the trunk, closed it, and replaced the lantern and the book. He carried his drink back to the bathroom and took another deep swallow. With his comb he made another swipe through his hair, staring into the mirror at his dazed face.

Could he have given the Colt to Sugarman and somehow forgotten? Had it been stolen by one of the people passing through that room in the last twenty years? It had been that long since he had even raised the lid on the trunk. Maybe he had gotten it out in his sleep, walked out across the sparkling water of Lake Surprise, and dropped it in the exact spot where Dallas James had died.

Thorn parked the Fleetwood and sat for a few minutes with the headlights blaring at the side of Kate's house. Finally, he pushed in the light plunger and sat there, breathing in the darkness. There was a thunderstorm out in the shipping lanes, explosions of lightning muffled inside black cumulus. The wind was beginning to quicken already, blowing the mosquitoes back into the Everglades. And the stand of tall Australian pines was moaning. Clouds sped past the moon.

If Kate's friends wanted to assemble and eulogize her, it was fine with him. But this part was his. He got out of the car, the wind filling his shirt, and he carried the cardboard box of her remains down to her dock.

He set the box on the fish-cleaning table and checked the lines on the *Heart Pounder*. Two of the clove hitches someone had made were loosened, and the bow had swung around and was grinding against one of the pilings. He hauled the boat back against the dock and snugged the lines.

He stepped aboard and stood for a moment next to the fighting chair, gripping the back of it. The boat was rocking in the rising wind. There was the smell of pine cleaner.

Inside the cabin the smell was stronger. As he looked out through the cabin windows at the dark, choppy flats, he could recall the feel of the *Heart Pounder* as it had ridden in rough seas. It wasn't a fast boat, but it could level out the heaviest chop.

He gripped the cold rim of the wheel and pulled himself into the captain's chair, swiveling it to look backward out the cabin door. Trying to imagine Kate's last night and trying not to.

For a while he was still, listening to the boat creak. His mind as blank as he could make it. Then he reached out and touched the instrument panel, the throttle lever, ran his hand across the teak drawers. Searching for some vibration left behind. He stood and dusted the surfaces of the cabin with his fingertips. Nothing there. Sterile.

Outside in the cockpit Thorn gazed out at the dark, felt a drop of rain against his face. The sky overhead was still clear, but the air was charged. He jumped back across to the dock.

He hefted the cardboard box. It was a square box, might have held a clock or a softball, but it weighed at least six pounds. Six pounds of pulverized bone and char. Thorn held it in one hand, breathing the airless breeze. He steadied himself against the fish-cleaning table and opened the flap of the box. From the faint light of a new moon he could tell the dust was whitish. Flecks of coarsely ground meal mixed into it.

Then he looked up at the stars, made a slow circuit of the bright sky. Nothing up there to pray to but a plane, too high for its engines to be heard. Thorn watched it slip through the stars.

He stepped out to the edge of the dock and swallowed a good breath.

"I'm here," he said to the dark. He waited. "I'm trying," he whispered.

The wind continued to build.

Thorn touched his finger to his tongue. He dabbed it in the open box. And brought the grit back to his tongue.

21

Thorn climbed the grassy terrace up to the house. The porch swing was banging. He hooked it back, then sat in one of the wicker chairs to catch his breath, taking the rain-scented wind almost straight on.

When the first fat drops exploded against him, he went inside and began turning on lights, working his way through the house. Even the pantry light and the small tensor light above Kate's bed. Sending the shadows back to wherever they came from.

In the refrigerator he found a carton of strawberries webbed with a blue mold, probably a cure for something by now. Thorn threw them in the empty trash can. There was also a six-pack of Busch. He opened a beer.

Drank half of it down in a swallow. He stayed in the kitchen till he'd finished it. He walked back into the living room, opening another beer.

Kate's desk was empty. The contents had been examined and returned and were still in the sheriff's cardboard cartons. Thorn sat at the desk, sipping his beer, gathering himself for this. The wind was sealing the house now, bellowing at the windows, bringing the rain against the tin roof with that roar Thorn had always found so comforting.

The first box took him an hour to wade through. He was thirstier for facts than he'd imagined, reading her tax forms straight through since 1958. And reading letters he and Ricki had written from Sea Camp in Grassy Key when Thorn was twelve, Ricki ten. "Your little camper," Thorn had signed all his letters. Ricki had just demanded over and over that Kate forward her snorkel and mask, water gun.

For another hour he worked through the second and third boxes. Reading every word, adding up sections of her checkbooks, balancing her statements. Trying to interpret the deviations in her signatures. Recalling what he could about every month her records covered.

Two hours and he'd read her history. All he knew now was what he had known already. She was a careful woman. She had spent a great deal of time saving things. Possibly for just such a night as this.

Thorn repacked all the cartons and looked again through the drawers of her desk. He pulled each drawer all the way out, set it aside on the floor, peered into the desk for spillage.

He was down to the last two drawers when he found

it. A partition in one of the drawers, separating off about an inch of space at the rear. The DEA boys had pulled it out one inch short. In that slot Kate had placed a file folder.

The folder was thinner than the others. Thorn opened it, glanced at the newspaper clippings there and abruptly sat back in the swivel chair.

It was a file on Dallas James.

Thorn rocked his head back, grimaced up at the ceiling, scanned the cobwebs up there, let his eyes come gradually back to the desk.

There was the clipping about the first accident, the one Thorn had read at thirteen. He'd forgotten the headline. NEWBORN SURVIVES AUTO CRASH. There were three articles about Dallas's dying in Lake Surprise. An article from the *Miami Herald* gave just two inches to it. The local Key Largo paper had published two stories about Dallas's death, describing other accidents at that same curve in the highway.

Thorn hadn't seen those articles when they first appeared. He'd been in a kind of perpetual shock back then, waiting for a knock on his bedroom door, for a man with a badge to want to ask him a few questions. Kate and Dr. Bill had been fishing in Alaska when it happened. They hadn't returned until late in July that year. She must've heard about it when they returned and tracked down the articles. She might even have harbored suspicions all those years.

He read the articles twice, but little of it took hold. He rubbed his eyes, propped his face over the old newsprint again, and forced himself to see the words. LOCAL BANKER DIES IN WATERY CRASH.

And the photograph showed a smiling Dallas in his banker's suit. The smile looked sincere, but his eyes were bleary, strained. Local banker, Dallas James, was survived by his wife, Marilyn, and daughter Sarah Ann, ten.

The storm rattled the front door. The white curtains stirred. Thorn stared again at the photo.

Dallas's mouth. His bottom lip was full, and his top lip was almost thin. There was a dimple in his left cheek. It was a very familiar mouth. A very familiar set of lips, that hint of a smile, that haunted flicker in the eyes.

Thorn studying the newsprint mouth, blinking his eyes, trying for a better focus. He shifted in his chair, looked up at the sound of the wind rearranging the porch furniture.

Survived by Sarah Ann. A daughter whose mouth was grown up by now. A daughter who was old enough to let men kiss her mouth. To kiss back, with passion or something like it. She would be thirty years old. Old enough for almost anything.

A woman with a mouth like that might let a man grow fond of her, fond of kissing her and of talking with her. A woman with Sarah's mouth, Sarah Ann's. A man might eventually bare himself to a woman with a mouth like that. He might confide in her, confess his deepest guilt.

Thorn opened his eyes and peered once more at the dots of ink, the full lower lip, the thin upper, the wary half-smile. It was a beautiful woman's mouth, the kind of mouth that dead men probably dreamed about when they were wishing they could return.

Southern Bell information had four M. Jameses in Miami. Thorn asked the operator if one of the parties happened to live in Coral Gables. Yes, sir, 3535 Anastasia Circle.

It was eight-fifteen when Thorn hung up the phone at Kate's and nine o'clock when he pulled into the driveway of Marilyn James's Spanish-style house. He parked where the '64 Buick had once been parked.

Thorn rang the chimes and waited. In a minute she pulled the heavy oak door open against a gold chain.

"I'm Bill Christian," Thorn said, his voice only a little shaky. "A friend of Sarah's from law school."

She showed no suspicion, but no warmth either. Thorn hoped for a moment that it was all wrong. This woman had never had a daughter in law school.

"I'm just in town for the evening, and I couldn't seem to locate her phone number."

"She's changed her name," Marilyn James said.

Thorn took a slow, even breath, waved a night bug away from his ear.

"Let me guess," he said. "I bet she uses Ryan now."

"Yes, that's right," she said, surprised. "That was my name."

Thorn said quietly, "I probably shouldn't have dropped by like this, but Sarah talked about you so much I just thought . . ."

Her face relaxed, and the door closed. The chain came off, and she swung the door open.

"You can come in if you like, Mr. Christian."

Thorn thanked her and stepped into the bright foyer.

She was Sarah's height but thinner, more brittle. Sarah's straight nose, Sarah's wiry black hair, going gray, held under tight control. An ankle-length navy blue sundress. Her skin as white as Sarah's. But the corners of her mouth turned down, and her eyes were red and desolate as though she had stared too long into the sun.

Looking past her into the living room, Thorn said, "You have a very nice home." There was a fireplace, a burgundy rug, highly polished cherry furniture.

"I'm afraid everything's terribly dusty," she said. "I just can't keep up with all the work."

Thorn followed her into the living room, his heart revving.

Over the mantel was a painting of Dallas and Marilyn and Sarah, dressed as though for Easter services. Dallas stood behind the two of them and tilted his smile upward in what might have been patriarchal pleasure. Or maybe, Thorn thought, he was drunk.

Marilyn offered him a glass of beer, some coffee, a real drink. Thorn refused everything, saying he was unfortunately short of time.

"I never get to meet Sarah's friends," she said, seating herself on the gray herringbone couch, making an empty smile. "You say she talked about me?"

Thorn sat opposite her in a wing-back chair, making sure to plant himself on the edge of the seat. Young man in a rush.

"She told me about the accident," Thorn said, nodding up at the painting.

"Did she?" Marilyn said. "But then I guess she would."

Thorn said, "She seemed to take it very hard."

"I've tried to snap her out of it," her mother said, "done everything I know how. But she doesn't listen to me. Never has."

"She *did* seem a bit . . . I don't know what it was."

"I believe it's known as an obsession," she said. A cold burn crossed her face. Thorn sat still and watched her choose another face, a hostess smile. She brushed at the lap of her blue sundress.

Thorn said, "Maybe losing her father like that gave her a purpose, a drive she might not have had otherwise."

Marilyn stiffened and brought her face together into a frown. She looked up at that painting, leaning back from it the way one might measure the height of a mountain.

She said, "You know, it's terrible, but I think sometimes that Sarah was competing with me over this. Who loved him more, who was hurt more. She acted it out her way, and I, I've done it another way. It's a terrible thing to admit, but I won't even drive the car anymore. I have a girl who does my shopping. I stand here and watch the golfers go by and I paint and that's my life. That's my entire life."

Thorn was silent, watching the face come apart, mouth forming an apologetic smile, but the eyes staying back there, flirting with anger and despair. She was lacing and unlacing her fingers, looking at Thorn. She shifted on the couch. She seemed to be inviting him to comment on her miserable lot.

When he said nothing, she said, "When I was

thirteen, I lost my father. It took me forever to forgive him for dying. Maybe that's how Sarah feels, I don't know. She might feel anger at him, and that makes her feel guilty." She paused and appraised Thorn. He tried to look sympathetic. "Forgive me," she said. "I've spent a lot of time thinking about this. I hardly do anything else."

Thorn edged an inch farther back on the chair.

"Black lung," she said. "That's how *my* father died. I never knew him when he wasn't coughing. But that I got over. I didn't make it my life's work."

"Lately," Thorn said, "has she been any better?"

"Sometimes I think so. And then I don't know," she said.

"She might be getting over it," he said.

"She's maturing, I suppose."

"If she were in love, finding someone to love," Thorn said, "that might help."

She eyed him. Thorn feeling safe behind this mask, Bill Christian.

"I suppose it's possible she's found somebody," she said. Her mouth made a motherly smile. "But I wouldn't let that stop me from looking her up."

Nodding toward her easel in the corner of the room, Thorn said, "Before I go, maybe you'd show me some of your work."

Marilyn James turned her eyes shyly to the floor.

"You're kind to ask." She rose, and Thorn followed her across the room to a pair of French doors leading out to the patio. He glanced out there. It was exactly as he remembered it. The same furniture, high-backed metal chairs, webbed chaise longue.

Marilyn drew off the cloak covering an oil painting she had half finished. If showed a gray weathered one-story house with a tin roof and a ramshackle porch facing a barren field. A single naked tree stood beside the driveway up to the house. The house glowing golden, the sky and field stark white.

"My old Kentucky home," she said. She stepped away from it, appraised it for a moment. "I'd probably go back there to live. But it's not there anymore."

"It looks like a nice fire's going inside, spring on its way and all that."

"Well," she said. "I think of it as November. I'm calling it *First Freeze*. That's what I'm working on now, putting the frost on the grass."

"It must be hard," Thorn said, "to look out at the golf course and paint a scene like this."

"No, not at all."

She let the cloth back down and led Thorn onto the patio. He ran his eyes over it all. Nothing out of place from his memory. The same half circle of furniture facing the golf course. Even a whiskey glass sitting on a metal table beside the chaise.

"That's her place," Mrs. James said, pointing at a light across the dark golf course. "She seems to be home."

"I should call first," said Thorn.

"No, no. Go on, surprise her. She needs to see somebody from back then." Her hand went to her forehead, pushed back some strands. "She needs somebody now."

Thorn asked her why. He watched her staring at Sarah's light.

She said, "Sarah's just lost somebody else. I'm afraid it was somebody she cared a great deal about."

He parked the Cadillac two blocks from Sarah's garage apartment, in the parking lot of the Church of the Little Flower. As he was working through the bushes onto the long fairway, the rain began. It had none of the vigor of a storm, a listless summer downpour. By the time he reached Sarah's, he was drenched.

Her apartment was part of a large walled estate. The main house was a bulky two-story modern Spanish. Spotlights shone on its white stucco walls and the patio, pool, and Jacuzzi were lit up from within. The rain came straight down, so light it was almost soundless in the trees around the house.

By the time he reached her place, her lights were out. He stood in the rough and looked at her darkened windows and then across the sloping fairway toward Dallas James's house. Just another house now. A house in need of a good dusting.

He worked through the bushes to the edges of the lighted estate. He climbed the wall where it joined the garage and let himself down onto the thick grass.

Her Trans Am was in the drive. And a dark Mercedes parked close behind it. Two other cars were parked in the garage. He climbed the stairway, the rain thickening.

The door to her apartment had glass jalousies, slanted open. Thorn stood on her porch, his ear close to the door. Hearing nothing but the rain now, creating its warm hush in the pines nearby. Trickles splattering from the roof to the driveway.

He pried back the aluminum frame holding one of the

glass slats in her door. Bent it back just far enough to slip the glass free. He repeated that with the slat above it. He set them quietly on the porch beside him and felt along the edge of the screened inset until he found a slight tear. He widened that till he could slide his hand inside the door.

There was a dead bolt, but she'd left the key in it, so Thorn squatted down and curled his hand around and opened the bolt. He turned the doorknob carefully until it was open. He drew his hand back and stood there, breathing hard. Rain flowing across his face. Still no lightning or thunder. Just the steady hum of the shower.

He drew the door open and stepped inside. His feet were squishing in the boat shoes, so Thorn stepped out of them, leaving them on the doormat. The security lights of the main house were lighting up her apartment.

There wasn't a piece of furniture in the living room. Just a polished oak floor, bamboo screens. Bare walls. He stood dripping on the floor, wondering if perhaps he had come to the wrong place. No sign of her anywhere in that room, no sign of a tenant at all.

There were two closed doors and a small kitchen. Thorn tried the kitchen first, carefully drawing open the refrigerator door. The quiet suck of its seal, the light inside. Mangoes, skim milk, a bowl of grapes. He closed it carefully.

The first door he tried was the bathroom. White cold tile floor. Her vials, her toothbrush, her shampoo. A copy of *The New Yorker* beside the john. He used her towel to dry his face, patting his damp shirt as well. He caught a trace of her scent there.

He went back to the living room and stood, looking

at the bare floor, the naked walls. His pulse was up again. A twinge of vertigo. Once when he was still in high school, he had picked up a hitchhiker and the guy had been reading a paperback book, tearing off the page he'd just read and tossing it out the window. Page after page, out the window. When Thorn asked him about it, the guy said he liked to travel light. When you're on the road, the guy had said, even too much money can slow you down.

Her apartment looked that way, as if she'd ripped all the pages out. This wasn't Thorn's spareness, his jailhouse purity. This room was stripped back to the spine. Sarah, on her way somewhere and in a hurry, all baggage a nuisance.

The door to her bedroom was cracked open an inch. Thorn stood before it, listening to the rain swelling outside. His throat was dry.

He nudged it open and stepped into her bedroom. There was a man lying on the bed, sleeping on his stomach, one arm dangling over the edge. He snored softly, the light from the main house shining off his balding head.

Sarah was sitting up, watching Thorn.

He came across the room and stood at the foot of her bed.

She had pulled the covers across her chest, and Thorn could see the dark sheets rise and fall with her breath. Her eyes, more her mother's than her father's. He saw that now. The glaze of hurt.

"I know who you are," he said quietly.

She nodded, closing her eyes briefly and reopening them.

"I see that," she said.

"It doesn't matter," Thorn said. "It doesn't change anything for me."

The man beside her stirred, pulled his arm back aboard, and dug deeper into his sleep.

She said, "I have no choice about this. I hope you know that."

"I don't know that any of us has much choice," Thorn said.

He stood there for a moment more, trying to pour himself into her eyes, give her a reason to rise and come to him. But she stayed there, watching him, the rain pattering outside.

He turned, walked back to the living room, slipped into his wet shoes, and left.

22

Irv watched Amos Clay leaning over the fender of his old red pickup. It was Tuesday morning, about ten o'clock, July 23. Irv had decided to get the rhythms of this place where he was going to pull his major score. A week or so early, and Irv was already getting high, a regulation zonk, just thinking about that cash.

He'd built himself a campsite in the mangroves. A tarp on the damp ground, a pair of binoculars, some pistols, three grenades. He'd left the bug spray home, confident that his garlic intake would keep the bugs away.

He'd come this morning dressed as Ho Chi Minh, in black silk pajamas and a black scarf around his head.

He'd dug up an eyepatch, too, to remind himself of Milburn. Sort of penance. The sucker was itching like crazy as he watched this old man, Amos Clay, dinking around in his truck. Irv could see now why Milburn had bitched about it. Looking out at the world with only half his brain.

He also wore Vietnamese rubber sandals and his Rolex. It was a great outfit, and Irv felt like he was cruising now, creative juices pumping; the madness or passion or whatever it was was warming him up, giving him an edge again.

He needed to get the lay of this location if he was going to give a first-rate show. He saw this as moving from off Broadway onto Forty-second Street, and you didn't just show up on opening night, no rehearsals, and expect to get raves.

Irv didn't mind waiting out here for two weeks to make this happen. Once he got the picture, wrote a script for this, he'd go home and get the rest of his supplies and return and just do a camping-out thing. Get tuned in to the place so well he wouldn't even have to wear camouflage, he'd be a mangrove. Work up a good funk of sweat and mud. Eat fruit and shit under rocks.

Sometime this week he'd take off a day and locate this Thorn guy, stamp his passport, and there it was. Next stop his new life. Oh, Grayson had told him Thorn was for some reason off limits, at least until after the transaction had been halted. But hell if Irv was going to let Grayson make up his schedule. Swat Thorn, get the million, jet to the Coast. One, two, three.

It was right that the million-dollar score should cost more of him than usual. The guys bringing the money, the ones he was going to quash, probably were a step up from the meatballs he'd been doing in lately. These guys no doubt had professional training, batting coaches, all the advantages. Irv couldn't just lark his way through this one.

Near as he could see, this old man, Amos, wasn't much of a mechanic. He seemed to be changing the oil in his truck, but it was taking him about an hour to do it. Frail old fart couldn't seem to budge the drain plug. Irv thought about walking out of the jungle and helping the guy twist that wrench, say hello, then walk off. Freak the guy.

But no. That was bush-league stuff. Irv had to be careful. He didn't want to piss on himself in front of the big boys. So he stayed there, squatting low, assuming eternal patience, Zen empty mind. Following his breath into egoless silence.

Thorn lay with his hands behind his head, watching the light reconstruct the room. A couple of squirrels scrambled across his tin roof. In his woods a wild rooster was celebrating an early-morning conquest. The Frigidaire's compressor heaved back on.

Through the French doors he could see a frigate bird suspended high over the bay. A man-o'-war, it would hover till it spotted some gull with a finger mullet in its mouth. Then it would drop, slash the bit of fish away, and ride the thermals back up into the blue atmosphere. Survival of the shittiest. Just the kind of thing that discouraged Thorn from counting too much on nature to guide the way.

Someone had trashed his house. When he'd gotten

out of the Cadillac last night, he had smelled the gunpowder. It looked as if they'd used a shotgun. All the windows gone. Dr. Bill's chairs shattered, his desk on its face. Buckshot holes in the front of the refrigerator. They had tried to set his bed on fire, but it had smoldered a little and gone out.

They'd torn his books in half, broken the lanterns, dropped his customized vise off the porch onto a protruding ledge of limestone. He hadn't gone down yet to see the damage. Some of his clothes were in the toilet. His one-burner had been set on high, and they'd laid a squirrel pelt across it to catch fire. The house stank of singed fur and charred flesh.

Thorn lay there listening to the highway noise. There was nothing to think about. There was nothing to do anymore. You do all you can, fix your bait carefully on the hook, and you lay your finger on the taut line and wait. It's not up to you anymore. You can do only a few things anyway. Choose the correct tide and pattern of wind. Be at the right place, not make noise or else make the right kind of noise, make a careful presentation. The rest was luck.

He heard a motorboat arriving at his dock, and he pulled himself up and went out there.

It was one of his regulars, a retired minister from Michigan. A man who had told Thorn once that bonefish were not nearly as elusive as what he was used to back home. What things are those? Thorn had asked. The minister had merely turned his eyes up to the sky.

Thorn shook his head as the minister coasted up to the dock.

"Gone out of business," Thorn said.

"You can't do that, son. I've just found the hottest patch of flats from here to the Bahamas. Best congregation I ever saw."

Thorn smiled. "Got to," he said. "Got to get back to fishing before I forget everything I know."

"Well," the minister said, "if it's a higher calling, you've got to follow it."

Thorn waited till nine, and when Sugarman didn't show up, he decided to drive over to his place. He stopped off at the 7-Eleven down the road from his house and bought a cup of coffee and drank it in the parking lot, sitting in the Cadillac. He watched a pretty woman talking on the outdoor phone, two black men drinking beers in a lawn service pickup truck. Thorn wondered who they'd killed, who wanted to kill them.

Nothing he saw looked familiar this morning. Or no, it wasn't that exactly. It was more that it all looked like a set, a flat thing set up to fool the eye. Like when he used to take the skiff out at dawn on a windless morning, the water so clear and flat that he skimmed over it and saw perfectly through it to the bottom, the water not there. Thorn seeing it both ways at once, having to force himself to settle for the way he knew it was. That's how Sarah was this morning. There, not there, lover, hater. Thorn's choice, flipping back and forth, comparing this new version of what the last year with her had been with the solid shape of his memories.

Sugarman lived behind a blanket store at mile marker 103, two blocks off the highway. A little block house with a bamboo screen fence. Shady lot, big oaks and banyans. A teenage boy was riding a three-wheel cycle in the vacant lot across from Sugarman's. Seeking out ruts, plowing across debris. Someone nearby was using a chain saw.

No one came to the door right away. Thorn couldn't tell if the buzzer was working with all that other noise. Finally, Sugarman swung the door open, a towel around his waist. His face prepared to dispatch a Mormon missionary.

"Sorry," Thorn said. "I should've called."

"Come in." Sugarman stood back out of the way, looking grim. "I been expecting you."

"Well," Thorn said. "Here I am."

"Man, you look like week-old shit." Sugarman padded across to the kitchenette.

Thorn followed him, saying, "Hell of a lot better than I feel."

Sugarman waved him onto one of the wooden stools at the breakfast nook. "Jeannie's come back."

"Is that good?" Thorn said, and glanced back down the hallway of the little house. In a full-length mirror at the end of the hall he saw Jeannie's reflection. He swallowed and cut his eyes back to Sugarman, who was pouring two glasses of orange juice. Jeannie was hanging back there, naked, upside down from gravity boots. Ankles hooked to a chinning bar in the bedroom doorway.

"Yeah, I'd say it is." The scent of anger. He said, "I need to have a talk with you."

"So talk, I'm here."

"Good grief, Thorny, don't get pissy on me, man."

"Sorry," he said. He thought for a second about telling him about Sarah, then said instead with more feeling, "Sorry."

Sugarman put the orange juice in front of Thorn and swallowed down his own. It wasn't right, but Thorn had to do it. He shot another look back there. The mirror was empty. Thank God.

"You been home yet?" Sugarman asked.

"My home?"

"Yeah, how many you got?"

"What? You know what happened over there?"

"I waited around for you till about midnight last night. I figured you had other plans, so I left. But we got the guys that did it at the jail."

Thorn stood up. "I want to see them."

"Sit down, sit down. What're you going to do, strangle them through the bars?"

"I want to see them, Sugar."

"OK, you'll see them, you'll see them. I'll take you over there in a little while."

Thorn sat back down. He heaved out a breath.

"It wasn't any police work on my part," Sugarman said. "I was coming by to see you, to tell you some other things we've developed, and kaboom, kaboom. These guys were dove hunting in your living room."

"Thanks," Thorn said.

"Five minutes later and the house would've been history. But as I say, man, it was only a piece of luck."

"So, who are they?"

"A couple of bozos with Armistead Construction. I guess they build them all day, tear them down all night."

Thorn shook his head. He raked both hands back through his hair. He glanced around at Sugarman's living room. The walls, the tables, everywhere he looked there were framed photos of Jeannie's family. Her mother. Her father. Sisters and one brother. White people. White people everywhere.

"You don't seem surprised," Sugarman said. "If I came home and found this house shot up like that, I'd register it somehow."

"I'm not surprised."

"Well, that upsets me, then. 'Cause I've been hearing things around town. Things about you, Thorn. Going around telling people you're pulling the plug on Allamanda. I thought what I'd heard was just so much bullshit. But I guess not, huh?"

"Don't lecture me, Sugar."

"OK," he said. "I'll just tell you something. This is going to stop. Right here. Right now. No more. I'll put you in jail, buddy. Material witness. Spitting in the ocean, whatever it takes. I'm not going to have you drawing fire like this."

"You came over last night to tell me something," Thorn said. Holding it in. Looking straight into Sugarman's rigid face. "What is it?"

"I mean it, buddy. I'll put you in jail."

Thorn asked him again what he'd found out.

"It's a bunch of medical mumbo jumbo is what it is. But it translates into something fairly interesting." Sugarman settled across from Thorn on another tall stool. "Apparently it was like I thought. Kate got in a couple of licks. She got one of them in the eye with one of those graphite rods she had. The blue ones?"

"Yeah, I know the ones."

"Well, she got it in pretty good." Sugarman picked up a small spiral notebook from the counter in front of him and read from his notes, "The cornea was pierced and the anterior chamber was entered. A blood vessel was broken in the iris. It's called hyphema, blood in the interior. The rod glanced the lid and removed samples of tissue and hair."

"So what does that tell you?"

"We now know the guy drives a brand-new white BMW."

"Oh, come on, Sugar."

"No, no. Not from this iris stuff. From some tracking I did afterwards. These guys are not real bright. They walk into Dr. Brimmer's office the next day like they were normal people. I called around to all the local eye doctors and found Brimmer. He'd treated a wound like the one we were looking for."

"Good work, man."

"Once again, it's just falling in my lap," he said. "It's just that these guys don't seem to give a shit. Anyway. Here's what the receptionist and the doctor gave us together. White new BMW, one short white male about five-five and one thirty-five, with two good eyes, dark, kinky hair, and a Spanish accent which the nurse said sounded phony. One six-three ugly son of a bitch with longish brown hair, goes over two hundred and has one hurting eye. They paid cash and left a phony address. At least they were doing something to make it harder."

"I don't believe this," Thorn said.

"What?"

"Nothing."

"Thorn," he said. "I'm telling you. You're that

close to jail right now. Don't push me. If you know something . . ."

"I think I saw these two. A big guy in an eye patch and a little guy with him. Both of them in Hawaiian shirts at Vacation Island. The other night. But shit. I don't remember anything about them. I'd been drinking." Thorn tried for a sincere look.

"You know," Sugarman said, pouring himself more Tropicana, offering it to Thorn. "That's interesting. There's a couple of lady tourists made a complaint about two guys who fit this same description, placed them at Vacation Island, when was it?"

"Last Wednesday night. Yeah, that's them. They were with two nurses. I remember that."

"These are either real fuck-ups or they're awful lonely," Sugarman said. "They left their dates out on Pickles Reef. Nurses were out there all night. They were in very bad shape."

"What does that mean, lonely?"

"Yesterday afternoon, the one with the eye patch washes up on Big Pine Key. Got a bullet in him that entered the neck from the rear; the guy was definitely done in up close. First, this little guy doesn't do something as simple as driving his partner up to Miami to have the eye checked out. That would've made it a hell of a lot harder to track down right there. And then it looks like he and his buddy might have had a little marital dispute, and I mean there are places to dump a body where it doesn't get found all that fast, and he didn't pick one of those. I mean, the guy's smart enough to try the marijuana thing on the boat. Make it look like something it isn't. So he's not a total fuck-up. So I call that lonely. Looking for love. Crying out."

"Maybe he thinks he's invincible," said Thorn.

"Or invisible," Sugarman said. "Well, we got a guy at the jail right now I know would be happy to love this guy. Make a hell of a cell mate."

"Jesus."

"Not so loud with that," Sugarman said. "Jeannie." He nodded toward the back of the house.

"Is that it then?"

"Well, the big guy was half shark-eaten when he came in. We sent his teeth to Tallahassee. I'm told by county medical the guy had some first-class bridgework; pathologist said he'd never seen anything like it. Stuff like that can turn out to be as good ID as fingerprints. Can be hell to track down, but it's a place to get going."

Jeannie called from the back of the house, "Are you talking about me, Sugarman?"

"I want to see these guys that did my house," Thorn said.

Sugarman said, "I'll meet you down there in half an hour."

" 'Cause if you are," she called out, "I want to hear what it is you're saying about me."

At the door, hearing Jeannie banging around back there. Thorn said, "I just want to look at them, see their faces."

"Sugarman!" she called. "Close that door! Those mosquitoes are carrying me off."

Sugarman tightened the towel around his waist and

said, ''You know, until she came back, I was thinking of leaving.''

''Leaving Key Largo?''

''Key Largo. Florida, all of it. Going up north. I was thinking about New Jersey.''

''New Jersey? Nobody goes to New Jersey.''

''I still might,'' he said. ''I've heard it's nice there.''

''This is your home, Sugarman. You were born here. You can't just chuck it like that. These are your roots.''

''What kind of place is this? It's like living in a damn airport. Everybody's got a suitcase, Thorn. Somebody you've never seen before is sitting in your spot at the diner. I hear they got basements in New Jersey. I'd like to see a basement for once.''

Thorn shook his head.

''Sugarman!'' Jeannie called. ''You shut that door or I'm calling the police.''

''I'll see you down there,'' Thorn said.

Thorn walked out to the Fleetwood, hearing another rumble louder than the three-wheeler or the chain saw. He looked over his shoulder up into the trees. It was Jerome making his mid-week run, trimming the tree-tops, driving the senile war veterans under their couches. Spreading his cancerous relief.

He got into the Caddy, started up the V-eight. He watched the blue smoke filter down, probably mixed now with African dust. He took in a lungful of that gas. Holding it in like dope smoke, getting high on the poison, holding in the pinch of someone's dried-up homeland.

He looked around the shady neighborhood. Every-body standing around with their rakes, their lawn mowers, their sponges and hoses, letting that haze break apart before they got back to it.

Thorn waited on the sidewalk outside the jail on Plantation Key. Sugarman arrived, wearing jeans and a plaid shirt. His eyes looked sore and heavy, but Thorn didn't ask him about it. He'd heard Jeannie's voice.

Sugarman led Thorn inside and back to the holding cells. The other cops glanced at Thorn and nodded at him. Not a member of their club, maybe, but no longer just one of those others.

"These guys," Sugarman said as they waited for a door to be unlocked, "they picked up their morals on their lunch break. Getting stoned and listening to outlaw music."

The two guys in the cell looked a lot like redbeard's friends. Wore their hair in ponytails. One of them had a little dot of gold on his earlobe. Thorn stared at them. And they, sitting on the edge of their cots, smoking cigarettes, stared back at him.

"They didn't kill her," Thorn said. "She would've tossed these shits overboard."

23

Thorn watched Sugarman pull his van into traffic and start home. He waited until the van was well up the highway, and he got out of the Fleetwood and went back into the county building.

Janice Deels was at the counter for car and boat registrations. She was on the phone but covered the mouthpiece and whispered to Thorn she'd be right with him, rolling her eyes at the person on the line.

He stood next to the water fountain and watched her talk. He felt as if his blood were glowing. Sarah was Dallas James's daughter. The eye patch guy and his partner had killed Kate. The two of them were connected with Grayson and Ricki. Sarah and Kate had been bringing in dope. Kate was dead. Eye patch was dead.

Sharing the same air, breathing in, breathing out. All that air, all those molecules endlessly passing between us, along streams of air, connecting us, converting us. In this hothouse, this closed system, breathing in the expelled breath of men long dead, breathing out molecules that will outlive us. Caught in a plot too complex for any one mind to hold. Quentin and Elizabeth breathing out, Dallas James breathing in, Dallas exhaling, Sarah inhaling. Thorn, standing beside the water fountain, trying to breathe.

"I'm awful sad about Kate," Janice said, taking his arm and turning him to the door. "I hope you're doing OK." Her arm in his, she led him outside to the shade of a banyan, her brown paper sack in her left hand.

"I'm getting better," said Thorn.

"Well, good!"

Janice had been a cheerleader. He remembered how she'd cried after losing games. He remembered her giving speeches in the auditorium about pep.

They sat on the grass under the banyan, and Thorn accepted one of her pieces of fried chicken and held it while she ate.

"I'm glad you came to see me," she said. "I think about you."

Thorn nodded. Holding his chicken. Breathing in, and out again.

"You know," she said. "I hear about you. I hear you're dating a girl from Miami."

"I need your help, Janice."

She wiped her mouth with a napkin, leaned across and took hold of his arm, and smiled at him earnestly. "Whatever I can do, Thorn, you know that."

"Irving David McMann," she said in a hoarse whisper, and wrote it on a pad. She typed in another command, watched her screen for a moment and whispered, "He lives at Coral Reef. 110 Barracuda Lane. Apartment A." She wrote that down. "Is that all you want?"

"You can't let anyone know I asked you for this."

"Don't worry," she said, glancing over her shoulder at the woman working at the desk behind her. "I like my job."

"I appreciate it, Janice."

"*Perfect Execution*. What is this guy, a friend of yours?"

"He owes me something," Thorn said.

She stood up and leaned across the counter and pecked him on the cheek.

"Perk up, Thorny." She squeezed his biceps. "Did you know the prayer group has been praying for you?"

"Don't stop now."

"I'm in the book," she said.

Thorn slipped the note in his pocket and left.

Irv was getting the classic late start. He'd overslept because the electricity had gone off and on sometime during the night and his digital clock was just blinking to be reset. Then he'd had to track down a key to

Milburn's condo, where they'd stored the heavy ammo. He'd decided to go paramilitary on this. He'd hyped himself to a paranoid, full-tilt rage, picturing the kind of delivery boy who carried a million dollars.

Then the BMW wouldn't start, so he had to call the Reef Exxon station to come tow it in. And then he had to pack the rest of the grenades, the Uzi, and the sawed-off shotgun into a pack, something he could strap onto the Kawasaki 650.

So, it was one-thirty, hot as shit, humidity 105. Irv always said it wasn't the heat, it was the stupidity. If he had any goddamn sense, he'd be spending the summers in Mendocino. Like his old man, the chicken franchise king. Johnny Chickenseed, Irv called him. Never to his face. But when Irv had that million safe in municipal bonds, shit, he'd call the old man any damn thing he pleased. Usually Irv just did a month in the winter at Coral Reef Club, then back to Manhattan or the family house at the Cape. But this year things had been happening, and he'd just coasted on into the summer. Never again.

Irv was astraddle the motorcycle, about to crank it up, when he remembered the photograph of the guy Thorn. An extremely familiar guy, not much of a haircut, but a good jaw, good wide chest. The photograph was of this Thorn guy and Ricki standing outside Sloppy Joe's Bar along with the old lady charter boat captain. Irv liked having a photo of her. Like an old lover, you look at it, and some of the memories come floating back up. Yeah. Like her throwing fucking chum in his face.

Irv thought maybe he should buy a Polaroid, snap a

shot of all his victims from now on. Something to remember all this by, something for his weird little grandchildren. He'd sit in his rocker and tell them, This is before. And this with the blood is after.

Irv went back in the condo. He'd stuck the photograph on the front of his refrigerator with one of those little magnetic vegetables. A brussels sprout or was it a broccoli? Irv didn't eat shit like that, so he wasn't sure.

The plan was, he'd go back to the mangroves at old man Clay's house. Stay there for a while, get nasty, starve himself a little, and when his blood was cooking, he'd cruise on down the road to where this Thorn lived. Isolated spot, it looked like on the map Ricki had drawn. Perfect place for a little explosion. Irv McMann's Carnage à la Carte.

After two hours out in the golf club parking lot, baking in the Fleetwood, wondering if anyone was watching him, calling in to security, Thorn saw the short guy come out of his town house and watched him open the door of the small attached garage and try to kick-start a big red motorcycle. Finally it caught and filled up the garage with oily smoke. Thorn slumped down.

He waited till the guy had rumbled out to the main road; then he started the car and pulled out. Following a quarter mile back, Thorn wound through the Coral Reef streets, feeling conspicuous as hell in that rusted boat. But at the same time his heart was light and fast. He'd found the guy, found where he slept, where the asshole lay down and dreamed.

Past the guard gate the cycle went straight ahead at

the four-way stop, still pumping out blue smoke. The guy was wearing a chunky pack, army regulation. And black, shiny long pants and a black, shiny shirt, a red helmet. Thorn couldn't tell much about his face. But he was short, five-four or -five, and he'd come out of the town house, 110 Barracuda Lane, apartment A. Had to be him.

When the bike slowed to about forty, Thorn thought maybe he'd been spotted, and he passed, watching in the rearview mirror as the guy pulled off onto the shoulder, just down from the entrance road into Amos Clay's. Thorn drove on, thinking, Oh, boy, oh, boy. You get enough chum in the water, things start happening.

He drove on up 905 for another couple of miles, then stopped and turned around. About two hundred yards before Amos Clay's drive he pulled off onto the shoulder. He got out and cut into the woods, heading north to the spot where he'd seen Irving McMann enter the jungle.

It took him almost half an hour to cover the half mile. Stepping carefully, and halting. Listening. Moving ahead another few yards, prying through the tangle of brush, his eyes scanning for any movement, the flash of that shiny black outfit.

Thorn was about fifty feet from Irv's camp when he saw him. Pressing his back against an oak, he watched, through a mesh of vines and Florida holly, Irving David McMann clean his Uzi. He had it broken down and spread out on a clear plastic tarp, and he was running a brush in and out the barrel. Amos Clay's place was two hundred yards to the east, just a glimpse of it visible through the dense bush.

On his toes, Thorn retreated, taking his bearings. North of a giant gumbo-limbo. Maybe a stone's throw from the highway.

The mosquitoes had discovered Thorn. They were sending their straws into his neck, his shoulders, his arms. Sipping. Stoning themselves on adrenaline.

24

Sarah was waiting at Thorn's place, sitting in her Trans Am in the shade of a sea grape tree when he returned. He parked the Caddy beneath the stilt house and went over to her car and got in.

She didn't look rested. Her madras blouse was wrinkled. She didn't smell fresh.

"My place is a mess," he said. "Let's do this at Kate's."

She drove. Her window open, her hair tangling in the wind.

"So where's the cash? Where do you keep it?"

She didn't look at him.

"OK," he said. "Then let me try this, tell you a

story. Stop me if I you don't like it.'' He rested his hand on her shoulder. Patted her once. Relax.

He said, ''Once there was a little girl, ten, eleven years old, having a so-so childhood. And one night she wakes up out of a deep sleep because she thinks she hears something, or maybe it's just some slight barometric change that wakes her. She follows her instincts out to her front porch, and she sees a teenage boy holding her father up against his car. And the boy rears back and hits her father. And she sees them drive away together. The next day she wakes up and she thinks maybe it's all a dream. Right away after that her mother comes in her room and tells her that her father has been killed in a car accident. He'd been drinking, out for some weird midnight drive.

''Maybe then the mother goes on and tells the little girl about that other accident her father'd been involved in a long time ago, happened in the same spot where he died. Maybe he'd even had others.

''But the little girl can't forget her dream. She grieves over her father's death and keeps her dream to herself. Sometime later, maybe she's a teenager by now, she finds out the details of that other accident, eighteen years earlier, there in Lake Surprise. The father had killed a young couple. Their baby had survived. This baby would've grown up. He would've been a teenager about the time the little girl's dream comes to her. And she—she maybe suddenly knows it all. She knows how this boy felt having his father and mother killed. She knows all of a sudden what loss, hatred, and obsession he might have known.''

Sarah kept her eyes ahead. The road was empty, but she was hard at work driving.

"How is this so far?"

She looked at him, a grudging softening of her face. "You're on a roll."

"Well," Thorn said, "so now our little girl is feeling what the boy felt. Maybe even identifying a little with his anger. This burn that won't stop. She forces herself to eat, to sleep, to hold a pencil and pay attention. She manages to get through high school, and by now, maybe she's thinking, No, it couldn't be. This is crazy, why am I screwing up my life like this? It was just a dream anyway. Maybe a quirky touch of precognition, a little ESP dream or something. However it happened, she gets through college, and she goes on to law school. Maybe somewhere in here it starts haunting her again, and she decides—"

"No," she said. "You're straying now."

"Ah, OK." Thorn closed his eyes, pressed his hand to his forehead, consulting his muse. "I got it. She never skips a beat. Always haunted. Never lets it go."

"That's better," Sarah said.

"Yeah, yeah. And then there's law school. That was to bring the guy to justice. Find out about legal rights. All that stuff. 'Cause basically our young woman is civilized. Go into her living room. Speak to her mother. The little girl had a good life, moral training. Maybe her emotional training was a little cold, a little half-hearted, but basically she has scruples. She wants to nail this asshole, but nail him legal if it's at all possible.

"So, now, she's out of law school, and she knows the law isn't going to help her any on this. She takes a job, a perfect job for somebody feeling guilty about this murder fantasy she's been having, and she starts driving down to Key Largo on the weekends, sniffing around. Scene-of-the-crime stuff. Maybe she'd already done some of that in high school. She knows the guy's last name from the newspaper article. Key Largo's a small town, so she finds out fairly quickly. But there's one hitch. She's not absolutely sure. There's a shadow of a doubt.

"And she might imagine it, showing up on this guy's front porch and saying, 'Hi, I'm the daughter of the man who killed your parents. Want to talk?' That wouldn't work. So she decides to go undercover. She starts using her mother's maiden name. She reads about Kate in the newspaper, all her environmental battles, and our lawyer decides it's a good time to develop an interest in wood rats."

Sarah turned off the highway into Kate's driveway. Thorn was quiet till she'd parked beside the house. The sky was darkening in the east. Another storm, more Sahara dust.

She turned off the motor and drew a coil of hair free from the corner of her mouth. When she turned her eyes to him, he said, "She and Kate spend some time together, and she starts to like it. She's not that hot about wood rats, but Kate, Kate she likes.

"Then girl meets boy. Over here. Boy comes over one night, I think it was a weekend in September, to cook his specialty, Dolphin California, for Kate, and this lovely woman is there. Whose idea was that?"

She said quietly, "It was destiny."

Thorn chuckled and said, "So then, there we are,

practically up to the present. Woman tracks down man she thinks murdered her father. Takes him to bed. Tries out special new truth serum. But lo and behold, instead of confessing that he killed her daddy, he's smitten. He invites her along to his little ceremony, as she called it. He's ready to confess to her all his dirty little secrets, and what's she do? She's swimming out there, splashing around.''

''She never splashed,'' Sarah said. ''You think that wasn't hard for her? You think she could step into that water knowing what had happened there without feeling . . .'' She gripped the shift lever. ''She didn't splash.''

''OK, so she didn't splash. She swam without splashing. But the mood was all wrong. Maybe, and this is just coming to me now, maybe she was starting to worry. Maybe she didn't want to hear him admit it after all, and so she pretended she was all light and upbeat and smartass so that this guy wouldn't spill his guts.''

''Maybe she was,'' Sarah said. ''Maybe that's exactly how she felt.''

Thorn took Sarah's hand from the shifter and held it lightly in both of his.

''Now why would she not want to hear the truth? Now why would she have spent so many years searching for this fellow, and then, when she senses the asshole is finally going to expose himself, she backs off, makes jokes, takes her clothes off, and swims? Why would this woman do this?''

Sarah said, ''Maybe she's confused. Maybe she's desperate and worried and confused.''

''Well,'' Thorn said, ''then I know how she feels.''

* * *

They went into the house, and while Sarah used the bathroom, Thorn located a bottle of wine in Kate's pantry. Nothing great, a New York grocery wine. He poured some into fragile cognac glasses and took them into the living room.

Sarah appeared out of the darkness of the back of the house. She came into the living room and sank into the couch opposite Thorn. She picked up the glass of wine, held it aloft.

She said, "To well-told stories."

Thorn said, "To swimming without splashing."

They drank, and Thorn smelled the faint sweetening of air from the approaching storm. The light drained away, and neither of them rose to turn on a light. Thorn leaned forward and refilled her glass and his own.

As the first breezes of the storm stirred through the room, Thorn stood and came across to her. Her lips parted slightly, and she made room for him beside her. He sat. She lowered her eyes and leaned her head against his chest. He held her. She nuzzled in, holding him now. His breath in her hair, breathing in the herbal scent of her shampoo, her own odor, a richer, darker, heavier thing. He lingered there, kissing the part in her hair. She gripped his ribs tightly.

The wind had begun to keen in the Australian pines. The odor of electricity, the white curtains stirring. Thorn rested his chin on her head and watched the pages of Kate's files flutter off her desk. Sarah burrowed deeper into their embrace.

She stood beside his boyhood bed, and Thorn unbuttoned her blouse. He slipped it off of her and let it fall and reached around her to unfasten her bra. The rain was coming now. The wind trembling at the windows, the gusts probably ripping away loose petals, carrying them off into the dark.

He shaped her breasts, molding his hands around one, then the other. Then brushing them lightly with his open hands, each nipple tickling a palm, tracing with the puckered tips of her nipples the edges of his outspread fingers.

"You don't trust me, do you?" Sarah said, her eyes closed.

Thorn brushed his fingertips down to her upper ribs, the roots of her breasts.

"I trust you more," Thorn said, "now that I know your real name."

His hands were slipping down her ribs, his thumbs brushing the sides of her breasts, sliding in under them, the hot fold. Down her narrowing waist, thumbs against her hip points. At the brim of her shorts.

Sarah said, a hoarse whisper, "I'm afraid of what may happen."

They unsnapped each other's pants in unison. And Thorn dragged her shorts and panties together down past the swell of her hips, her very full bush. Sarah unzipping him.

"You're afraid you're going to kill me," Thorn said.

Sarah stepped to the side and, with her toe, tossed her shorts aside. She gripped the tails of Thorn's cowboy shirt and in one sudden opening of her arms unsnapped all the pearl buttons. She pulled his jeans down, and Thorn stepped out of them.

"It's crossed my mind," she said.

She held his shirt by the yoke and slid if off him.

Thorn said, with sudden laryngitis, "I don't recommend it."

"I've fantasized about it," Sarah said, "for such a long time."

She pulled his Jockey shorts down, forcing his erection to ride down with them. It sprang back, and she gripped it.

"In your story," she said, "you were wrong about something." Her hand trickled up and down him there, and she said, "It was always more than truth serum."

"Thank God for that." Thorn, his eyes closing involuntarily, hardly able to speak, said, "If you kill me, we can't do this anymore."

Her eyes were cagey and lustrous when she leaned forward and kissed him hard. Teeth clicking. He sucked her tongue in deeper. Hurting it with the pressure. She drew it back slowly, and he skimmed it with his incisors.

They both let go at once. Stood apart, breathing. Both of them slick with sweat. Thorn reached out and touched his fingertip to her hardened left nipple, circled it. Let his nail rake across the wrinkled flesh.

"If you don't kill me," Thorn said in a whisper, "is it because you might love me?"

"The official statute of limitations has run out on you, Thorn," she said. "But mine, it's still running."

They lay on their sides on the bed. Thorn reaching to her knees, stroking, and sliding his hand back up to her thigh, running a finger around the rim of her vagina, tangling in her long black secret hair. She cocked her left leg up to give him access, and Thorn continued a moist, slow circuit.

"Did you steal my pistol?"

She said yes.

"That's perfect," he said. "Perfect."

"You asked me," Sarah said, eyes drowsy, "where the cash was."

"The cash?" Thorn's finger slipped briefly into the dark quick. "Oh, the cash."

Sarah patted the mattress behind her, her legs spreading more. "Kate put it inside here."

"We're making love on a million dollars?"

"Nine hundred thousand." Sarah's voice husky, her eyes tight, head digging back into the pillow as Thorn's finger found a gentle pressure. "One trip left to go."

Thorn tried to hold on as the orgasm took her, gradually at first, then whipping through her, electrocuting her, his finger driving her. Watching her grimace.

When it was finished, Sarah lay still for a few minutes.

"This's the most money I've ever made love on," Thorn said.

"You're catching on to it," she said.

They lay and listened to the rain lashing the tin roof, a shutter tapping an SOS against the kitchen window. Her hand coating and recoating his erection with sweat.

She rolled up and swung a leg across him and eased herself down onto him. She raised herself and came down again, settling her stickiness against his, a small twitch, a subtle grind, and then she went back up.

He took two handfuls of sheet and mattress cover. Crucified. Her breasts shimmying, sweat trails running between them.

He dragged her down, still inside her. And from the

side they cooperated, found a rhythm and stayed with it, nudged it gradually faster. She rolled back on top, and another roll brought him there. Thorn couldn't tell who was the bandleader here, who wanted to be on top, who on bottom.

She broke the connection, rolled onto her stomach, and tipped her bottom up at him. Edging forward on his knees, he entered her and held to her hipbones as she wriggled and gasped and shook him. He leaned across her back, finding her breasts again. She reached back around and gripped his buttocks and pulled him tighter against her.

And as he felt the burn rise inside him, she clamped her vagina tight, a fist, locking the sperm in its corridor. Thorn shook his head, and a high groan, then a howl, broke from his throat. She seized tighter, shaking her head again, the last remnants of her chignon come loose.

"Let go!"

"I am, I am, I am."

Thorn yelled at her now, bruising her with his grip on her waist. "Let go, goddamn it!"

"I am!"

She shivered, shook her bottom, and dropped flat onto her stomach, bringing him down hard onto her back, and Thorn released, the sap flooding now. A lancing pain firing through him.

They woke several times, and each time it was still raining. Thorn mounting her, or Sarah mounting him. Top, rear, side, on the floor, bent across his desk, where he'd solved geometry problems, but nothing like this. The rain coming listlessly all the time. They lay holding each other for the times in between, alternating fetal curls.

No more conversation. She spoke only in the growls of hunger. And he tried to answer her. As the darkness dwindled and Thorn looked groggily at the drizzling dawn, he knew he was free of something. He felt it as a lightness in his chest. A cavity in there where there had been thickness and weight. A clearing, a lessening of swelling.

Sarah was awake beside him.

"It's still raining."

"I can see that," she said. She sat up, puffed up the pillow at her back.

He debated it a moment and said, "Who was the guy the other night?"

"Who are they all?"

He rolled up on an elbow to see her.

"Me, too?" he asked. "I'm your daddy, too?"

She looked for a moment at the rain smearing the window, then turned to him.

"You more than anyone."

He nodded, waited a moment, and asked quietly, "Who was he?"

"Nobody special."

"Does he know that?"

"Yes."

"Just your sleeping pill?"

"We're each other's sleeping pill."

"Well," Thorn said. "You weren't asleep when I came by."

"It's not working anymore," she said.

* * *

When Thorn was asleep again, his breathing deep and raspy, Sarah inched to the edge of the bed. She set her feet on the wood floor and stood. As she crossed the room, she looked back at Thorn's motionless sleep.

She'd left the Colt Python in her straw bag beside the living room couch. She padded out there, the thick rush of rain covering the creaking wood floors. The revolver was wrapped in a black camisole. Sarah unwrapped it and opened the cylinder quietly to make sure it was loaded. She carefully clicked the cylinder closed.

Thorn was on his stomach, his face mushed into the pillow. Sarah came back into the bedroom, crossed to the bed, and stood beside him. His left arm was draped over the edge of the bed, his fingertips touching the floor.

She stood beside him, looking down at him silently. She cradled the revolver against her chest. Her face was lax; her breath came slowly.

"Who's going to save the wood rats," Thorn said, his voice muffled in the pillow, "if I'm dead and you're in jail?" He had one eye barely open as he turned his head to peer back at her. "Anyway, it's not your style to shoot in the back."

"I can wait till you turn over," Sarah said.

Thorn was measuring a roll to his left, hit her in the knees, grab the wrist the way you grabbed a rattler behind the head.

"Was I that bad in bed?" Thorn said, lifting his head for a better look at her. Poised for the grab.

"You're not going to try to stop me, are you? Not taking this seriously."

"I tried all last night, best I knew how. If that doesn't work, what can I do?"

"You could do me before I do you."

"No," Thorn said. "I have a thing about killing people I love."

Sarah's eyes were fogging, her forehead beginning to clench. "You don't love me," she said. "You love somebody we cooked up between us."

"Close enough," Thorn said.

Sarah said, "No. You're right." She sat down beside him on the edge of the bed. Thorn feeling his muscles unknot. "Wood rats come first. Our debt to Kate."

Turning over onto his back, Thorn released a long breath. Sarah brushed a strand of his blond hair off his forehead with her free hand. Her eyes in long focus, staring out the bedroom window, her hand absently combed through his hair.

25

Sarah was sprawled on a towel, on the front deck of Thorn's bonefish skiff, across the live-bait wells and the icebox. She was covered up against the sun, in one of his long-sleeved workshirts, Kate's fishing hat, white jeans, and tennis shoes. Thorn glanced at her off and on, wondering what it signified, her having to hide from the sun like that.

She'd called in to work that morning, told someone she had to take some emergency annual leave. Back in two weeks. Have Stanley take over her cases. Got some static, gave some back, and hung up.

Thorn cast a weighted fly out to the reef patch, using one of his ultralight spinning rods, the reel no bigger than the fist of a baby. The fly had just enough weight to carry about twenty feet, maybe twenty-five with the wind at his back. Five feet of water, a mile off Kate's place. Sunday morning, the sun just easing up out of the Atlantic.

"How'd you figure it out?" she asked.

"I have powers," he said. "I can hear what's happening inside you."

"Can you hear this?" She gave him a look.

"It's not that simple. I have to be enjoying an intimate connection with the subject for it to work."

"When we're like that, I don't *have* any thoughts."

Thorn told her about finding the newspaper photograph.

When he'd finished, she was quiet, watching as Thorn climbed up on the observation stand mounted above his outboard. He cast out the port side, glancing back at her.

"You think Kate knew who I was?"

"It's possible," he said. "But I doubt it." He squinted at the shadows a few yards inside his lure, maybe bones, maybe jack, maybe just a school of mullet. "If she'd suspected, she would've mentioned it to me."

"Not unless she suspected what you'd done," Sarah said.

"Maybe she knew everything," Thorn said, "but didn't tell anybody anything 'cause she saw how you felt about me, knew you and I would work it out."

"If she knew how I felt about you, she was better than clairvoyant. 'Cause *I* don't know."

Retrieving his bait now, nudging it in front of those

shadows, he said, "She'd been suspicious, she would've confronted you, something. She didn't like liars."

"I never lied to her. Or you."

"Hell of a difference between nothing-but-the-truth and the whole truth."

The leading shadow surged forward and hit his lure. The reel whirred. Whistling, Thorn held his tip down, pointing toward where the jack was running, out to sea, darker water.

"What is it?"

"Just a jack," Thorn said as he reeled back some line. It took him about five minutes, but he brought the jack next to the boat. A jack crevalle, went about four pounds.

"You just release it?" Sarah was standing, watching the dazed fish drifting unhooked beside the boat. Its grogginess passed, and it flicked out of sight.

"Yeah, torture and release."

"Noble sport," she said. "I can see why you gave it up."

"I'm rekindling my enthusiasm. It sure tunes up the reflexes."

"Cranking in a fish, that tunes your reflexes? I can't see it. Maybe if you're going to eat them."

"Why don't you try a nap, take a load off your puritanism." Thorn said.

He cast as far as he could, not a shadow in sight, and began a slow retrieve, jigging it every now and then. He said, "I think our relationship is better off when our feet are waving around in the air. We get in trouble when we try to compare the lengths of our morals."

Sarah stood up and came around to the swivel seat. She sat and revolved it so she was looking at Thorn.

"Do you feel remorse, Thorn? Any remorse?"

He looked at her, back out to the water.

"I do," he said. "And I don't."

"You can't have it both ways."

"You know. I got two-pound test line on this. I have to special order the stuff. You use this thread to tie buttons onto shirts. It breaks if you think about it too hard. That's where the sport is."

Sarah said, "Giving them a chance. Making it hard on yourself."

"You can't lift a soggy slice of bread out of the water with this line. I'd say it gives them a damn good chance."

"You'd give them more of a chance if you didn't use anything, just wait out here and see if they'll jump in the boat."

"They give me something, I give them something back." He finished reeling in the line and cast it immediately. He'd spotted something. A ghost, hovering, moving ahead, hovering again. He twitched the line.

"What could you give them?"

"Knowledge," Thorn said. "I'm improving the gene pool, making them more wary."

The bonefish smacked the lure. Thorn lurched, caught himself, watched the line sizzle off the reel. He had wound four hundred yards of that narrow-gauge thread on his reel, four hundred yards of monofilament dragging through the salt water, resisting the powerhouse fish. But that was all that would tire it, because Thorn had taken the drag off. If the line didn't slow him, it'd be free in a few more yards, roaming for a week or two with a rusting hook in its lip.

There was only a turn or two of line left on the reel when the run stopped. Thorn won back a few yards of it, delicately cranking. Alert. Holding his breath, that fragile line taut. Even the slightest twitch of the bonefish while he was reeling in would snap it. Thorn tried to send his mind out to the creature, anticipate its reviving energy, its next spurt.

He cranked, paused. Cranked a few more turns, paused longer. Even a puff of wind, rocking the boat against the tension of the line, would rupture the connection.

Sarah said, "I wonder if it knows what's happening, that it's being sacrificed for the higher good? Satisfying the spiritual needs of the ruling species, all that."

"It knows."

He ate up a few more yards, his reel now a quarter refilled. The finest, sheerest awareness awakening. Threading a miniature needle, sighting a hummingbird through a long-distance scope, tuning in the faintest shortwave signal. Every inhalation straining the tensile strength of his line.

"If I had a pair of scissors," said Sarah. "If I had a razor blade."

The next run came with the reel half full. But even if Thorn had had a thousand yards of line, that fish would have spun it off. The reel singing, Thorn smiling inside himself.

"Good for her," said Sarah.

"Good for all of us," said Thorn.

* * *

Thorn fished until noon, aiming at shadows. He anchored the skiff at different angles around the perimeter of the scattered patch reefs. His casting skill returning. With Kate in the last few years, he had only fished for meat, drop a line beside the boat down a hundred feet and haul up a mutton snapper. His sure hand, the carefully calibrated toss had deserted him, but now, after four hours of it, the muscles were remembering.

At noon they ate the cold chicken and pickles and potato salad that Sarah had picked up at the Largo Shopper.

Thorn put his empty beer can in the bait box. He said, "Couldn't you change things, have Amos meet us in some lawyer's office for the closing?"

"You kidding? Amos in a lawyer's office?"

"Yeah," Thorn said. "I guess you're right. Well, anyway. You better bring along the Colt."

"I was planning to," she said.

Thorn cast his fly at a sparkle twenty yards away. Hit it. Retrieved. Cast at a blade of passing turtle grass. Direct hit. A few more days and he'd be able to lay a number two hook on a barracuda flashing by at thirty miles an hour.

Sugarman had been sitting in the pro shop behind a rack of golf pants for three days, staring at the row of town houses across the street. He was very polite, moving aside when one of the rich geezers was passing down the aisle, looking for a new plaid Sansabelt. But he knew he was getting on the pro's nerves.

Sugarman sure didn't like it any more than the pro did. But it was what was going to crack this thing. An address of a guy who was a friend of a guy whose teeth had washed ashore. The eye patch guy who had come in with the tide had once had a root canal done on a rear molar. He had three other teeth rot away and had needed the Brooklyn Bridge to keep things together in there.

Sugarman had trotted the X rays from Key West to Key Largo to every dentist in the county. He'd sat in so many waiting rooms now he'd memorized the July *Reader's Digest*. Finally a dentist in Islamorada had said it looked like the guy had suffered from internal resorption. Teeth were rotting away from within for no apparent reason. Sugarman almost told the guy, oh, yes, there's a reason all right. The guy was a damn killer.

So anyway, this dentist recommends a doctor in Fort Lauderdale who specializes in internal resorption. Sugarman calls, the guy's on vacation, he tracks him down long-distance in North Carolina, gets the name of another dentist who is also a specialist in this area, an office in Boca Raton. So Sugarman takes a day and drives up to Boca, and this guy takes one look at the X rays and says, "Stillman. Dr. Roger Stillman in Palm Beach." So it's back in the van, and all this is on his own time, back in the van, up to this fancy Palm Beach dentist, and there's Sugarman sitting in the waiting room with chauffeurs holding poodles and rich old guys in white suits and bow ties.

Finally Stillman's nurse looks over the X ray and says, "Yeah, we know this guy. Spends a good deal of time with us." Sugarman lighting up, not tired anymore, coasting back to the Keys with a photocopy of this guy's folder.

Lesley Allen Milburn, address at Coral Reef Club. Just your all-American neighborhood hit man. Forget about calling in somebody from Chicago. This way you didn't even have to pay travel.

Back in Key Largo it didn't take him long, asking around at the Coral Reef pro shop, the gas station, the restaurants, to find out his pal was a guy by the name of Irving David McMann. A good match on the description the eye doctor had given, and there you were. Both of them living off their daddies' cash flows.

Sugarman had tried for a warrant. Just go into this guy's town house, give Sugarman ten minutes, he'd find something that connected Milburn and McMann with Kate's last fishing trip. But the judge had taken a look at the influential address and told Sugarman to find some other way to gather his information. Sugarman pleaded, even gave the judge a short history of Dr. Bill and Captain Kate. But that sealed it. This judge was a landowner, a pretty significant one, and Kate Truman's name made that white-haired protector of rights glow red.

So the wheels of justice bounced along. Sugarman sat in a canvas director's chair, watching the door of that quarter-of-a-million-dollar one bedroom apartment. A Bible in his lap. He was becoming a damn Bible scholar so he could counter Jeannie's hundred quotations. He knew his own point of view was in there somewhere. Stuff about honoring your husband, holding no one else before him, not even the goddamn minister, not even if he did look like Robert Redford.

* * *

Irv McMann painted another green *S* on his cheek. This one interlocked with another *S* and a *C*. He checked his face in the little camping mirror. No, it wasn't there yet. He was trying for a camouflage effect. Yellows, greens, his tan would take care of the brown background. But Irv was getting something else, something goofy. He was glad Milburn wasn't here to pooh-pooh him.

He could hear it. You look like you been dunking for turds.

Irv was out here for good now. He'd planted his little surprise package for Thorn. All that taken care of. And now he had his water, some beef jerky, nuts, a few radishes to wake him up. He had his sleeping bag and his weapons and his binoculars and his paperback book, *The Story of O* to keep his dick hard. He'd read somewhere about some tribe, Zulus or some shit, who ran into battle with hard-ons. He liked that a lot. Scare the bejesus out of your enemies. They're all shriveled up, creeping around, and here you come rushing out of the trees, a spear in your hand and one between your legs.

Irv loved being out there with the mosquitoes and possums with the slimy bugs crawling around his supplies. He felt himself climbing down a rung or two on the evolutionary ladder, actually starting to like the stink growing in his armpits. He was leaning back against a banyan tree, its roots hanging down around him, hiding his little grotto.

Irv put down the mirror. The camouflage was good enough. He picked up the novel again and read some more about O, how much she was starting to like all these guys slipping it to her. Confirmed what Irv had always thought about women. He touched himself through the black pajama bottoms, keeping his stiffness alive. It was like tending a fire through the night to hold off the bears.

On Friday morning Thorn went back over to Dr. Bill's house to meet Jerome. He hadn't been there all week, and he thought he might be ready to clean up the place.

Jerome was waiting for him in the bash-mobile when Thorn drove up in Kate's VW, top down. Jerome gave him a quick wiggle of the mouse ears and got out.

"I heard about this," Jerome said, waving up at the house. A woodpecker fluttered out of the broken bathroom window. "You been hanging around the wrong types."

"Interior decorators ran amok," he said. "Had to fire them."

"I heard." Jerome dug his toe into the thick grass. "Listen, man. I was out of line about what I said about Captain Kate. It was none of my goddamn business."

Thorn patted him on the back and handed him Dr. Bill's keys.

"Jerome, you going to drive up to Miami with that goddamn rug on backwards?"

"That ain't the problem," said Jerome. "My head's just not on straight."

Thorn led him to where the Cadillac was parked under the stilt house. Jerome got in behind the wheel and asked him if there was anything special he should know about driving the thing.

"No," Thorn said. "I haven't driven it lately. But just last month I had the ears tuned up, the whiskers rotated."

Jerome said he'd forgotten a magazine he'd brought to read in traffic. He climbed out.

"You be careful now, Jerome," Thorn said, moving to the stairs. "You can squash a normal car in that yacht and not even know it."

"You bet," Jerome said. "Let me at 'em." Jerome hurried back to the bash-mobile for his magazine, while Thorn went on upstairs.

He was halfway up to the porch when Jerome started the Cadillac. A rush of scalding air blew Thorn thirty feet backward into some hibiscus shrubs. And the concussion of the blast put him deep asleep.

When he woke, the volunteer ambulance was blinking in front of him, Sugarman leaning over him. Thorn turned his head and saw the Frigidaire lying a few feet away. It wasn't chugging anymore.

"You're all right, man," Sugarman said. "It was car bombers this time."

Thorn heard himself say, "Jerome?"

Down a long, narrow pipeline Sugarman shook his head.

Thorn was wheeled across the rough ground and slid into the back of the ambulance. He caught a glimpse of Dr. Bill's house before they shut the doors. Just a couple of the telephone pole stilts remained. He could remember the house was a mess, but he hadn't remembered its being that bad. It made him sleepy thinking about it. A nap might be just the thing.

Sarah held his hand. Sugarman sat for hours across from his bed. Thorn lay there, in Mariner's Hospital, hovering just outside his body. He knew he was all right. The young black nurse had told him nothing was broken, that his paralysis was probably just a form of shock. Some deep bruise in his motor system.

But Thorn knew why he couldn't move. He was afraid if he got up, moved around, somebody else would die.

He had a string of visitors, Janice Deels, tears coming the whole time, shooting looks at Sarah. And Jerome senior came to tell Thorn it struck him as being for the best, Jerome junior going quick like that. Sammy from the liquor store came and told Thorn all the guys were cheering for him. Sugarman stayed next to Sammy the whole time like he was ready to drag him away if he made any wrong turns. Some of Thorn's fishermen friends stumbled in and stood smiling at him, sunburned and gawky.

Late Monday night, while Sarah was sleeping in the chair beside the bed, Thorn sat up. It was worse lying there, while the stream of friends stood at the foot of his bed trying to joke with him, than getting up, getting back to it.

He dragged one leg out from under the sheets, then the other, swiveled and put his feet back on the cold linoleum. He stood.

"Raptures of the deep?" Sarah said, stretching, rubbing sleep from her face.

"What month is it?"

"Still mosquito season," said Sarah. "Still a few shopping days left."

His feet were tender, and his lower back, shoulders, neck, and butt ached. But he could move. He gathered in a breath and hobbled across the cold hard floor to where Sarah stood waiting.

By Tuesday he could bend over and touch his knees. He could turn his head a few degrees, raise his arms above his head. All the necessary skills.

On Tuesday morning, the thirtieth, Thorn started dialing around nine and got no answer at Grayson's office. His home phone was unlisted, so Thorn kept redialing the office number off and on all morning till finally at eleven-thirty Grayson himself picked up the receiver.

"It's the bugman," Thorn said. "Remember me?"

Grayson was silent. Thorn listened to the hundred miles of empty line echo between them.

Thorn said, "I heard something. A guy talked to me, and I thought you should know."

"A guy talked to you," Grayson said.

"I was talking to some people I know at a bar, talking about Allamanda, arguing, you know, about wood rats, saving the land, all that bullshit. Conversation was getting a little heated, and I may have said your name out loud."

"You said my name."

"You know, making a point about Allamanda. I might've taken your name in vain. Not in a bad-mouthing way, but saying, like you were one hardass son of a bitch. I meant it respectfully, with admiration, but right after that this guy walks over to me, taps me on the shoulder. Wants to buy me a drink in a booth. He thinks we have an enemy in common. You."

"Can we get through this part, to what this is about?"

Thorn loved it. In the hospital he'd had this conversation in his mind, putting in the one missing piece, getting Grayson down from his penthouse. But all the times he'd run through it, it hadn't gone this well.

"This swarthy fellow, he acts like he knows you, says he's helping you out with a little problem involving some land deal. I get all perked up."

"I don't believe this," Grayson said. "I don't believe I'm having this kind of conversation."

Thorn said, "This is a very verbal fellow. This is all late at night; the guy's obviously under the sway of some mind-altering chemicals."

"Without the close-ups," Grayson said. "Just tell it."

"Well, this guy is planning to knife his boss in the

muscle. Once he gets home with a certain sack of money, he's going to call his boss, tell him he wants double what he's got in the bag to keep him from making a few phone calls. Is this an old story or what?''

"I don't fucking believe this,'' Grayson said. "What kind of scam is this?''

Thorn gave Grayson a few seconds to stew. He leaned against the kitchen wall, looked out at Sarah on the porch. Hands in her lap as if she were just snapping a few beans. He could see what she was doing, though, cleaning that damn Colt. Cleaning it, out there on the porch.

Thorn said, trying to make his voice reproachful, "Look, the only reason I didn't tell this guy to piss off was I thought this might be of some help to you.''

"I'm listening. Have I hung up? Even though I'm not believing a word of this.''

"Well, the fact is, I laugh at this guy. I go, 'You? A wahoo like you blackmail a guy like that? Come on.'

"And he makes these eyes at me. Like he's got some spicy thing he knows, one phone call to the newspaper, another call somewhere else, and the asshole keeps grinning at me like he's used to being underestimated, cat-with-the-canary look.

"OK, so I'm there, digesting this, and now all of a sudden the guy's coming on to me, saying, well, the reason he's invested so much time in talking to me is that he can use some help with this. He hears how I feel about this guy, Grayson, running him down out in public, so he proceeds to offer me a job, says he's used to working with a partner. And his regular partner is out sick. Guy offered me ten thousand dollars to be his driver, keep his car running and drive him home. Maybe one or two other things he didn't specify.'' Thorn paused, a little dizzy at how easily he'd slipped into this act. ''Kind of destroys your faith in the working class, am I right?''

Grayson didn't respond for a few moments. When he spoke again, his voice was hoarse, full of bile.

''And what do *you* want from me?''

''Not a thing,'' Thorn said. ''I'm content being your feelers. Wave around, see what I can pick up. It's like I figure, when Port Allamanda gets built, you'll probably need a full-time bugman. Don't you think?''

''Yeah, I guess I will,'' Grayson said. He paused. ''You wouldn't be interested in some other work before that, would you? Exterminate some other pest?''

''Oh, no, no, man,'' Thorn said. ''It's got to have at least four legs.''

''Not even for a million dollars?''

Thorn said no. Then swallowed hard.

''Yeah, well, OK,'' said Grayson. ''I appreciate the call, bugman.'' Thorn could hear half of some other conversation, a woman's faint voice carrying on a business call. Talking about medical insurance premiums. ''Hey,'' said Grayson. ''You wouldn't have an address for this guy, would you?''

''A man who works for you, you don't know where he lives?''

''I usually make it a point not to,'' said Grayson.

''I happen to know, yeah,'' said Thorn. ''I bought

our friend a few drinkies, and we go back to his place, so I know just where it is, yeah.'' Thorn thought, *drinkies*? Where in hell was this coming from?

''So?''

Thorn told him the address at Coral Reef.

''Jesus, there?''

''Guys you deal with are very upper-crust. Got Saudis for neighbors.''

''I guess I'm in your debt, bugman,'' Grayson said.

''Be careful,'' said Thorn. ''Lot of bozos out there. Lot of yammering people under the sway of this or that chemical.''

''Right. I'm very aware of this.''

When Thorn hung up the phone, he shook his head, kept shaking it. He went out to the porch, and Sarah asked him what in the hell he was grinning about; but he just kept shaking his head.

That evening while Thorn warmed up the *Heart Pounder*, Sarah was inside the house, packing the money. A squall had passed through after sunset and had scrubbed the sky clean. He found himself yawning as he gazed up into the bright field of stars. The false drowsiness of fear. As he had done so often as a boy when he felt this way, Thorn let his mind travel out into the sky.

Out there in the dark prairies of the atmosphere, that chilled unreflective vacuum, Thorn considered what vast forces were at work. Nuclear eruptions, the clash of meteors against stark moons. But all of it still somehow hanging together, glued by laws and forces no one could quite describe.

Maybe what was wringing sweat from Thorn's body, what was pumping his heart at such a pace, was some shadowy stray vine worked loose from the vortex of some black hole, a quark or quirk, leaked through the lid of the earth's sky, that had twisted down into Thorn's body. And with every pulse and twitch of that puppeteer's finger, Thorn's world quaked.

He wished he could still believe something like that, something grand and complicated that surrendered his fate to the sky. But the truth was, he was scared shitless. And the stars, the moon, all of that had nothing to do with it. It had been Thorn who had wound the springs tight, and now it was his time to stand close by and watch it make its freakish topsy-turvy spin.

When Sarah came aboard, they didn't speak. She stowed the gym bags with the cash inside the live-bait wells, loosened the lines, pulled them aboard, and coiled them neatly. Thorn eased the boat forward into the channel.

They made it to Carysfort Reef by midnight and Thorn killed the motor and they drifted for a while, looking up at the stars. Listening as the flying fish hummed past, chased by something big. There were a couple of other boats out there, fishing for yellowtail, one group drinking and whooping as it reeled up its fish. The wind had lain down, and the moon was nearly full again.

When they had drifted off the reef, back into the quiet dark, Thorn started up the engine again and headed the *Heart Pounder* out to sea.

* * *

"What is it now?" Sarah asked him.

"Four-thirty," Thorn said. "Looks like we've been stood up." Sarah, at the wheel up on the tuna tower, was staring south into the darkness. The loran flickered green in the dark. Thorn's hand on the rail beside hers.

"See if I made a mistake," she said. She pointed the penlight at a scrap of paper she'd opened on the control panel.

Thorn peered at it and said no, that's where they were. The numbers matched.

"They ever been late before?"

"Not this late," she said.

"If it was me, I'd split," Thorn said.

"It *is* you."

"It's both of us," Thorn said, "and Kate."

"Five more minutes," Sarah said.

The swells were regular and deep, rocking them against the railing of the tower stand.

"Let's go in," said Thorn. "The deal's off." A school of flying fish broke out of the water off their bow, skimmed along for twenty yards, and cut back into a wave.

"Damn," said Sarah.

Thorn said, "It's OK. I don't see why we can't go ahead with the other part of it. Go on to Amos's."

"A hundred thousand dollars short?"

"Amos strike you as a real reliable counter? Think he can count to a million?"

"You don't know, Thorn. He could have invited a lawyer, a relative, somebody else who was a good counter."

"You got another suggestion?"

"This is all falling apart, Thorn. I knew it was going to, I felt it."

"You sure the appointment was for three A.M.?"

Sarah said yes, unfortunately, she was sure of it.

She cranked up the big Chevy and stood aside for Thorn to take them back in.

"The deal's dead," Sarah said. "Even if Amos did believe it was a full million, soon as he goes to put it in the bank or in stocks or anywhere, the whole thing would come to light. Banks, they count money pretty carefully. They'd miss a hundred thousand."

"Amos? A bank? I'm telling you, Sarah. If it's over ten thousand dollars, Amos is going to believe he's a millionaire. You get his signature on the contracts, as far as we know later, he lost the hundred thousand, or spent it or gambled it away."

She said, "I like straight lines, things sticking together. I've never been much on making it up as you go." Sarah shook her head. "But at this point I guess we don't have much choice but try it your way. Con the old coot. Shit, shit, shit."

Thorn was lowering the anchor at Carysfort Reef, a place he knew on the outer bank, where it dropped to sixty feet. Ledges down there and a scattering of staghorn coral. He'd dived it plenty of times. There were big grouper lurking around under the ledges. As long as Sarah insisted on this part of the routine, they might as well get supper, tempt one of those drowsy giants out with a jumbo shrimp.

As the anchor chain ran out, Thorn looked out into

the fading dark. A searchlight panned the water about a mile to the east. It swung around and made another arc.

Thorn hauled up the anchor and secured it quickly. He hustled back to the cabin, climbed the tower ladder.

"Let's go," he said.

"We're clean," she said. "No problem."

"Almost a million in cash on board. That's pretty damn dirty, Sarah. Let's go before they decide to hail us."

Thorn spun the wheel, easing the throttle forward, heading due west, the shortest route to shore.

The spotlight swung back and forth another time. Still too far away to tell if it was a private vessel or not.

Thorn powered the boat up onto a plane, both of them watching the boat behind them. Its searchlight went out. Thorn took a compass heading, Sarah still looking back toward the lightening horizon.

She said, "We're probably overreacting."

The searchlight came on again, aiming toward the *Heart Pounder.*

Sarah cursed, and Thorn kept his eye on the compass heading.

The marine patrol boat gained on them gradually over the next two miles. Sarah banged her ribs against the railing of the tower as Thorn plowed at right angles into the light swells.

"If they really want us, they'll radio for an intercept."

"Maybe not," said Thorn. "They're spread awful thin out here." He mashed the throttle lever down for any trickle of extra juice.

By the time they were in the channel off Garden Cove, the marine patrol was five hundred yards behind them. A man's stony voice came over a loudspeaker, warning them to stop immediately.

"Stop, Thorn," Sarah said. "It's over."

"Cut your engines, Chris-Craft!" came the voice again.

"Just a little farther," Thorn told her.

They were slowing to make the hard left turn into Crawfish Creek, back into the mangrove canals, no more than fifty yards of visibility in that dusky light. Thorn took them into the turn, the marine patrol now just two hundred yards from their stern, riding their wake.

He gripped the throttle with one hand, the wheel with the other. Told Sarah to hold on.

"No, Thorn, come on. It's over."

"I used to play boat tag back here," he said, watching the mangroves fly past. "This is my second home."

He whirled the wheel to the right and hit the throttle lever, cutting into an opening in the mangroves that was half the width of the *Heart Pounder.* The branches scraped the hull, crashing against the railing, but Thorn forged through the narrow canal. Thirty yards of that, and they broke out into a small lagoon. Thorn could hear the other boat back there, slowing, looking for his wash.

Three small creeks led out of the lagoon. Thorn chose one and forced the *Heart Pounder* into it. The engine almost stalled as the prop dug through the mire, churning up a trail of silt behind them. He powered through mangrove roots, the Chevy chugging now, strangling on the muck.

Sarah ducked the lash of a branch, bumped her nose against the tower rail.

"You OK?"

"Just push this sucker, Thorn. Push it."

He smiled and made it through the last ten yards and out into a main channel. A twenty-three-foot Mako with some Cuban fishermen was cruising past. They saluted Thorn and Sarah with Budweisers. Dawn beers.

Thorn ducked into two more inlets on the way back to Kate's. Bulldozing mangrove roots, ramming ahead through passages too narrow for a boat half their size. At one narrow crook of the canal they surprised a couple of teenagers fishing from a little plastic boat, almost capsized them.

Thorn said, "This thing was due for a hull job anyway. I must have scraped a few barnacles off her."

"Off me, too," said Sarah. Her face ruddy, a spark in her eyes.

Sugarman recognized this guy, but he couldn't place him. He sat there with the Bible opened to Ecclesiastes, thinking who this guy was. Fairly short, and nicely dressed. A suit, John Kennedy haircut.

He'd walked into the town house in question at about 1:00 P.M. And Sugarman had been trying to make him for the last hour. He'd narrowed it down to Key West. The guy was a Key Wester, but beyond that, all Sugarman could call up was haze. Key West, Key West. John Kennedy haircut. A suit. Like a banker or some kind of hotshot. A doctor, lawyer, haberdasher. No, in Key West, Hart Schaffner & Marx were probably a gay comedy team or a bunch of Communists.

Sugarman stepped out of the way of an old red-faced guy carrying some bright pink golf pants and went over to stand by the entrance to the pro shop, staring at the town house. The slick haircut from Key West had driven up in a gunmetal gray Volvo, very conservative, like his suit. He'd opened the front door of the condo like he had a key. That or the guy was one hell of a locksmith.

The hell of it was, this guy didn't match the description he was going on. A little too tall and with straight hair.

He debated it. Go over there, frisk the guy, frisk the whole condo. Violate everybody's rights. Peek in the window? Catch somebody with his zipper open. Or just stay put in the golf shop, drive this young pro into scream therapy. Damn if Sugarman couldn't use a little scream therapy himself at this point.

Sugarman glared at the condo. Dead quiet over there. He'd wait it out. Be patient. He wasn't sure if he was being very professional about all this. He could feel a clench building in his throat.

"Twenty, twenty-five pounds," said Thorn. "I pictured it weighing more. You hear about a million dollars, you think it must take up a whole motel room."

"In five or tens, it might," Sarah said. "The people we've been dealing with, they like hundreds."

Thorn put the gym bags with the cash into the bait well. Sarah stepped aboard, put her purse on top of the bait well lid. The *Heart Pounder* was tied up on one side of the dock, Thorn's skiff on the other.

"You got everything?" Thorn nodded at her purse.

Sarah gave him a lost look. "I think so."

"Well, I guess it's judgment time."

"I wish you'd stop being so damn upbeat. This is serious."

"Is that what I'm being?" He turned, yanked the starter rope, and the motor caught. "I'm sorry. Hey, I'm just trying to keep my tongue from sticking to the roof of my mouth."

27

For Irving McMann it wasn't the million dollars anymore. It wasn't owning Vacation Island or going to Hollywood, meeting Jack Nicholson or becoming a movie star. By now he'd stared so long at that coral house with its tin roof, at the glimpse of ocean beyond it, at the crotons and sea grape and hibiscus that were planted next to the house, that Irv was sick of this neat little scene, just wanted to make wreckage of it, some absolute over-the-top mayhem.

He was itchy and tired and smelled like he was decomposing. He knew he was slipping into another stage. His thoughts were just coming willy-nilly, nothing connected, a jumble of wild images flowing past.

One minute he flexed his biceps and gave it a good feel; next minute he'd slipped the oily barrel of the .44 in his mouth and sucked.

Just that morning he'd been digging with his hands in the sandy dirt, at first thinking of making his campsite into a foxhole, but he'd gotten to limestone in about three inches. So what he did was, he tried a pinch of dirt. Tasting it, connecting with this sacred place where he was about to become rich. Saying to himself that he didn't want to be Ho Chi Minh anymore. He didn't even know who Ho was. Thinking maybe what'd be the ultimate challenge at this point was to be Irv McMann. A guy who killed people for his occupation.

His watch showed three o'clock. The thing was going down in the next couple of hours if he could hold on. He was sick of *The Story of O*, bored by the torture. It was all so polite, her master always asking her before he whipped her if it was OK. Irv had lost his erection. For the last few hours he'd massaged it and squeezed it, but the thing was gone, just a flap of flesh. Dead *carne*. That scared him a little.

But then, on the other hand, being scared was giving his blood a tremble, a cold burn that Irv thought might just make the whole episode better. He'd pictured two or three burly guys, carrying suitcases of money. Maybe one guy with the suitcases and two big, ugly Italians carrying the automatic weapons. Irv'd run through it over and over, trying to make a movie of it. He comes charging out of the bushes, wipes out the weaponry first, and then, as the guy with the suitcases goes for his gun, Irv leaps on him and chews his throat out.

Irv McMann lay on his belly, peering at Amos Clay's

house, mosquitoes feasting on his neck, his cheeks, the backs of his hands.

Thorn made the skiff fast at Amos's dock, a slipknot instead of the usual clove hitches, cinching it up close to the rotting post, for a fast exit.

"I'll be up there in a minute; you go ahead," he said.

Sarah wasn't sure. She stood on the bank, her leather briefcase under her arm. Regarding Thorn. He dragged the gym bags out of the bait locker and carried them over to her.

"You can handle these, can't you?"

"Of course." Still staring at him, sizing him, trying to read the poker face.

Thorn said, "I'm just going to snoop around a little first. See who's in the bushes. Go on in there. I'll be in to witness in a few minutes."

"You want the gun?"

"No, you hold on to that."

Sarah went ahead, walking up the slight knoll to the front door. Thorn watched her knock, wait. The door came open. Amos standing there in overalls, a baseball cap. She looked back at him, said something to Amos, who looked at Thorn, too. Thorn waved to them. Neither waved back.

Sarah went inside.

Thorn retrieved his short-shaft blue rod, the reel reloaded with ten-pound test. A lure he'd named Crazy Billy was tied on. He'd created it the night before, the first fly he'd managed in what felt like months. He'd pulled it up from the void, only a vague idea at first of what he was after. But he had quickly caught the old sizzle.

It was a heavy lure, with brass treble hooks, a wisp of blue Mylar for a tail, broken points of two lead pencils glued on for eyes. The body was a rubber eraser. An obscene lure. No fish alive would strike such a thing. But Thorn didn't intend it to bring up fish.

He walked toward the house, his eyes swiveling, his tread lightening. Drifting into the quickened senses of bonefish stalking. He came right up to the front door, then melted off to the right, crouching as he went, choosing a route through the dense trees and vines.

The gumbo-limbo he'd taken a sighting on was about a hundred feet behind the house. So Thorn swung wide and started a slow trajectory back to where Irving David McMann waited. Get behind him. Watch him watching. Hook him in the face or eye with Crazy Billy, and then, while he was fighting with the hook and pain, subdue him. Thorn's chance to bring his man in alive this time. His moment come 'round again.

He seemed to be making too much noise. Poling across the flats was one thing. Slipping the pole in, not stirring the marl, drawing it out without a wake or a flutter of water. But this was a harder thing. Every cobweb seemed hooked to a rattling seedpod; every bed of decaying leaves hid the crunch of a stick.

Thorn brushed mosquitoes from his face. He had already inhaled a bitter insect, lodged now like an aspirin in his throat. His dark green T-shirt damp with sweat.

He felt his pulse ticking in his chest.

Twenty yards into the jungle, Thorn caught himself

mid-step. Drew back. A voice was speaking just five, six yards to his right. Beneath a young banyan tree. Closer to the house than he'd estimated. He was speaking to himself, as if he were trying different voices, or different intonations, saying the same thing:

"Milburn, I know it's you, man. Milburn. I *know* it's you, man. *Milburn*, I know. It's you."

Thorn had to step a foot closer to get a clear path to McMann. He was standing there in black pajamas, holding an Uzi in his right hand, peeking out from behind the banyan, looking toward the house. From his position the guy had a view of the driveway, but it seemed to Thorn that his view of the dock was obstructed by the house. Thorn wasn't sure, but it might be that Irving David hadn't seen them arrive.

Thorn opened the bailer on the reel, held the line with his finger. He edged forward, blocked from Irving's peripheral vision by a stand of buttonwood saplings. Irving chattered on, washing away the mosquitoes in front of his face.

Thorn stepped into a strong cobweb, the fine wire gluing to his cheek. He felt the spider scuttling down the back of his T-shirt. He held still while it fled.

One more step forward, and Thorn was standing in an aisle that led through the brush to Irv's encampment. At Thorn's feet there was a sudden flurry in the weeds. He stiffened and drew back. Fewer than ten thousand of them left on earth and he had crushed a nursery of woodrats.

He watched two of the adolescents burrow under a pile of sticks and leaves nearby. And he stepped forward into that lane again, avoiding the nest this time, took quick aim, and cast his lure at Irving David McMann.

The lure ticked against one of the stringy roots hanging down from the banyan branches and fell to the ground. Thorn reeled it back carefully. The treble hooks caught in a pile of sticks. Thorn paused, took a new grip on the rod, and flicked the line up to shake it free.

"Milburn!" Irving hissed. "Milburn! Show your fat ass."

Thorn traced the path he wanted and then cast again, underhanded this time to get it beneath those dangling roots. As the line played out, Irving stooped over, began searching through the rest of his supplies. The Uzi still in one hand.

Crazy Billy caught on Irving's ear. Thorn hauled back on the rod with both hands, raising the tip then, and cranking hard.

Irv howled and came up firing the Uzi. Spraying the tops of the trees as if he were trying to bring down a sniper. Thorn gave the rod another ripping jerk. The treble hooks tore loose.

Irv kept screaming and spun around, firing rounds from the Uzi till it was empty; then, still screaming, he bent down, scrabbled through his pack, and came up with a grenade. He was crying when he pulled the pin and lobbed the thing toward a tree twenty yards to the left of Thorn. Thorn flopped flat, the blast sending whistles past his head.

He listened to Irving crashing through the brush toward the highway. Thorn stayed down, the trunk of an ironwood tree between him and where the grenade had hit. It was all right. Let him run. Thorn knew where he lived.

Sarah's voice came from the house, calling for him. He heard a motorcycle rev up, rev way, way up, missing first gear, revving probably past red line, catching the gear; then off it went.

When Thorn emerged at the edge of the clearing, Amos Clay was standing beside Sarah, aiming his shotgun at him. Sarah with her hand inside her purse.

"It's Thorn," Sarah said to Amos. "Thorn."

Amos continued to show Thorn the dark double barrels. Thorn still listening to the whine of the distant cycle.

"What're you doing shooting on my land, boy!"

Sarah asked him if he was hurt, coming across to him, between those barrels and him.

"I'm OK," he said. He held up the pole for Amos to see. "You should've seen the size of the son of a bitch."

Amos said, "First goddamn fish I ever heard of shooting back."

They went inside the house. Amos still watching Thorn with a cagey eye. The shotgun in both hands, port arms.

When they were all seated in the living room, Thorn felt a rush of nausea rising inside him. He drew in a breath, held it. Both of them watching him. His ears alert to any noise outside.

Sarah said, "Amos has decided he wants two million dollars."

"And I'm going to get it, too," he said. He'd sat in a chair across from them, tilted by the sag in his floor. He still gripped the shotgun by the barrel, its stock on the dirty rug beside his chair.

"Says taxes will take half of it, so he needs two million to be a millionaire."

"That makes sense," said Thorn.

"Thorn," Sarah said.

"No, I agree with you, Amos. Goddamn Uncle Sam's gonna steal half of it to pay some idiot not to plant corn, or to pay some other idiot so he can lay around and watch TV all day. I don't blame you at all."

Amos shook his head at Sarah. See there, I told you.

"But you know, what it is, Amos, is that two million is all we brought with us, so if you start hanging on any other charges here, this whole deal is gonna fall through."

"What were you doing out there, boy, shooting on my land?"

"I thought I saw something," he said. "It wasn't anything."

"It sounded like the godblamed Second World War."

"I got carried away, is all. But shit, Amos. You're gonna be John D. Rockefeller. You should be thinking about that. What're you going do with all of it?"

"Buy a condo," he said. "Up in Daytona Beach. I got a girl friend up there."

Sarah had crossed her arms across her chest, her head down, not believing the bullshit she was hearing.

"Daytona's nice," Thorn said.

"Daytona's the shittiest town I ever seen. It's worse than Miami," said Amos. "I'm not going there 'cause I like the place. I'm going there 'cause that's where my girl friend's at. And you can bet your ass I'm glad to be leaving this rock, too. I been here for forty years, getting sucked dry by the bugs and burned dry by the weather. If you keep this land like it is now, you're the damnedest fool I ever heard about, and if you build some goddamn concrete hotel or whatnot here, I'll come back down here and have your ass ground up for chum."

Laying his shotgun down on the floor, Amos said, "Well, now, let's see the color of this money."

"You can't do this, Thorn."

"Can't do what?"

"The contract won't be—"

Thorn stood up, waving Sarah quiet. He brought the gym bags over to Amos and unzippered them.

"Hundreds," Thorn said. "Thousands of hundreds."

"I remember that trout you caught," Amos said. "On a mirror lure at night. I never seen a mirror lure so mangled up in my life, and that sucker still caught fish."

"Yeah it was a miracle lure," Thorn said, winking at Sarah.

"Daytona Beach," Amos said. "What she said was she wouldn't marry me less I was a millionaire." The man smiled, his dentures stained, the sun rising behind his dull blue eyes.

Irv turned the bike around at the guardhouse at Coral Reef. He did a wheelie and roared back toward Amos Clay's, flattening himself against the seat, out of the wind. His ear was leaking down his shirt, blood all over his hands now. His own fucking blood. Irving McMann's fucking blood.

He was still shivering, but his brain had cleared. Milburn was dead. He'd shot him. Down in Key West. There wasn't any Milburn, not back there in the woods, not anywhere. Irv couldn't believe it, how he'd come unfastened like that. Started hearing things, and then the bat or owl or whatever the fuck it was that had clawed at his ear. He'd thought it was that fat sack Milburn, running a goof on him, like old times. A fat smartass ghost.

Now, there he was, a banshee on a Kawasaki, flat out in fifth gear, ninety-five on that empty narrow highway.

This time he didn't go slinking into the woods, hiding like some Cong scum. He braked hard at Amos Clay's drive, and then downshifted to second, revved up the drive, hitting the potholes, hammering his nuts, getting angrier with every hurt.

It didn't matter to him now if there were five, ten, a whole army of them. He had the Uzi still on the shoulder strap across his back, and he'd just wade into them, get his money, and fly. It was his money. Maybe it hadn't been at first, but after a week waiting in the woods, wiping his ass with his left hand, and all the rest of it, it was his money.

There was nobody outside the house. Nobody in the clearing. Irv didn't bother with the kickstand, just let the bike fall, and swung the Uzi over his head, rammed in another magazine, and walked over to the door.

In the week he'd been living in the woods, thinking of himself as a Zulu warrior, he'd wanted to scream a dozen times, and now, as he threw open that rickety door, a scalding howl came from his throat.

There was his money. All spread out over a long table, bundles of it held by rubber bands. And there was the old man Irv had been watching come and go all week. The old man was on the other side of the table, standing there, staring at Irv with his Uzi.

The old man reached out and picked up his dentures

that lay next to a bundle of hundreds. He popped the choppers in his mouth.

Irv watched the old man shrink up, as he got the picture, his dentures probably coming loose. Irv screamed at the man. He waved the Uzi at the old fart, telling him to back away.

This was it. Not much of a goddamn audience, but what a fucking part. Playing Irv McMann, killer, millionaire. The million cash dollars lying there. Sunlight still coming strong, a warm breeze. Life was still good. Everything was going to be possible. Playing himself. His own fucking self. That's all Jack did, after all. Why shouldn't Irv get famous playing himself?

Irv aimed the Uzi now. The old man raised his hands, a feeble squint, a quiver in his face. Like he was bracing himself for the noise the Uzi was going to make.

Irv inched around the perimeter of the table. The old man turned to face him but didn't back away. Irv didn't like the way this old fart was standing there now, like he was sassing him, challenging him to go ahead and shoot.

"You know me?" Irv asked him. "You know who the fuck I am?"

"I been knowing you was coming," said the old man. "I been waiting all my life, knowing you was on your way."

"Who am I!" Irv screamed at him. "Who am I, you dead fuck!"

"You ain't getting me to say it. Not out loud I won't."

Irv let off a three-round burst and pinned the skinny

old fart against the wall. Amos started to slide to the floor, but Irv stapled him with another burst and another one. Kept him up there, jerking against the rough wood wall. Twitching, bucking, like somebody had hold of his prostate.

Sugarman had found a good line. It didn't have anything to do directly with Jeannie and the minister or marriage, but it scared the shit out of him and might just, in a general kind of way, make Jeannie see how serious things could get. In Jeremiah. Chapter 19, Verse 7, the Lord is talking, saying, "I will cause their people to fall by the sword before their enemies, and by the hand of those who seek their life. I will give their dead bodies for food to the birds of the air and to the beasts of the earth. And I will make this city a horror, a thing to be hissed at, every one who passes by it will be horrified and will hiss because of all its disasters. And I will make them eat the flesh of their sons and their daughters, and every one will eat the flesh of his neighbor in the siege and distress."

He liked it because it was God-the-avenger. Not Jeannie's picture of God, some sexy white guy with a beard who wanted everyone to screw and moan and have orgasms day after day. This God was one serious guy. When he says, "Honor thy husband," he can back it up. A God using cannibalism to make his people mind him, this was a serious God.

The golf pro was whistling at him. Sugarman looked up and followed the pro's pointing finger over to the condo. His man had arrived. Dressed like Hugh Hefner home from a night of mud wrestling. Carrying two gym bags. Was it enough probable cause that a guy was riding around on a motorcycle in his pajamas? Sugarman thought it probably was.

He watched the guy open the front door, go inside. He'd let Irving mix with his buddy in there for a while, let things coagulate; then he'd go over and see what was going down or what was coming up.

28

Through the bright, hot sun Thorn steered the skiff the five miles up to Coral Reef Club. He wound through the network of creeks and canals and finally into the main channel. Past the marina full of yachts and schooners, their masts and rigging tinkling in the midday breeze, and into the residential canals. At no-wake speed he guided them past the private docks, most with their fifty-foot Hatterases, Bertrams, like glossy stallions dozing behind their masters' condos.

Thorn was listening to the Evinrude burble, tuned a little rich maybe, but still, all in all, he'd done a damn good job getting that thing going. It was a goofy time to feel it, but Thorn, with Sarah on the seat before him, her head tipped up a bit to let the breeze run down her neck, and his motor behind him going fine, felt happy.

There wasn't a bigger or smaller word for it. This was where he wanted to be, what he wanted to be doing. And he was with her, the only one who knew who he truly was, down to the muck and mire no one else had ever known.

Of course, the fact that she might want to murder him took some of the fine edge off his pleasure. He felt the way those abandoned soldiers must feel who finally work their way out of the jungle after twenty years, happy to be standing in the clearing, but not sure if that first person they see is going to embrace them or rattle bullets their way.

He slowed to barely above an idle, scanning the line of yachts. When he saw it, the red Scarab, *Perfect Execution*, he cut into the slip, bumping up beside it.

Sarah said, "I know this boat. These guys. They were the ones acting like DEA men, scared the hell out of me."

"They're scary guys," Thorn said. "They did Kate. It was about Allamanda. And Ricki, she was mixed in it, too, somehow. Judas, maybe."

Sarah asked him if he was sure.

"I'm sure about the little guy. Absolutely sure." Thorn tied up to the Scarab.

"You have a plan?"

"Sort of."

"A sort of plan, for guys like this? I don't know, Thorn. You got to have some idea, some strategy. Maybe it's time to call Sugarman."

"No," Thorn said. "I'm the one stirred the dragon up, I'm the one to go in the cave."

"Take the pistol then at least." She held it out to him by the barrel.

"No," he said. "You keep it. What plan I got doesn't include that."

Sarah drew in a long breath. Nodded her head in agreement. She gathered the hair on her shoulders with one hand and lifted it off her neck. Holding the Colt still by the barrel, letting the breeze cool her briefly, she looked lonelier than Thorn had ever seen her. Gone inward, eyes unplugged.

Thorn said, "You stay here, and don't let anybody come tearing out here and try to get away in that boat. Do you hear me, Sarah?" She came awake in there, met his eyes. "Can you shoot that thing?" he asked.

"Yeah," she said vacantly. "I've been practicing."

"Wonderful. That's wonderful." He headed on down the dock.

"Thorn," she called out. He stopped at the end of the dock. "We could both just let go. We could just drop this, the whole goddamn thing. Walk away."

But he heard in her voice that she didn't believe herself. He stayed there for a moment, watching her, bracing himself against a piling. He watched her sigh and drop her head.

She raised her eyes to him, waved him away. "Go ahead, go on."

He moved up the terrace to the condo, swung wide around it and around to the front door. A golf cart hummed down the shimmering avenue. Thorn nodded to the old man and his wife riding in it. They drew up to their garage, two doors down from Irv, still watching him.

In the shadow of Irv's stoop he pressed his ear to the door but heard nothing. Carefully he tried the handle. Locked. He brought his ear back to the door. There was only the hum of the air conditioner.

He circled the building, and as he came around behind Irv's patio, he glanced down at Sarah, pacing the dock, her gaze out to sea. The patio was surrounded by a high wooden fence. Thorn lifted the latch to the wooden gate and slid inside. He pressed his back against the cedar planks. There were marijuana plants growing there in large stone pots.

A thick curtain was drawn across the sliding glass doors. He brought his face against the glass and squinted into a small buckle in the curtains, but he could see only the corner of a white chair. He waited there for a few moments, a light fog from his breath building on the glass.

As he was drawing back to leave, he caught a flash of shiny black. Those satiny pajama legs. He brought his eye quickly back to the window. He couldn't see above the knees of those black pants, but that was high enough to catch the glint of the long silencer, pointing, for now, down to the floor.

He edged out of the patio and jogged around the row of town houses and across the street to the golf pro shop. He caught his breath outside the door, patted for his wallet.

The clerk was a young blond woman. She looked up from her *Cosmopolitan* when Thorn asked her if he could use the phone. She checked him out silently and then pushed the phone on the counter over to him.

Jerome senior answered on the first ring.

"I got a problem, Jerome."

"Insect problem?"

"You could say that." Thorn smiled at the clerk, who had put her magazine down and was listening to this. "Same bugs that stung Junior."

"Yeah? Is that a fact?"

"I'm out here at Coral Reef, a short row of town houses across the street from the golf pro shop. You know it?"

"I believe I do."

"Know it from the air?"

"Yep," he said. "Squeeters get awful bad up there this time of year, don't they, boy?"

"They surely do," said Thorn.

After he'd finished setting things up with Jerome, he shopped for ten minutes. Bought a red polo shirt, parrot green long pants. A shiny white leather belt. A blinding yellow sports coat. He stood in the middle of the triple mirrors. There was something missing. He splurged on a red-and-white-checked porkpie hat.

As he was counting out Grayson's money, $340 for the whole outfit, the young woman clerk asked him if he didn't want shoes. Thorn looked down at his scruffy tan boat shoes.

"That might be overdoing it," he said. He glanced around the shop. "But, ah, I *do* need a driver."

She'd closed her magazine, her eyes resigned to deal with this nuisance.

"Walk in here a fisherman, walk out a golfer," she said. "Why not?"

"What do you recommend in a driver?"

"The Daiwa's a big seller, with the fiber glass shaft, high impact through the power zone." She gestured toward a display rack nearby.

"Something more traditional," Thorn said, thinking about Dr. Bill, his heavy leather bag, long afternoons at Homestead Country Club. That one summer when Dr. Bill had experimented with landlubber games.

"You got your Ben Hogan, Ram, Jack Nicklaus."

"Ben Hogan," Thorn said.

"Balls?"

"Got to have 'em," Thorn said, picking up a large box from a shelf. He thought about it for a moment and took a second and third dozen.

"Those are illegals," she said. "Hot Dots."

"How's that?"

"I don't know," she said. "They've got some space age stuff in them, makes them go farther. Can't play tournaments with them. But then I guess you're not looking to play tournaments."

"These'll do fine," he said. "And some, what do you call them, tees?"

She handed him two packages from behind the counter, and he counted out more of Grayson's money.

"You're all set," she said as she handed back his change.

"How do I look?"

She shrugged. None of her business if people wanted to dress like Martians.

Thorn walked back across the street, the stiff synthetics chafing already. Up on the stretch of fairway that ran behind the row of town houses, Thorn emptied each of the boxes of balls on the grass. There was a patch of creeping Charlie strangling the grass at his feet. Some golfer hiking out of the rough had tracked bad seeds into this virgin Bermuda.

Wishing now he'd bought the spikes, Thorn adjusted his feet, looking for the stance Dr. Bill had shown him one or two afternoons twenty years before. The fairway was skinned and scorched, as hard as a sidewalk where Thorn teed up the first ball. Lining up, shoulder down, head down, grip firm but relaxed. Hit down, ball goes up. Almost like casting underhanded. It was always a surprise how suppleness and snap got more distance than muscle.

Irv's place was done in black and white. White short shag, flat black walls. Checkered furniture. High-tech black counters. All the toys, the stereo, TV, disk player, polished black.

Grayson, wearing a suit, was sitting on the couch, rubbing at his swollen cheekbone, darkening eye. This black cop with long lashes sitting beside him. His holster empty. A ribbon of blood coming out of his kinky hair, wandering across his forehead. His fine, straight nose was puffy. But his eyes were fired up, Irv could see that plain enough. He thought that between the two of these assholes the cop was the better listener. So he talked to him. Fuck Grayson.

"You know, this guy, this lawyer, man"—talking earnestly to Sugarman—"he's one crooked son of a bitch. This guy figured he'd come in here, hide behind the couch, ambush me, and then steal this money and use it to buy this land he's so hot about. The fucker claims I'm going to blackmail him. Imagine that. Got the balls to sneak into my house and try to hit me. You don't shoot a shooter, man. Isn't that right, cop?''

Sugarman said nothing. Measuring angles, distances from here to there, flexing his feet, remembering how he could once explode into a slot between big blockers, remembering that surge out of a three-point stance.

''Irv, don't be a moron,'' Grayson said. ''I can get you out of this. It hasn't gone so far yet. There're still ways out. Can't you see what's happening here? I was conned. This guy Thorn concocted this whole thing. The son of a bitch ran one on me, turned me against you. But all we got to do is, we wipe out these two and it's all clear between us. You take the million and we walk.''

''I already *got* the million, you dork,'' Irv said. ''Guy like you should see he's got no bargaining power here. Trick to negotiating is you got to have something to trade, fuckhead. And you, man, you got nothing. Nothing.''

''I know the law,'' Grayson said. ''I can finesse us out of trouble here. You just calm down a second, you'll see that.''

The silencer made two pfftts. Twin bottle rockets launching. Grayson's head snapped back against the wall, and his body slumped onto Sugarman. Sugarman pushed Grayson away from him, and the corpse rolled onto the other arm of the couch.

Irv said, ''Shit! I meant to ask him where he got his hair cut.''

Irv rubbed at the black oil on his face. Smeared it. Scratched at his nose backhanded and sniffed. Brought his hand to his ragged ear and touched it gingerly.

He edged backward to the counter, patted his left hand around back there, and found a mason jar. He picked it up and held it up for Sugarman to see.

"I've been saving this," he said, "for a time I needed a little extra go power. Know what this is?" He smiled at Sugarman. "This is magic, man. This is a five-carat diamond and a ruby big as your eyeball, been marinating in this water all summer. I heard about this, man, it's like drinking a gallon of adrenaline. Diamond power, ruby power." Irv held the bottle under his gun arm and unscrewed the cap and took a cautious sip of it, watching Sugarman. He gasped and said, "Fucking superman, diamond power. Better than gorilla jism."

Glass broke from someplace nearby. Sounded like upstairs. Irv choked a little on the water. He moved quickly to the sliding glass door. Somebody was yelling now from two town houses down. The old fart down there having it out with his old fart wife, Irv guessed. Jeez, he was jumpy.

When he turned back, the black cop was standing up, holding his hand out like he was directing traffic, telling Irv to stop, going to wave on the other cars.

"Listen, fellow," Sugarman said, "if you're bright as I think you are, you'll just—"

Irv brought the automatic up, leveled it at Sugarman. He wiped his mouth on his sleeve and set the mason jar back on the counter. Outside there was a thwock, sound of a hammer cracking bricks. Irv glared hard at Sugarman as though he were up to something.

Irv waved the automatic at him. "You got a death wish, man?"

"No," Sugarman said, and stepped back, lowering his hand.

"Hey, now let's talk about you," said Irv. He smiled and tried breathing his heart back into regular pace. "I got this new policy. I don't wet strangers anymore. I got to get to know you good. Gourmet shit. Touchy feely. Heavy-duty emotions. California, acting school work-out. People getting into very good touch with their inner life and all that.

"Like, for instance, who the fuck are you, cop? And what in fuck's name are you doing in my home?"

"You're still standing there, so you don't know it yet," said Sugarman, "but they already split you open, doing an autopsy on your brain to see what kind of cancer you got up there screwing up your mind."

"Whoo-whoo," Irv said. "I'm pissing down my leg."

Irv was coiling that trigger finger, half a pound of pressure away from doing this guy when something whacked the picture window that looked out on the golf course. Irv did a jerky jig as if the floor were suddenly electrified, almost dropping the Smith & Wesson in the process.

"Place is quiet three hundred and sixty-four days a year, and today the old farts decide to go three falls, Texas no-rules wrestling."

Watching Sugarman, Irv moved over to the picture window. He had the curtains halfway open when another whack against the glass shattered the whole pane.

Irv screamed. He spun around and focused everything he had on Sugarman, sighting down that long silencer, shivering. And he screamed at Sugarman, nothing coherent, no words.

Glass all over the rug, the dining room table. The hot, sticky afternoon wind coming into the room. Irv breathing so hard he might've just carried Milburn on his back up six flights of stairs. But he blinked a couple of times, got the room back out of the mist. There was a golf ball rolling across the dining room floor.

"Get over there, Broderick Crawford," Irv said, motioning Sugarman toward the sliding glass doors, the patio. "Get your goddamn negroid hands up in the air." Another ball sailed through the window, hit the kitchen cabinets, ricocheted against the refrigerator, and wound up spinning around inside the sink.

Irv was thinking now maybe it was just the diamond water starting to take effect, heating up his blood. Maybe none of this was happening.

29

Thorn was down to the last dozen balls. But he was catching on. Three into Irv's window, the second one taking it all out. Before that he'd sprayed a few around, even sent one flying clear over the roof. That swing had felt particularly good. He tried to get his body to repeat that motion, but the next few stayed low, drilling into backyard fences. He made hash of the windshield on a white BMW. Somebody had left it around the side of the building, getting ready to wash and wax.

And the old couple, boy, he'd made their month, renewed their enthusiasm for living. The old guy had decided it was Dunkirk or Anzio or something. He'd found a deer rifle and was standing in his broken-out upstairs window, gesturing at Thorn with it, yelling at him. Was he crazy, hitting golf balls through civilized people's windows! Guess so, Thorn had said to himself, and cranked another one, this one hooking off to knock out somebody's security spotlight.

Sarah had shouted to him, too. Just his name, like she was calling down a long corridor at night, checking to see if it was him or some stranger. He didn't answer. It *was* some stranger. And now she was staying a safe way back, on the steps to the dock. Thorn felt the skin on his back lifting, wrinkling, bumps running under his armpits and down his ribs. Out there in all that sunlight, probably after five o'clock. High tide or thereabouts. Having chills on the fairway.

He wiggled his hips a little, the way he'd seen somebody do once. Maybe that was a baseball player. All these land games, he'd not paid enough attention. Set his feet again. Addressed the ball. Head down. He'd heard about the trick of tying a tight string from pecker to head. Try to bob your head up then. People could get serious about games, risking injury of that sort.

He had six or seven balls left when Irv came outside. Thorn was just getting set, adjusting his grip, straightening that left elbow. Sighting on Irv's busted-out window.

And goddamn if Irv wasn't prodding Sugarman in front of him. Sugarman, raising his hands, but only up to about his chest, peering at Thorn now as if he were trying to see through fog. And behind him was Irv, wearing camouflage goop on his face, and blood dried in a wavering trail down his neck. Though he couldn't see it, Thorn knew the silencer was back of Sugarman, that these were now the seconds that counted, that all the other minutes and hours and days had been narrowing into these moments. Glad for that. For any kind of finish.

He tamped the ground around the tee with the black flatsided driver. Gave another hip wiggle, brought everything in line, and let it rip. A slice, curved ten feet right of Irv and Sugarman and sailed out into the avenue, bounced along toward the pro shop. But Irv reacted as if a warhead had skimmed him, dropping to a squat, pulling Sugarman down by the collar, and shielding himself with Sugarman's bulk.

"Hey!" he screamed at Thorn. "Hey, cunt, what in the fuck are you doing? You blind or what? There's people out here, right in front of you!" He rose and dragged Sugarman up with him.

Sugarman sending some play calls with his eyes, but Thorn couldn't read them. Sugar darted his eyes over toward a sand trap that dropped off ten feet to his right. Thorn tried to say back to him, What? I can't tell what you're saying. Finally just giving a full shrug, face shrugging, too.

Irv screwed his face into a broad, unhappy grin and said, "I don't believe this. I don't believe what I'm seeing here." He brought the automatic out from behind Sugarman, stepped back a step, waggled the pistol at Thorn.

"You, man," said Irv, glaring at Thorn. "I know your ass, don't I?" Irv snorted and smiled. "Jesus fucking Christ, look who it is, Sugarbear. This is the guy I was doing for what's her name, Ricki. Is this something else or what? The guy with the dead mother."

Thorn pulled another of those hot balls from the

small pile, feeling comfortable now using the driver like a rake. He stopped, set the ball on the tee, straightened, assumed the position again, and tried to let his weight shift down into his hips this time. Give him twenty years, and he'd learn how to do this thing. Twenty years was about how long it took him on anything with any complexity to it.

"Look it," Irv said, inching closer now, nudging Sugarman with him. "How come you aren't dead, man? I heard you got exploded."

Sugarman said, "You got another guy. A friend of ours."

"Well, I'll be fucked, man." Smiling now, a wide, toothy smile, but his eyes seeming to Thorn to be dead, flat and empty. Thorn adjusted the grip again, decided to try hooking fingers the way he'd done back with Dr. Bill standing behind him, conforming his body to Thorn's, showing him how it was done. One of the few times the man had ever embraced him.

"Would you look at this shit, man? My hits are coming to me. I don't even have to look them up anymore. They hear I'm after their ass, and they go, 'Whoops, I'm dead. Might as well get over there.'"

The old man in the upstairs window was holding his rifle now at present arms. Thorn took a look around for Sarah but didn't find her. He came back to Irv, this wiry guy, trying so hard to be smartass, wanting Thorn to say something, anything, so he could top him. Worst thing you could do to a guy like this was give him nothing to feed on, passive-aggressive him. Irv was snaking his head out and back, like a disco duck, keeping a fast beat, watching Thorn. Maybe a little admiration had worked into his face for Thorn's loony performance, the clothes. Something this class clown could relate to.

"I love it," Irv said. "Don't you love it, cop? Guys I'm hired to kill are lining up outside my place, saving me the trouble." When Sugarman gave him no response, Irv poked him hard in the back. "OK, show's over. We're out of here now. Back inside, where we can have a good old-fashioned encounter session. Get out of these damaging rays. Guy in my business has to watch his skin."

Thorn heard it now. Not much louder than a lawn mower a block away. He really exaggerated the hip wiggle this time. Let the wiggle run all the way up his body so his shoulders were doing it, too. Give this guy something to watch. He let his neck go loose and wiggled his head, too. One of those kid's toys, held upright by a string running through its parts. You press the button in the bottom, loosen all the strings, and the thing collapses. That was definitely Thorn, a button push away from falling in a heap.

The noise building now, a drone. Thorn drew his club back a foot and brought it back to the ball, did that again. One to get ready, two to get set.

"Forget that, asshole, no more games," Irv said. "Put the club down. Fucking now!"

The DC-3 broke into view over the tall mangroves on Thompson Island, the huge thunder now, the rumble rising as if up through the hard earth. And Thorn went about his golf business. Nothing happening, taking a quick peek at Sugarman, who was leaning toward the sand trap. Thorn focusing everything on that ball, picturing its trajectory, a cartoon hole through Irv's forehead.

Irv screamed something, waved the pistol around, fired up at Jerome as he skimmed not fifteen feet above the fairway, dumping what must have been half his normal load for the whole twenty-mile island, all right there.

Though he could not see anymore, his eyes burning, Thorn found the rhythm again, cocked the driver back, and sailed one into the depths of that smog. Then he dropped to his knees, fanning for air, and hearing now the small poofs from Irv's pistol, and seeing a divot appear in the fairway a few inches from his right hand. He rolled quickly to the left. No visibility at all. Not a foot. He continued to roll, and then the real gunfire sounded.

One, two, three. Regular intervals. Very, very loud in that billowing blue-gray smoke. Four, five. And the rumble was returning for another pass. Jerome going above and beyond. The crescendo louder and louder. The concrete fairway quaked. It sounded as if Jerome had gouged holes in the mufflers before he'd left. Thorn felt the heavy whoosh of air before the plane came, the surge and suck of wind as it passed. And more diesel fuel, Malathion. Man, they wouldn't have mosquito troubles on this golf course for at least a month.

There was no sound for a while as Thorn lay on his belly, breathing into the short grass, getting sand on his lips, swallowing some. But in a few moments he made out a harsh click, the fall of a hammer on empty cylinders. A breeze was lifting the poisonous cloud, shredding it. Thorn crawled toward the noise, dragging himself on knees and elbows, hauling along the Ben Hogan.

He heard someone coughing off to his right, but he continued to pull himself forward toward the clicking noise. Getting a little buzz from all that poison, head swimming. He knew better than to attempt a normal thought and watch it dissolve or turn crazy. He kept his mind on that click and wriggled across the grass.

Then there was a shoe, the sole of a shoe in his face. It was a small foot, waffle-sole running shoe. Its mate was next to it, spread a couple of feet away.

A breeze lifted more of the gas, and Thorn was looking into the crotch of a pair of black shiny pajamas. Guy was just lying there, taking it easy, waiting for the mist to clear. Rolling suddenly onto his side, Thorn got his other hand on the club's rubber grip and took as much of a swing as his awkward position would allow, bringing Ben Hogan thudding down on that shiny crotch.

"Too late," he heard Sugarman say.

Thorn up on his knees now, cocked for another swing.

The last of the fumes carried away on the easterly. There was Sugarman, prying the Colt out of Sarah's hand. Both of them standing above Irv, Sarah staring down at the body, a spasm in her trigger finger. Click. Sugarman pulling the fingers open, click. Click.

It was almost sunset when Sally Spencer had finally taken the bodies away and Danny Sterling, Monroe County homicide detective, had finished giving Thorn and Sarah and Sugarman a lecture on their irresponsibility and their luck and the incredible amount of shit still stuck to their shoes. The three of them stood on the dock beside Thorn's skiff.

Sugarman said, "You're a hell of a shot, counselor, especially in all that bug spray. Though I think there's going to be some questions about those last few rounds. One extra they usually give you. Four more, that's pushing it."

Sarah nodded, miles from the dock, from that stifling summer evening.

"And you, Thorn," Sugarman said, "you ever going to tell me how you wound up at that condo?"

"Probably not," he said. "No."

"Yeah, well, I'm sure you'll dream up something entertaining for the sheriff." Sugarman touched the shiny bill of his hat, nodding at Sarah. "I'd like to stay longer, have a nice chat, but I got to get over to the funeral home," he said. "I got an autopsy I want to see."

30

"Where to?" Thorn asked her when they'd gotten back into the skiff.

"Where do you think?"

He tried for a moment to see behind her blue eyes. But she'd taken them out of action. Dazed or determined, it hardly mattered at this point.

Thorn took the skiff back down the coast, skimming past Kate's, down past Garden Cove, into Crawfish Creek, and into Largo Sound. Past the mangrove canal where that morning they had eluded the marine patrol. Through Adams Cut and over to the bay and then back up the coastline, north through Blackwater Sound. Sarah sitting up front, facing into the wind, Thorn standing out from behind the windscreen, also taking it full in the face, steering with his left hand.

He called out to her, "This what you had in mind?" She nodded, without turning to look at him, that it was.

He slowed as they came through the narrow inlet into Lake Surprise.

"Out there," Sarah said, and pointed to a spot a hundred yards from the highway. She snapped the cylinder back in place on the Colt. Held it in her lap.

Thorn made for her spot.

"Anchor?" he asked her when they'd reached the place.

She shook her head no.

Thorn looked down into the clear water, six, maybe seven feet. The turtle grass bending with the incoming tide. When he looked up again, she had moved forward and was sitting on the bait wells, facing him. The revolver in both hands still in her lap.

Thorn said, "Haven't you already bagged your limit for today?"

Sarah stared at him, the arteries in her temples working hard. "I *do* love you," she said.

"But you still want to kill me," Thorn said, stealing a look at the pistol. "It'd be a typical modern marriage."

"Being flip," she said, "that's not changing anything."

"What'd you save my life for back there? So you could be the one to pull the trigger?"

"I'd like to pardon you," she said. "If you'd let me."

Thorn said, settling his eyes on hers, "We could pardon each other." He took hold of the railing around the console, for leverage if he had to lunge for her.

"You give me a rosary to say, I give you three Hail Marys, and we call the whole thing even."

She kept looking at him from a long way off, unamused.

"That's close," she said, the revolver rising from her lap, hovering. "I want you to take your clothes off, Thorn."

He squinted at her, puzzled, started to smile, felt it disappear.

She raised the Colt, let him stare at that a moment.

"Take everything off."

"What? You want to do that out here, now?"

"Not that," she said. "Something else."

"Sarah," he said, trying to shake her awake. "Sarah!"

"Do what I tell you."

Her face seemed to be under fierce control, her mouth clamped, eyes straining. The veins in her arm had begun to show.

Slowly he began to peel out of those stiff, bright clothes, glancing once out at the highway. When he turned to her again, she was shivering. Not used to killing guys the way he was, not taking it like a pro.

She said, "You come out here, Thorn, once a year, stare at it, run it all through your mind, feeling sorry for yourself. You brought me out here, I could've been anybody. Going to tell somebody, this stranger, so you'd have it off your heart finally. That's nothing. That means nothing. *Looking* at it. Telling your secrets to strangers. Exposing your shame to somebody you didn't even know. That's nothing."

"Whose fault was it I didn't know you?" Thorn shook his head, trying to untangle this. "I thought I knew you, I thought I loved you. I'd never been tempted to confess to anybody before.''

From a rental shop on the south shore of Lake Surprise two jet skis blared to life. A gang of kids in bright clothes razzed the two riders who were mounting up.

Thorn looked back to her. ''Listen, what're the words you're looking for? I apologize? I'm sorry? I wish it hadn't happened? What is it you want?'' He edged around the center console, gave her the clearest of shots. ''When it happened, I was nineteen years old, for godsakes.''

''Nineteen is old enough. You knew what you were doing.''

''Did I?'' Thorn said. ''Think who you were at nineteen.''

''I'm still nineteen,'' Sarah said. ''In here.'' She tapped her left breast with the butt of the Colt. ''Nineteen. Ten. All of it.''

The two teenagers chased each other across the calm water, circling thirty yards around the skiff. The girl whooped as the boy pulled alongside, swerving close to her, making a theatrical grab for her. The girl, seeing Thorn standing naked, slowed.

''Come on, Sarah,'' Thorn said. ''We're past this point. Things have changed for us. Promises you made when you were a little girl, they're not binding now.''

''Listen, Thorn,'' she said, a roughness in her voice, ''somebody's got to stop this thing. Somebody's got to break the cycle.''

The two kids on the jet skis were creeping closer to the boat, whispering.

"I want you in that water," she said. "If I have to shoot you and throw you in, I want you in that water."

He wasn't feeling detached anymore. His ears were still thumping from the gunshots earlier. He wanted badly to tell her what he saw now. That they were joined. By thin, invisible umbilicals, hooked together. Every pinprick made the other wince. Her stricken face, the panic in her eyes at what she might do, was a replica of his face. Her exhalation came with his inhaling. Twined. Something more powerful than love binding them. It was a marriage consecrated by a '65 Buick, by a lifetime of regret and loss and anger.

The sun seeped into the horizon's edge behind her, and her shadow fell onto him. He wanted to tell her this, show her this fact. That they were halves of one whole, depending on the other. If he sank below the surface, she would be dragged down too.

He said instead, his voice surprising him with its calmness, "I did it. I killed your father. I killed him, and I've had no rest since."

She nodded, turning her eyes to the deck.

Holding onto the gunwale, Thorn slipped overboard. The water was bath warm. He held to the skiff, his breath coming with difficulty. The wake from the jet skis was rocking the boat. She waved him away from the side of the skiff with the Colt. Her mouth was open, her eyes muddy.

He turned, let go, began to breaststroke toward the spot where it had happened. Where he had made it happen. The water, thicker than water, warmer than water.

And he knew she was right; he had just been looking

at it. He had come out there and sat and stared and said the same things to himself. The appearance of penitence. He'd rehashed the story to himself a hundred times, and though a deep hurt came to him when he recalled it, that pain had not changed him.

Thorn was twenty yards from the skiff when he stopped swimming, paddled around, and faced her. She had skinned out of her clothes and was standing naked now, holding the pistol by her side. The teenagers had slowed to a crawl thirty yards away, staring on, their machines muttering.

Thorn waited there, treading water. He could feel the tickle of the turtle grass against his feet. The drag of the tide, already hauling his body toward shore.

She found a good grip on the barrel of the Colt and slung it out into the lake. He'd never seen her throw before. She had a damn good arm.

She slipped over the side of the skiff and glided through the water toward him. Thorn released the breath he'd been holding and pushed ahead against the swelling tide toward her.

THE #1 PHENOMENAL BLOCKBUSTER
PRESUMED INNOCENT
A NOVEL BY
SCOTT TUROW
(A35-098, $4.95, USA) (A35-099, $5.95, Canada)
The remarkable, unforgettable novel of a chief deputy prosecutor charged with the murder of his colleague and lover.
"Mesmerizing."—Cosmopolitan
"Spellbinding."—The New York Times
"Splendid."—Chicago Tribune
"I haven't recently had this much fun."—Newsweek
"Who could ask for anything more?" —Washington Post Book World
A MAY 1988 PAPERBACK
Warner Books P.O. Box 690
New York, NY 10019
Please send me the books I have checked. I enclose a check or money order (not cash), plus 95¢ per order and 95¢ per copy to cover postage and handling.* (Allow 4-6 weeks for delivery.)
___Please send me your free mail order catalog. (If ordering only the catalog, include a large self-addressed, stamped envelope.)
Name